What readers are saying about previous books by

PEGGY STOKS:

"Heart-wrenching, heartwarming, honest, and pure."
—Johanna Asmi, Washington

"Ministered much to my soul. So encouraging, so real."
—Twila Simonson, Minnesota

"Oh, how I wished it had been longer! I don't ever recall reading another book that has held my attention like this one."
—Edna Bell Winland, Ohio

"Written from the heart, written beautifully. Captivating and real, and I believed every moment."
—Terri Gross, Minnesota

"I'm keeping this book to read again and again. Thank you."
—Rachel Donahue, Oregon

"I laughed, I cried, I rejoiced. It was wonderful."
—Sattie Jo-Ann Trusiak, Pennsylvania

"Couldn't wait to get to the end—then I was disappointed it was over."
—Ruth Bennett, Minnesota

"You can't stop now—you must write another book!"
—Pat Doocy, Minnesota

"Thank you so much for the great entertainment you have given me this week!"
—Lee Ann Cline, Missouri

HEART
QUEST®

romance the way it's meant to be

HeartQuest brings you romantic fiction
with a foundation of biblical truth.
Adventure, mystery, intrigue, and suspense
mingle in these heartwarming stories of
men and women of faith striving to build
a love that will last a lifetime.

May HeartQuest books sweep you
into the arms of God, who longs for you
and pursues you always.

Elena's Song

PEGGY STOKS

HEART QUEST®

Romance fiction from
Tyndale House Publishers, Inc.
WHEATON, ILLINOIS

Visit Tyndale's exciting Web site at www.tyndale.com

Check out the latest about HeartQuest Books at www.heartquest.com

HeartQuest is a registered trademark of Tyndale House Publishers, Inc.

Edited by Kathryn S. Olson

Designed by Jacqueline Noe

Scripture quotation in author's note is taken from the *Holy Bible,* New Living Translation, copyright © 1996. Used by permission of Tyndale House Publishers, Inc., Wheaton, Illinois 60189. All rights reserved.

Library of Congress Cataloging-in-Publication Data

Stoks, Peggy.
Elena's song / Peggy Stoks.
  p. cm. — (HeartQuest) (Abounding love series ; bk. 3)
ISBN 0-8423-1944-1 (pbk.)
1. Adult child abuse victims—Fiction. 2. Separated people—Fiction.
3. Women singers—Fiction. 4. Michigan—Fiction. 5. Actors—Fiction.
I. Title II. Series.
PS3569.T62237 E44 2002

813'.54—dc21   2001006403

Printed in the United States of America

07 06 05 04 03 02
9   8   7   6   5   4   3   2   1

For Denise and Lora:
Your voices lifted in song have filled me with pure joy
and ministered so deeply to my hurts.
I cannot count the number of times I have wept
for the sheer pleasure of hearing you sing.

❦

Chapter 1

Detroit, Michigan
Autumn 1885

"Brava! Brava! Brava!"

The audience was on its feet, chanting and cheering, wild with excitement. Never before had Crawford's Opera House been shaken in such a manner. Flushed with success, trembling, and exhilarated, Elena Breen joined hands with her handsome leading man, Jesse Golden, and took a bow.

With even greater volume, the crowd erupted with cries for an encore. From the wings, manager Stephen Villard looked on, a pleased smile curving his lips. Catching Elena's eye, he nodded with satisfaction, his expression fading into something sharp and unpleasant as his gaze shifted to Jesse Golden. Though she told herself she hadn't really seen what she thought she had, anxiety curled in the pit of Elena's stomach nonetheless.

"You were magnificent," came Jesse's voice as they took another bow, his words meant for her ears alone. How her heart thrilled at his touch, at the warmth of his fingers laced through her own. Though they had met only months earlier, having been cast together in the musical production If Not for You, *she felt as if she had known him forever. As often as possible, they stole away and spent whatever moments together they could. Once upon a time she thought she had been in love, but since meeting Jesse, she knew her previous experience was only a shadow of what could exist between a man and a woman.*

Affection, tenderness, friendship, ardor. With Jesse, she had known all these things to a measure which she'd never reckoned.

Suddenly a loud wail split the air, followed by wretched moaning. More such sounds ensued, drowning out the cries of the theater patrons with a dissonance of whimpering, sobbing, and mutterings of madness. Where had the crowd gone? The orchestra? What had happened to the curtains?

Where was Jesse?

No longer did her beloved have hold of her hand. With fingers of ice, Stephen Villard had snatched Elena's wrist and pulled her away. Hopelessness filled her as she realized she would never escape, never be free. How she longed for a void of blackness to swallow her whole, to put an end to the misery her life had become.

But from her left came another shriek, making it impossible for her dark wish to be fulfilled. The woman's name—Beth—came to Elena's mind, though she did not want it to. Covered with putrefying sores, Beth had been admitted to the Hospital of the Benevolent Sisters of Mercy a few days previously and been placed in the cot next to Elena's. Before Screeching Beth, a shriveled old woman had lain in the same berth and silently submitted to her mortality.

Poverty, sickness, pain, and death: the sureties of life.

"Sister Therese, Sister Antonia," called the short sister with the musical voice. "Help me turn our friend; then let us call upon the Lord for mercy."

Pulling the scratchy wool blanket more closely over her shoulder took all the strength Elena possessed, but she did so, unwilling to open her eyes and view the dismal surroundings that swathed her like a burial shroud. Certainly she had no wish to view the grotesque spectacle beside her.

Skirts swishing, the tireless sisters converged at the cot next to her own, efficiently caring for the agonized woman. In the split-second pauses between Beth's cries, Elena heard snatches of the graceful notes Sister Evangeline hummed, which caused her far more wretched feelings than did the screams of her neighbor.

Listening to such a lovely voice was akin to having spirits poured into an open wound.

"That's better now, isn't it?" came Sister Evangeline's gentle entreaty as Beth gradually quieted. "Most holy Lord Jesus," she began, and Elena stopped listening.

How could they do this, day after day? Never had she heard a cross or impatient word pass from the sisters' lips, and all the time they prayed. If they weren't interceding aloud for one of the twenty-some inhabitants of their small, one-room hospital, they were engaged in wordless prayer with a pitiless higher power who never responded to their pleas.

They were fools. Wasting their lives in a disease-ridden hovel, they poured themselves out upon the sick as rare oil from a priceless decanter. Didn't they know their vessels would one day empty once and for all? That they might succumb to the same dread illnesses which they now tended? With all that was in her, Elena would never understand how anyone could choose to spend her life in such a manner.

Beth was now quiet, and the sisters continued praying calmly but fervently for her healing, her comfort, and the salvation of her soul. Over the past several days, such prayers had been uttered over Elena's cot as well, for naught. She was going to die—she *wanted* to die—and no one or nothing could change that fact.

How long ago had it been since she'd pilfered that bottle of opiates from a pharmacy? The days ran together in an endless smudge of gray. For so long she'd had no food, no shelter, no money. Her life lay in ruins behind her, and there was no reason to go on. Anything of value had been stripped from her . . . she had been cast aside like so much debris.

You'd best take to your knees, Elena.

With the clarity of a tinkling bell, a voice she hadn't heard in more than a decade rang through the recesses of her memory. Accompanying the admonishment was a vivid picture in her mind's eye, causing her to recall the remarkable woman to whom the voice belonged.

Adeline Esmond had been a talented country healer as well as grandmother to one of her two best girlhood friends. After sustaining the loss of her daughter and son-in-law, the God-fearing widow had consequently raised their daughter, Olivia Plummer, near Elena's home in the outskirts of St. Louis.

Gentle, kindly Olivia, together with dark-haired Romy Schmitt, had been Elena's comrades from her earliest recollections. The three girls had been inseparable, passing many hours under Granny Esmond's watchful eye. Elena recalled that the older woman had done as much talking about Jesus and praying as these wimpled, gray-skirted sisters.

It had been much the same at the Schmitts'. She remembered Romy's mother as a nearly permanent fixture of her generous-sized farm kitchen, turning out hearty stews, mouthwatering pies, and golden brown biscuits. Whether family, guest, or hired hand, anyone who sat at Johanna Schmitt's table was fed well. Often lengthy prayers preceded mealtimes, filled with thanks for God's blessings, God's provision, and God's generosity. The Schmitts' reverence for the Lord seemed to penetrate every area of their lives.

It was hard to say which of the two homes was her favorite, Olivia's or Romy's. Both were warm and welcoming, a far cry from the dreary house Elena shared with her father and brothers. Her mother's death had changed the cheerless Breen dwelling into one in which Elena could hardly bear to live. Though neither Olivia nor Romy were ever so impolite to say so aloud, she knew they vastly preferred their own homes to hers.

Elena's father and three older brothers were unpleasant men. When her younger brother Gene, who had for much of her childhood been her friend and confidant, began following the example set forth by his older siblings, she viewed it the final familial betrayal, the justification that had propelled her out the door to seek a future of her own making.

A racking pain in her stomach caused her to draw her knees up to her chest and stifle a moan. Her arms and legs were cold, her movements weak, and her heart thudded slowly in her ears.

She recognized she was thirsty, but she would not ask for water. It would only prolong the inevitable.

"You suffer so greatly, little one, and yet you do not have to."

Sister Evangeline's words preceded the gentle sweep of her fingers across Elena's temple. "A few spoonfuls of soup would ease your distress and make your body ready to take more nourishment."

"No," Elena croaked, with a slight shake of her head.

"I do not even know your name, yet I worry for the state of your soul. I wonder if you would believe how much I have been praying for you. I see you try so hard not to look or listen, but I know there is a spark of life inside you still."

"My soul is dead." *And soon I will be too.*

A soft sigh soughed across Sister Evangeline's lips. Kneeling at the bedside, she reached beneath the blanket and took Elena's hands in her own. "Your flesh is as cold as winter itself. You are starving, you know."

Powerless to stop herself from opening her eyes, Elena was taken aback by the depth of feeling in her caregiver's dark gaze. It at once drew and held her, not allowing her to turn away.

"Would that I could rescue you from the fate you seem to be intent on accomplishing. But I must leave that to our almighty Father in heaven . . . and to the choices you must make."

"Why . . . do you care?" A curse upon the person or persons who had found her after she'd drunk the entire bottle of painkiller and brought her to the Benevolent Sisters of Mercy. Why hadn't she been allowed to die as she had wanted?

"I care because you are created in God's image, little one, and because he loves you most dearly. It grieves him to watch you destroy yourself."

"If God exists, he doesn't care about me." Acrimony dripped from Elena's words, which were surprisingly forceful despite her diminished physical state.

"Oh, but he does." Matching passion blazed in the sister's

bottomless gaze. "I assure you he exists and that he wants you—every bit of you—for he loves you in a way you do not understand." Drawing Elena's hands forward, she pressed a kiss upon her icy knuckles. "Tell me your name. Tell me how you came to be here, and perhaps I can help you."

Seeing, talking, feeling—these were things Elena had denied herself for so long now. Life didn't hold the same clout, she had learned, if one refused to engage these senses. But what was it about Sister Evangeline's eyes that held her? How did the middle-aged sister's voice have the power to cause such torture inside her?

"My name is Elena," she whispered despite her desire to die a nameless death. At this point, did it really matter? "And if you knew anything else about me, you wouldn't want to be holding my hand."

"Oh?" Sister Evangeline's eyebrows rose like the wings of a graceful bird. "Perhaps you would be so kind as to permit me to be the judge of that. Tell me, Elena, what has made your life so difficult?"

Though Elena had thought it impossible that she should cry ever again, moisture grew in her eyes, and a lump formed in her throat. And still she could not look away from the gaze that held her with an invisible potency.

"May I begin?" spoke the older woman. "I know you have borne a child. When I bathed you, I saw your mother's marks."

At that, a keening cry left Elena, and she was overcome by a wave of grief so intense she could scarcely bear its onslaught. When, some minutes later, she ascended from her anguish just enough to realize the small sister still held her hands, she tried pulling them away.

"No, no, dearest one," chided Sister Evangeline, her modest strength more than a match for Elena's weakened state. "Let me be your companion as you think of these things that hurt you so. You have lost your child, I take it?"

With a barely perceptible movement, Elena shook her head. Memories of little Bobby swam in her head . . . his head full of tousled blond curls, the sweet smell of his neck, the feel of his baby-soft cheek against hers. He was a year old the last time she'd seen him, toddling about on sturdy little legs. Four long years ago. How foolish she had been to travel to Detroit in the vain hope of seeing him one last time.

"I had no choice," she somehow uttered though her chest was so hollow it felt as if it might cave in.

A subtle sadness fell across the sister's countenance, yet it seemed as though the dark eyes regarded her with an increased measure of compassion. "Did you procure an abortion?"

"No, Sister." Elena's words were barely audible. "I gave him to his father."

There was more—much, much more that would never be told—but for some reason, Elena needed her benevolent caregiver to know that she could not harm a child of her own flesh.

"Ah, his father," Sister Evangeline repeated in an assessing manner. "I suppose you will not tell me his name."

"No." Elena's voice gained strength in her refusal. "It's better this way."

"Well, then tell me more about your life. Were you engaged in an occupation?"

"I sang." Elena could not help the bitterness that escaped with her words.

"A singer!"

"My voice was my curse," Elena interjected acridly, knowing the damage that had been done.

"How could a beautiful voice be a curse?"

"Because of it, I lost everything."

"Your son?"

"More than my son; I lost everyone and everything I ever cared about. And in the end, I lost my voice too. I can't sing anymore." She gave a short, humorless laugh. "Bobby's gone, and so is Jesse, and I no longer have any means to support myself. So please tell me, Sister, if you will, what reason I have to live."

"You live to display the glory of God."

Shocked by Sister Evangeline's bold, unhesitating words, Elena felt a flash of anger course through her, and she spat out an unclean phrase.

Sister Evangeline did not so much as flinch, not even when Elena snatched back her hands from the warm, comforting grasp. How could this religious woman dare to preach such nonsense when she had no idea what it was like to make her own way in the world? No doubt she had grown up in a stable, loving home, and from there gone straight to the shelter of the convent. Sister Evangeline didn't wonder where she would be sleeping any given night, nor where her next meal might come from.

It's not as if you didn't have choices, Elena, a dissenting voice spoke from inside her. *What about Olivia and Romy? You just stopped answering their letters. Why didn't you look them up and seek their help? You know either of them would have opened her door to you.*

And then there was Jesse. For just one second, though she had made repeated, regretful, sobbing promises to herself that she would never do so again, she permitted herself to think of him. In the next instant, as her heart was impaled by pain, she realized what an unwise decision she had once again made.

As she lay here in these abject surroundings, it seemed impossible to believe that she had ever been happy. In love. Beloved. Oh, how she had loved Jesse, and loved him still. She knew it would never be possible for him to understand why she'd had to leave him, but she hoped he might one day forgive her for doing so.

Though Jesse Golden had been a relative newcomer to the stage when she had met him, he possessed a natural theatrical presence and a well-trained tenor range. In just a short time, he went from being an unknown talent to one very much in demand by audiences.

At odds with that, however, was his pious upbringing. Elena learned he had pursued his stage career against the wishes of his widowed mother, and as time went on, she also became aware of how frequently he wrestled with the tenets of his faith on matters of morality. Once he became the father of little Bobby, this struggle inside him had only intensified.

For Elena, the months following Bobby's birth had been everything from wonderful to terrible. She knew other performers who managed to maintain stage identities while raising children, but frequent travel, rehearsals, and exhaustion took their toll on her . . . on Jesse . . . on them.

After a year of that, Jesse had decided he'd had enough. Casting aside his flourishing career in musical theater, he made plans for them to travel to Michigan, back to the home in which he'd been raised. He wanted to return to the faith of his upbringing, and he wanted that life for both her and their son as well.

Though Elena's belief in a loving God was dubious at best, she had not been opposed to leaving the stage and settling down. Yet in one dark moment, Stephen Villard, her manager, had effectively seen to it that she had no choice in the matter. None whatsoever. Jesse and the boy might go, but she would stay . . . for as long as he said. She was trapped, with no alternative, no way out.

Well, now she had her way out, and the last laugh had been on Villard, who had exploited her voice to such a degree that she had become worthless to him.

"Please go," she whispered, realizing Sister Evangeline continued to kneel beside her, regarding her with that limpid, humane gaze.

"I would leave you in exchange for six spoonfuls of broth."

"No."

"Five?"

"I will eat nothing. I want to die." With a deep sigh, Elena tore away her gaze and stared at the ceiling.

"I see a spark in you, dearest Elena, the tiniest little flame that burns yet within your heart. I do not know what happened with the father of your son, but your eyes revealed much when you spoke of your child. For him, I think, you would choose life."

"I'll never see him again."

"Sister Therese comes now with the soup kettle. Today you will try a few swallows."

Elena shook her head, the picture of Bobby's cherubic face fixed in her mind. Behind him was Jesse, his countenance filled with pain. Hotness burned in her eyes, and her heart felt as though it might rend in two. Surely death was the only answer to a suffering this great. *God, if you hear me, take my life.*

"Three little mouthfuls of soup," pressed the tender voice. After some moments, during which Elena did not reply, Sister Evangeline began singing a haunting melody, the purity of her tone surpassing any performance Elena had ever heard. The Latin words were unknown to her, but the humble passion of the sister's voice caused gooseflesh to raise on her arms. Curiously, though the pain in her heart did not diminish, it unfurled into an exquisite yearning . . . for what? Why did she hold her breath?

Remember, Elena?

This experience was not completely unknown to her. From the deepest alcoves of her being, she recalled memories of breaking bread at the Schmitts' supper table . . . of helping Olivia and Granny Esmond fold bandages. Their homes were different. *They* were different.

They had something she knew she could never have.

As the final notes of the sister's offering rose to the sooty, cracked ceiling and perhaps beyond, Elena became aware that the urge to fight this determined woman had left her.

"I will have one taste of your soup," she heard herself say, shocked and surprised because she had not planned on speaking at all, much less asking for anything to eat.

"Perhaps one will be so good, you will wish to enjoy two— or more," negotiated her caregiver, a smile hidden in her gentle banter.

Elena didn't reply as Sister Evangeline called to Sister Therese for a half cup of soup. A single spoonful wouldn't prolong her life even one day longer, she reasoned, so what was the harm in humoring this kindly stranger who had given her the gifts of her time, attention, and song?

Studying the ceiling, Elena renewed her resolve to depart this life. Overhead, the network of blackened cracks spanned nearly from wall to wall. If there was a way to view her heart, she was certain its appearance would be much the same. Soon it would be incapable of functioning, and her existence would come to an end.

She shivered as she waited for the spoon to be brought to her lips, wondering how much longer it would take to die.

❦

"Papa! Papa! There is a messenger at the door!"

"Get your nose out of the window, Master Robert," Frances Golden admonished from the kitchen, clucking her tongue. "A messenger? This time of the evening? Why, it's long past time for decent people to be indoors." With a sigh, she untied her apron and began pulling it over her head.

"I'll get the door, Mother," Jesse Golden replied, looking up from his writing at the dining-room table. "It could be about one of my plays. I've sent out several now."

"Well, if that's the case, I have serious reservations about anyone who would choose to contact you this time of night," she said with a pained expression, retying her apron.

Ruffling his son's blond curls as he walked past the window, Jesse wondered if possibly the messenger carried the kind of news a playwright longed to hear. After pouring his heart and creativity into writing nearly two dozen plays, he had yet to experience more than moderate success. Were the underlying themes of virtue and righteousness and faith in God too out of vogue for today's popular culture?

How many more rejections would it take before he could accept that he was yet again off course? To date, his life consisted of a series of wrong paths traveled. How many more times would he charge out headlong to follow his own plans, only to end up surrendering the wreckage to the Lord and praying belatedly for direction and grace? Would he never learn?

He was barely providing for his son and mother, and to do so he was rapidly depleting the savings he had accrued during his few years in the theater. As returning to that type of livelihood was not an option for him, he had begun quietly researching other types of employment.

To whom much is given, much is expected, his mother had admonished over the years, cautioning him to seek God's will in using his natural gifts and blessings. From his earliest years, Jesse knew his singing voice was one people loved hearing. His easy success in the theater only underscored that point, but it had also gone to his head, causing him to fall away, for a time, from his faith in Christ.

If nothing else, that experience had sparked his long-deferred longing to create, eclipsing even his desire to sing. He wanted to write plays that clearly proclaimed and honored God, envisioning how they would not only touch audiences but also the actors and actresses who performed them. He dreamed for his work to soften hearts, change lives, and even save souls.

Reaching the door, he sighed, remembering the first time he had seen Elena Breen and heard her magnificent voice. If he were to be completely honest with himself, he had to admit that after all that had passed between them, she still possessed a piece of his heart. His gaze traveled to Robert, their son, and he saw in him her eyes, her blonde curls, her infectious smile.

Though it hurt less to think of Elena these days, it still hurt. Where was she? he wondered. What had become of her? Did she still believe that she was the master of her own destiny, and that God, if he existed, didn't care a bit about her? He prayed for Elena every night, and somehow through the years his pain and anger had faded to . . . acceptance.

"Mr. Jesse Golden?" inquired the deliveryman, who was really a boy scarcely old enough to shave his chin.

"Yes," Jesse replied, reaching into his pocket for a few coins as the youth handed him the envelope. "Thank you."

"What does it say, Papa?" Robert asked, scarcely before he'd closed the door.

"I don't know yet, Robert."

"Do you want me to read it for you? Nana says I am reading very well now."

"You are, indeed," Jesse agreed, kneeling down to enfold
his son in his embrace. "But I believe I will read this letter for
myself."

"What does it say?" called his mother, walking into the
room still drying a glass. Despite her gruff words a few minutes
earlier, a mixture of hope and maternal pride shone in her oval
face. Flushed by the heat of the kitchen, her cheeks were tinted
pink, making her seem like a young, excited girl.

"It says . . ." Jesse began, trailing off as he withdrew the
paper from the envelope and began to read.

"Papa! You're reading inside your head. We want you to
read out loud," Robert protested, tugging on the leg of Jesse's
trousers, with no objection coming from Nana Frances about his
behavior.

"Jesse?" came his mother's voice a few moments later,
slightly hesitant. "Do you have some good news to share with
us?"

"I . . . I'm going to have to go out for a while," he finally
managed to say, looking at his mother, though not really seeing
her.

"What is it, Jess?" she asked, sympathy filling her blue eyes.

"I'll be a few hours, I imagine," he said numbly, knowing
the tenderness in her expression would vanish if he were to
speak of the letter's contents. Reaching for his coat, he added, "If
you want to wait up for me, I'll have more information when I
get back."

"Papa, where are you going?" Robert called, looking back
and forth between his father and grandmother with confusion.

"I need to attend to some business, Robert," Jesse replied.
"Will you be the man of the house while I'm away and make
sure things run smoothly for Nana?"

"Yes, Papa," Robert dutifully replied, going to his grandmother's side. Her hand settled around his shoulder, then moved up to cup his cheek.

"Good night, then," Jesse bid, turning away and stepping out into the night. The letter he'd received burned in his hand, while the name *Elena* roared through his mind and heart like a firestorm.

Chapter 2

Jesse stood in the vestibule of the small hospital, the smell of sickness threatening the tenuous strand of composure to which he clung. A wimpled sister wearing a dark gray habit had answered the bell and let him in, then bidden him to wait for yet another sister, the one who had written the letter. Pulling the envelope from his vest pocket, he withdrew the folded paper and read the words yet one more time.

> *Dear Mr. Golden,*
>
> *I am not certain you are the gentleman I seek, and I beg your forgiveness for troubling you if I am in error. However, there is a patient at our hospital who speaks of her son, Bobby, with such sadness and longing. She will not tell me more than her first name, Elena, and that she once sang for her living. If you have knowledge of this woman, I pray you will do whatever our heavenly Father would impress upon your heart.*

It was signed by a Sister Evangeline, followed by the name and address of the hospital in which he now stood.

Oh, Ellie. To what end have you come?

After replacing the missive in his breast pocket, he quickly wiped his eyes with his handkerchief and tucked that away as well. Beyond the doorway that led deeper into the hospital, he heard cries and groans. Was one of them Elena's? The very thought pierced his heart. Why was she here?

He pulled in a deep sigh and released it, allowing himself to glance around the area in which he stood. A shabby, unattended desk and chair sat against one wall of the entry. The walls were clean and white, adorned by only a simple, wooden crucifix and a pair of wall sconces that cast dim light.

"Good evening, Mr. Golden. I'm Sister Evangeline. I didn't expect you this quickly," a smooth female voice greeted him.

Turning, Jesse took in the small woman. The cloth covering her head, chin, and neck matched the plain dark fabric of her robes, exposing only the pale features of her face. How old was she? At first glance, it was impossible to determine whether she was in her twenties, thirties, or even forties.

"I have not yet prepared Elena for the possibility of your visit," Sister Evangeline went on, clasping her hands before her. Pausing, she sought his gaze and held it for a long moment. "It also saddens me to inform you of her grave condition."

Grave condition? Jesse felt another blow strike his heart. His Ellie could be lots of things—stubborn, determined, even downright disagreeable—but she was always strong. He used to marvel at her command of will, until her independent nature had been the object of their destruction.

"What's happened to her?"

"Undernourishment, starvation, despair . . . attempted suicide."

The sister's directness penetrated Jesse's sense of unreality like sharpened arrows. Elena starving? He only vaguely heard the rest of the woman's words as he pictured Elena when he'd last seen her; she had been thriving. With her new stage name, lavish costumes, and burgeoning popularity, she had appeared to be in need of no one or nothing. Keeping track of her had been a desperate and foolish thing to do, and finally he'd stopped searching the papers for her name, realizing how much pain it caused him. Yet secretly a part of him continued hoping she'd come back one day, if not for his sake, for Robert's.

"Mr. Golden?"

The sister's concerned tone helped him refocus his attention on the present. He was grateful she continued on, for he feared if he were to try speaking, words would fail him.

"When I learned Elena had a son, I suspected she had come to the city of Detroit because he lived here. I made a number of inquiries before I found someone who recalled your Elena, or Ellie, as she was later known. It's odd. Her link to you was not well remembered and was more difficult to search out. I do not travel out into the world often, but it seems to me, Mr. Golden, that the theater is a fickle business."

Despite his painful emotional state, a wry smile twisted Jesse's lips, and he gazed at the kind-spoken sister with frank respect. "You have made a wise and accurate observation, dear lady."

"I learned you were once an actor yourself."

"I was." Jesse nodded, feeling his throat tighten. "And I learned that if a man's not careful," he said slowly, "that kind of life can swallow him whole. He might compromise anything he's ever held dear."

Sister Evangeline nodded. "Yes, I imagine so. But don't think that sort of thing happens only in the theater. Our little hospital is filled with women whose lives have borne out the truth of your statement."

"What has Elena told you?" he questioned, suddenly desperate for information. "Where has she been?"

"She has told me next to nothing about herself, only that she wants to die."

"She wants to . . . *die?*" he repeated, incredulous, numbly recalling that the sister had already told him Ellie had tried taking her own life.

Sister Evangeline's ageless features assumed an expression of profound sorrow. "Such is the case with many of our patients.

Either they have forgotten or have not ever known the One in whose precious image they were made."

"Can I see her?"

The wimpled head bowed in assent, and the sister turned. "Follow me."

Jesse observed that the lighting in the large, open hospital room was as dim as the vestibule. The building was well past its prime, and though the sisters no doubt made every effort to keep their infirmary as neat and clean as possible, its age and shabbiness showed. Too, the reek in here was worse: sickness, elimination, and the smell of decay mingled together in an odious bouquet that defied description. Jesse found himself taking shallow breaths through his lips, resisting the temptation to clap his handkerchief over his mouth and nose.

At least a score of iron beds stood in two neat rows. For each two beds there sat a small table between them, and about the room were scattered a few simple, wooden chairs. By no means was there a chair for each bed, and he wondered how many of the women here had visitors.

Moving with grace down the center aisle, Sister Evangeline led him to the space between the feet of two beds, then stopped. In the shadows, he could not read her expression, but he imagined her eyes were filled with the same compassion she had shown when she told him of Elena's dire condition.

When a loud howling set forth, he nearly jumped out of his skin. Sister Evangeline held up a finger, motioning him to wait, then proceeded to the head of one of the beds before them. Surely that wasn't Elena . . . was it? Her once-lovely voice sounded like something inhuman. Not able to help himself, Jesse slowly walked forward and peered over the sister's shoulder.

A face—a rictus, really—covered with dark sores stared back at him, and he recoiled in horror. *Ellie?* Bile rose in his throat, and he took a step backward. He was ready to turn and flee when a weak voice hit his ears.

"Jesse?"

At first he wasn't sure he'd heard his name at all, and so

continued backing away from the woman whose cries were slowly beginning to fade. Yet between the widening cycles of her shrieks, he again heard the one-word question, this time a little louder, from the bed to the left.

He stopped, his heart pounding as it never had before, then took a tentative step forward.

A woman, her pale hair hanging like a hag's, stared at him from the bed opposite the screeching woman. Everything inside Jesse rallied against acknowledging that this woman bore any resemblance to the Elena he once knew, but he knew at once it was Ellie.

It *was* her.

Her face was painfully thin, making her once-expressive dark brown eyes appear as enormous black sockets in the face of a living skeleton. From beneath the covers, a matchstick-thin lower arm appeared, bony fingers reaching toward him. Again she spoke his name, with incredulity and disbelief, as she tried raising her head from the pillow. The small effort appeared to be too much for her.

"It's me," he said, kneeling beside her and taking the icy cold hand in his own.

"Oh, Jesse. I thought I was dreaming. Am I in heaven?" A soft expression crossed her face, reminding him of the days when their love had been enough to overcome any obstacle.

Heaven? The sights, smells, and sounds of this place were surely reminiscent of just the opposite. Beside them, Sister Evangeline began singing a hymn, the splendor of her pure voice underscoring the dichotomy of beauty and ugliness, dreams and nightmares, and heaven and hell.

"Sometimes I hate it when she sings." The gentleness of Elena's voice was replaced by an almost brittle tone.

"What?" Shock wave after shock wave continued coursing through Jesse as he tried to take in the realities before him. Elena's eyes had closed, and her face was filled with pain until Sister Evangeline finished singing. Mercifully, the patient in the next bed quieted.

A moment later, Elena opened her eyes and repeated her initial question: "Jesse?"

"Yes, Ellie."

"Are you really here?" Elena's voice, once her striking hallmark, was now flat and dull.

"He is, indeed," Sister Evangeline spoke, having approached silently with one of the wooden chairs, which she set behind Jesse. "And you have me to either thank or hate for that."

"You never give up, do you?" Elena asked, her eyes darting to her caregiver while Jesse painfully straightened from his crouched position and took a seat in the chair. Despite Elena's weakened state, he noticed that her fingers did not loosen their grip upon his hand even a bit.

This was so far from how he imagined they might again one day meet as to be laughable. As a playwright, he would have a hard time surpassing such a scene in his own work. Elena Breen, the indomitable, fair-haired darling of the boards, lay in weakness and poverty, yearning for death. How could this be? What had happened in the years since their parting? Guilt overwhelmed him, and he wondered how things would have been different if he had found a way to convince her to leave the stage, as he had. Had he truly tried hard enough, or had he allowed his feelings of rejection to grow into stubbornness and pride?

"This isn't your fault," Elena whispered dully as Sister Evangeline moved away. How was it possible she still had the same knack of sensing his thoughts, even after all this time apart?

"Ellie, I don't—"

"Shh," she interrupted, clutching his hand even harder. "For whatever it's worth, I'm sorry. I made the wrong choice."

His heart contracted at the desolation of her words, at the desperation of her situation.

Without inflection, she continued. "I'll soon be gone, and that's for the best."

"Don't talk like that, Ellie," he cried, too loudly he knew, but unable to moderate his tone.

Her hand loosened, then slipped from his. "Please tell Bobby his mama loves him."

Was it his imagination, or did her voice catch slightly when she spoke Robert's name? With the back of his sleeve, he wiped his eyes and peered more closely into her face. Despite the firm set of her emaciated features, moisture shimmered in the inner corners of her eyes.

"Did you ever love me?" he whispered in return, his gaze searching her face.

"Don't." Her eyes squeezed shut, the dewdrop tears glinting like jewels in the dim light.

As he leaned over her, the scents of her body rose to him, a mixture of familiar and unfamiliar, pleasant and unpleasant. The aroma of lye soap lingered about her. Once she had smelled of damask roses, heady and sweet.

"Don't what? Don't ask? I need to know, Ellie." As if four years had not passed, the pain of their parting came back with stabbing freshness. His voice broke. "Why? I need to know why."

A sob shook Elena, and her face contorted in agony.

"Did you ever love me?" he asked again, his voice raw, determined to have an answer to the question that had tortured him for more than a thousand days and nights.

"Yes" came a reply as pitiful and mewling as a kitten's cry.

"So you love Robert, and you're telling me you once loved me." His words ragged, Jesse persisted, needing to know that she spoke the truth.

"Yes," she cried hopelessly. "Now . . . please . . . go away. Let me . . . die."

"I'm afraid I can't do that," he said, taking her face in his hands.

"Why not?" Elena wailed, becoming more agitated. Her breath came in jagged, irregular gasps.

Jesse felt a light touch at his shoulder and turned quickly to see Sister Evangeline standing behind him. He knew his and

Elena's exchange was far from silent or private, and though he was upsetting Ellie and most likely other patients in the hospital, he had to keep going. Had to finish.

God Almighty, give me the strength.

"I can't let you die, Elena, because your son needs his mother."

"No! Leave me! Let me go!"

Though her words were reminiscent of her rejection of him four years earlier, he steeled himself against their serrated power.

"I can't let you die, Elena, because your son needs his mother," he said once again, bending so his face was only inches above her own. Beneath his fingertips her once-silky strands of hair were as coarse as straw, and her skin had lost its characteristic softness. Despite that, he continued, the vow and declaration he had once taken reverberating through his mind with increasing volume and clarity.

"Mr. Golden," Sister Evangeline cautioned, but Jesse pressed on quickly, before he lost the only remaining chance he would ever have.

"And I *won't* let you die, Elena, because you need your husband . . . and he needs you."

Chapter 3

The mantel clock struck twelve-thirty. In the stillness particular to this time of night, the tone of the last chime lingered on, fading slowly in Frances Golden's ears while she wondered how many more times the clock would strike before Jesse returned.

The house was dark except for a wall lamp burning in the sitting room, positioned above the chair in which she sat. Upon the oval table beside the chair rested her embroidery basket and the recent piece she had been stitching; in her lap lay a Bible, opened to the Psalms. Upstairs, Robert slept in his bed, sweetly oblivious to the fact that his father had not yet come home.

Sighing, Frances rubbed her hand across her eyes and tried once more to pray. It was useless to stitch, useless to read; she couldn't concentrate on either. Why did such a persistent feeling of doom cling to her? With her whole heart, she believed Jesse's repentance was true, and she believed he wouldn't do anything to jeopardize the son he loved so dearly. His short-lived occupation as an actor was a thing of the past, as was his affiliation with Elena.

She knew it was wrong to pin the entirety of Jesse's spiritual lapse upon one woman—especially one whom she had never met—yet she firmly believed if not for his dalliance with Elena Breen, he might have reclaimed his senses much more quickly.

Heaven above, her son had fathered a child with a theater woman of easy virtue and then, as a fool throws good money after bad, he'd married her.

Frances held no disappointment that Jesse hadn't brought Elena with him when he'd left the stage. In those first months after returning home, he had sorrowed bitterly over his wife's desertion of their marriage. In some ways, watching Jesse had brought back a shadow of the grief she'd experienced almost ten years before that time, when Gerald, her husband, had taken sick and died.

But whereas Gerald had been a God-fearing man and a faithful husband, deserving of a lengthy period of bereavement, Elena had evidently valued fame and its trappings over the noble callings of marriage and motherhood. She was not worthy of Jesse's grief, and Frances had prayed earnestly that whatever enchantment Elena held over Jesse would soon dissipate so he could reestablish himself and make a new life.

Making things more difficult was the towheaded, brown-eyed toddler who had come home with her son. Jesse's older sister, Sara, had already given Frances two grandchildren whom she loved more than she could put into words. In those early days, she wondered if she could feel the same about little Robert, whose flesh and blood came half from a capricious woman of the stage.

Despite her fears, it had taken no time at all for her and Robert to fall deeply in love with one another. While she knew it wasn't true, it soon became easy to believe that her youngest grandson had been created by Jesse alone.

Lately though, Robert had been asking many questions about his real mother. Frances tried persuading Jesse to tell Robert that Elena had died, but Jesse had put his foot down when she'd suggested the idea. "I don't know what I'm going to say, but I'm not going to lie to him," he'd averred in a manner that didn't invite reply.

"Maybe it's the truth," she'd reasoned again just last month. "She could be dead. We don't know anything about her.

Or do you know something?" she'd asked, sudden alarm going through her. One of her recurrent fears was that he would search Elena out; another was that he remained secretly in contact with her.

"No, Mother," Jesse had reassured her, "I haven't heard anything of Ellie in two years."

Ellie.

How Frances hated it when Jesse referred to Elena by that diminutive. After he and Elena had married, they had invented a new stage name for Elena: Ellie Lundeen. It had been against the advice of Elena's manager that Elena take Jesse's last name, so Jesse had written that he'd suggested Frances's maiden name, Lundeen, as a way for Elena to possess a name of his family heritage, yet keep peace with Elena's manager.

Frances still remembered the postmark of the envelope Jesse had sent informing her of this travesty: Denver, Colorado. She also recalled flying into a rage and having broken three plates and five glasses, not to mention bruising her foot because she had kicked the kitchen door with all her might.

If it hadn't been disturbing enough to know that her only son was squandering his God-given singing talents while living a life of debauchery, it was all the more upsetting to know that the woman who had given birth to a full-sized male infant six months after her marriage to Jesse now possessed Frances's heretofore unsullied maiden name. The thought could still make her blood boil.

Peace, dearest Lord, she prayed silently, letting out a long, steady breath. *I pray that you will fill me with your peace while I wait for Jesse to return. Please keep him safe. I lost him once to the enemy of this world, but you were faithful and saved him from the coils that had entangled his feet. Most gracious Father, I beseech you to set Jesse squarely on the course you have planned for him. Please reveal to him the perfection of your will for his life and—*

From the quiet street outside came the clip-clop of a team of horses and the clatter of a conveyance. She had not known where Jesse had gone, nor by what means he had traveled to his destination. Quickly, she set the Bible aside and hastened to the window, where she pulled apart the curtains and peered out in the very same manner for which she had earlier chastened Robert.

A carriage-and-two had stopped in front of their house, partially illuminated by its pair of hanging lanterns. Jesse didn't immediately alight the vehicle, and a few moments later, the figure seated at the reins climbed down and went to its door.

Fear gripped Frances by the throat. Was Jesse ill? injured? Amidst these awfulties another appalling suspicion clawed at her mind, one that led back to the nightmare of months when Jesse wantonly pursued a path of moral destruction. What if the message he'd received this evening had induced him to drown his sorrows at a local pub? Oh, heavens, what if he was drunk?

Heart pounding, Frances went to the front door and turned open the lock. The autumn air was cool, but she scarcely felt its chill while she observed Jesse's familiar form back out of the cab, carrying something large in both arms.

Without another thought, she was out the door and down the front walk. To her horror, she recognized that the thing supported by Jesse's strong arms was a human being. Her shock intensified as he turned and a fair-haired head lolled against his chest.

Her son carried a woman, and in the split second it took for her brain to register that information, she knew down to the soles of her feet that the woman's identity was Elena Breen.

"No," she whispered, bringing her hands to her face. "Oh no," she repeated, louder. "Jesse, no!"

"Yes, Mother, I'd like to introduce my wife, Elena," Jesse affirmed in a low voice. "She's quite ill, so if you'd be so kind to go indoors and turn down my bed, I'll be right behind you. I've already paid the driver."

Turn down his bed?

Speechless, Frances stared at the wan, blanket-swathed figure in her son's arms a moment longer before fleeing back into the house. As she ascended to the second story in the dark, she was unable to hold back the scalding tears that ran down her cheeks in torrents.

Elena was here.

For the past four years, Frances had lived with the secret fear that Robert's mother would one day appear. Adding to her worry was the fact that Jesse had never sought to have his marriage dissolved. Not that she believed in divorce, but surely some godly provision existed for a state of affairs such as this.

Reaching Jesse's room, Frances fumbled for the matches and managed to get the lamp lit. Already her son's heavy steps were nearly at the top of the staircase, and she turned down the covers just as he entered the room. Swiftly he moved to the bed and laid down his blanket-wrapped bundle.

A soft moan issued from the pitiful-looking woman, whose skin draped over her bones like a poor-quality fabric. Despite her shock and distress, Frances was flabbergasted at the so-called beautiful Elena Breen that had bewitched her handsome son. This woman bore no resemblance whatsoever to the description Jesse had written home of his wife.

Taking a half step closer, Frances noted that the creature in the bed appeared old before her time. How did Elena's color manage the feat of looking both pasty and blotchy at once? she wondered. An unpleasant odor emanated from the bed, and Frances dreaded to think of the disease and vermin Jesse had just carried into their home. A soft moan issued from the woman, and from his knees, Jesse soothed, "Just rest. You're home now, Ellie."

The gentle words her son spoke to that . . . that . . . unspeakable being struck Frances with the force of a blow, rupturing each and every one of her dreams for the future. Home? What would having Elena here mean for Jesse? for Robert? What would the neighbors say? their church community?

Each thought caused an invisible cinch around her chest to clamp more tightly, until the final conclusion robbed her of the ability to breathe: Jesse expected her to live under the same roof with the very woman who had beguiled him along a path of wickedness and sin.

Maybe she'll die.

The callous thought flitted across Frances's mind, at once horrifying her and giving her a fragment of hope to which to cling. Her eyes swept again over what she could see of Elena's appearance, finding the younger woman in dire health, indeed. Dull blonde hair hung in untidy hanks about her face, and the arm that had worked its way out of the covers appeared nearly skeletal. Surely a person so debilitated was not long for this world.

Elena said something then, her voice too low for Frances to make out the words, but from Jesse's reply, she ascertained that Elena had asked about Robert. Her son would visit her tomorrow, he replied, his words stirring fierceness in Frances's breast.

Slipping from the room, she found herself shaking with anger. What was Jesse thinking? How could he have done this to their family? Never would her grandson have a moment's exposure to an individual such as Elena Breen, even if she was his mother.

Never.

※

Elena's slow ascent toward wakefulness began with the familiar, deep aching in her joints, her belly, even her skin . . . yet at the same time, something was different. Even before she opened her eyes, the stillness of her surroundings struck her. Had Screeching Beth passed during the night? Where was the bustle and movement of the industrious sisters, the metal clank of the breakfast cart?

Taking a breath, she shifted slightly, noticing that her thin cot felt almost plush. Too, rather than irritating her throbbing flesh, the scratchy wool blanket seemed instead to caress her skin, its warmth releasing the warm, familiar fragrance of . . . Jesse?

Opening her eyes to the colorless tones of early morning, she was perplexed to view not the high windows and cracked ceiling of the hospital but the appearance of a modest-sized bedchamber. And slumped over in a chair beside her bed was the sleeping form of the very man about whom she so often dreamed.

She watched as he breathed, restful and even, wondering what new, cruel trick her mind was playing upon her. Long ago she used to gaze upon Jesse as he slumbered. Yes, she had marveled at his rugged male beauty, but more so at the concept that he loved her. Jesse Golden was a man like no other she'd ever known. Highly principled, kindhearted, considerate, self-less. And though he tried to deny it for a period of time, he was God-fearing as well.

What had he ever seen in someone like her?

Infatuations between people of the stage were as common-place as dandelions in the spring. Over the years, she had been plied with many ardent declarations and stolen kisses, but from the first moment she glimpsed Jesse and heard his marvelous tenor, she knew he was destined to be more than a passing fancy in her life. In fact, during their several months together, he—and tiny Bobby, their son—had touched the deepest places of her heart.

Many times she had asked herself if it was because Jesse had insisted upon wedding her once he'd learned she was preg-nant. Such gallantry did not exist in the circles she traveled, nor did men such as himself. She should never have allowed him to compromise himself in such a way, but she'd had such naive hopes that together they could overcome any obstacles they might face.

As it turned out, their love had not been strong enough to withstand the problems that pressed in on them from every side. Though Jesse doubtlessly believed she had fallen out of love with him or had never loved him at all, just the opposite was true. She loved him still. Insisting that he and Bobby leave the theater without her was the hardest thing she had ever done, but she knew they would both be better off for it.

Jesse was a good man . . . and she was what she was. When

he'd married her, he'd accepted that she did not hold with the idea of a loving Creator, nor did she have any interest in seeking the kind of faith her friends Olivia and Romy had possessed. Long ago, perhaps she had been willing to believe there was a God who answered prayers, but the events of her life had borne out just the opposite.

Then, after Bobby was born, Jesse had begun to wrestle with morals and principles so unfamiliar to her way of thinking as to be completely foreign. Though he swore he did not regret marrying her or having Bobby, he expressed remorse for having walked away from his devotion to Jesus Christ, likening himself to the prodigal son in the Bible. His pleasure of performing paled, and he began yearning to return to Detroit, to his home and family, and to his church.

How a man who regularly sent money to his widowed mother could regard himself dissolute was beyond her, but Elena was aware of the interior battle stirring—then raging—inside him. She'd also seen some of the letters Mrs. Golden had written, exhorting her son, in no uncertain terms, to repent of his wicked pursuits and pastimes. Though Jesse had never said so, Elena had no doubt Mrs. Golden considered her the root of Jesse's degeneration.

From what her husband had told her, it sounded as if their backgrounds were as different as night and day. Jesse and his older sister, Sara, had been raised in a stable, loving household in the city. Elena's upbringing had been rural, her domestic unit far from harmonious. Whereas Jesse talked about his home with a certain wistfulness, Elena had never once entertained a thought of returning to St. Louis. She had no idea if her father was still living or what had become of her brothers. In fact, she hoped each of them was roasting in hell, if there was such a place.

"Elena?"

The sleeping figure in the chair was no longer asleep. Jesse's blue eyes were open, regarding her with concern. Wrinkles furrowed his brow, and he reached out to touch her arm. "Do you remember anything about last night?" he questioned gently.

Last night? Closing her eyes, Elena breathed in deeply, wondering what type of delirium she suffered. Jesse couldn't be here . . . yet he seemed so real. In most of her dreams he looked the same as he did when they'd met, but in this dream he looked older and sadder, which made her feel sad as well.

"Sister Evangeline warned me you might not remember anything," the soothing, familiar voice went on, causing her to open her eyes again. He was still there in the chair; in fact, his whole body leaned toward her.

"Are you really Jesse?" she rasped, feeling the warmth of his hand on her arm.

A pensive smile crossed his face, and he nodded. "I brought you home from the hospital last night."

Home?

"And now that you've slept—much better than I did, I might add—it's time for some nourishment. Sister recommended you start with broth or a thin gruel." His troubled gaze dropped to her forearm after he'd explained how he had found her. "I'm also hoping to have Dr. Schrantz come by and look at you before the day is out."

Self-consciousness replaced disbelief as Elena's line of sight followed Jesse's. She was gaunt, ragged, ugly. Though her mind raced, it was at the same time foggy, her memory incomplete. Frustration grew, yet she was so weak that she could do nothing.

"Why?" she whispered, helpless tears filling her eyes.

"Because the doctor might have some medicine or advice that will help you get better more quickly."

"No," she whispered, trying to shake her head, wishing she could ask him a hundred questions all at once. Especially about Bobby.

"You don't want to get better?" he asked, misunderstanding.

Or did he understand more than she thought?

"Ellie," his voice caressed, bringing back memories of happier times, "no matter what's happened, the loss of your life is no kind of answer." His brows drew together, and he shook his head. "As your husband, I take full responsibility for your condition. I'm sorry, Elena, so sorry. It was wrong of me to walk away from you four years ago, no matter how much you insisted I do just that. I hope one day you can forgive me for failing you."

He thought everything was his fault? that he'd failed her? He couldn't be more wrong. Stephen Villard had been in control of her destiny, bringing her to nothing but ruin. She never should have married Jesse, burdening such a good man with problems and responsibilities he didn't deserve. She licked her dried-out lips and tried to speak, but he gently set a finger across her mouth.

"If my memory serves me, I know you're about to disagree. Allow me to finish; then you may say what's on your mind."

Elena remained silent while he moved his finger from her lips.

"Last night you admitted that you once cared about me." While her eyes grew wide with shock, he continued. "The good Lord willing, there will be plenty of time to discuss what went wrong between us, but this morning, we're starting anew." With a sigh, he released her hand and stood. "For a time I cast aside what I'd learned as a boy. Instead of making decisions based on Christian principles and prayerful discernment, I lived some years doing as I pleased. In my selfishness, I acquired a wife, whom I have failed to provide for and protect, and a son, whom I have protected, yet I have failed to provide for him a most essential ingredient of boyhood—his mother."

With scarcely a breath, he went on. "During the time we dwelt together as man and wife, Elena, we lived according to the world. I don't know what the years have done to your doubts of a loving heavenly Father, but no matter whether you believe or not, as a Christian husband I must now submit our marriage to him."

Before Elena's incredulous eyes, Jesse knelt at the bedside and took her hand. "Most holy and merciful Lord," he entreated, right before her, "this prayer is long overdue. I can't thank you enough for leading me to Elena before it was too late. Please heal her, and restore her to good health. Father, apart from you we are feeble creatures. Even together, Ellie and I were still not strong. We need you, for a threefold cord is not quickly broken. I acknowledge our weakness and sin, and our utter dependence upon you, and I ask your sovereignty over our lives and our marriage. Please forgive us for all our transgressions and give us your blessing. Amen."

During Jesse's prayer, Elena resisted the initial rush of softness that rose inside her at his plea for her recovery, allowing embarrassment and indignation at the remainder of his words to blend together in a flare of anger. He called her weak and sinful, then had the gall to ask God to forgive her? She opened her mouth to protest, but he was still not finished.

"We need to pray together every day, Ellie," he resolved, managing the feat of appearing earnest at the same time he issued his preposterous decree.

He wanted to pray with her every day? Did he think that because he'd rescued her, he could tell her what to do and when to do it? At that moment, her stomach contracted painfully, preventing her from telling him that he presumed too much.

His dark eyes filled with tenderness. "I'll see about your breakfast right away."

Three soft knocks, in rapid succession, came from the door.

"That will be my mother," he said softly to Elena before looking away, the sudden, subtle tension on his features speaking volumes about her mother-in-law's reaction to her presence.

The door opened a few inches, but Mrs. Golden did not enter. Instead, Jesse went to the narrow aperture and spoke with his mother in quiet tones. Elena could not make out the older woman's words, but the rapid flurry of speech followed by a sharp sigh only confirmed her mother-in-law's displeasure.

The door closed with no gentleness. The sound of retreating footsteps followed, becoming more faint as their owner, Elena guessed, descended a set of stairs.

"Mother is going to make you some gruel," Jesse said, turning back toward her. His shoulders no longer held the same proud bearing as they had when he'd sworn his—and her—fealty to the unseen God, and on his handsome face rested both worry and weariness.

A stirring of sympathy softened her antagonism toward Jesse and his high-handed new ideas. Struggling to rise, Elena succeeded only in lifting her head from the pillow. "I don't belong here. Take me back to the hospital."

"No, Ellie, I won't. You do belong here."

"Your mother doesn't want me."

"For now, that may be true," he allowed with a slight nod, "but your son would give up every one of his prized possessions for the chance to meet you. He's been asking so many questions . . ."

Her son. At the mention of Bobby, Elena's breath caught in her throat, and she imagined what her cherubic little boy must look like now.

"As soon as you're feeling up to it—"

"No," she forced out, her heart splintering with each successive word. "Take me away before he knows I was here."

"Ellie!" Jesse cried, shocked.

"Papa?" a reed-thin voice came from outside the door. "Papa, who are you talking to?"

Before Jesse could answer, the door opened, and a tousle-haired child peered inside. "Hello," he said to Elena, staring at her with unabashed curiosity. "Are you sick?"

"Master Robert, you are to stay away from your father's room!" a woman's voice reprimanded, growing closer as sharp heels clicked against wood in a furious tempo. "Come away from there immediately."

"Yes, Nana," he replied, sucking in a little breath as he glanced anxiously over his shoulder. Before departing, he looked once more at Elena, then quickly at his father, his eyes as large as chocolate candy buttons, before pulling the door closed and scampering away.

A tongue-lashing followed for the boy, muted by the solid plaster walls.

"Excuse me for a few minutes." Jesse moved quickly toward

the door, unease written on his face. "I . . . I'll be back soon with your breakfast."

In short order, the rumble of his deep voice had quieted the infuriated tones of his mother. Soul sickness gripped Elena as she wondered if Bobby was frequently subjected to this sort of attack. Worse yet, what if the woman boxed his ears or whipped him? The memory of his precious little face framed in the doorway would haunt her until she drew her last breath.

How could you have given up your son?

Regret and despair slashed through her vitals as a burning tear escaped her right eye. What had Jesse been thinking to bring her here? A woman who abandoned her family was not a fit mother, no matter what kind of pie-in-the-sky hopes her jilted husband entertained. As much as it hurt to realize, she knew Bobby would be better off with his father and harsh-sounding grandmother than he ever would with her.

As she had while in the hospital, Elena wondered how much longer it would take to die. She would refuse to eat, and it would soon be over.

What will your death do to Jesse? to Bobby?

Fresh pain mounted atop her agony, causing her to curl up on her side. Everything would have been easier if she hadn't seen Bobby, and if he hadn't seen her. Despite that, she ached to take the little boy in her arms and bury her face in those soft blond curls.

Why did you do this to me, Jesse? she cried from her heart. *Seeing you and Bobby hurts so much, and all I want is to stop hurting. I don't want to feel anymore. Why did you bring me here?*

Why, indeed? With all the time and pain separating them, why did he have any sort of desire to save her? Had he removed her from the hospital merely out of duty? obligation? Did he remain the dashing and flirtatious man with whom she had fallen in love, or was he now a zealot preoccupied with matters of God and guilt, trying to make good on a bad pledge? This morning he'd spoken of marriage and healing and togetherness, but he had not said he loved her. Not once.

Love! What did you expect? You're filthy and sick . . . and four years ago you rejected him, your child, and his God.

Another tear formed as she thought of his prayer. Jesse on his knees, beseeching an unknowable deity on their behalf, had unaccountably evoked the memory of Olivia's grandmother. A full half of all of Granny Esmond's speech had been directed to the Almighty, as if he stood invisibly right in the room.

Jesse came in then, interrupting her thoughts. How was it possible that the very sight of him still caused her heart to skip a beat? Shame washed through her as she considered who was the better person. She didn't deserve the concern she read on his features, nor any of his ministrations.

"Jesse," she began weakly. "I—"

"Shh. Robert's having his breakfast, none the worse for his wear." He took his seat in the chair beside the bed, holding a spoon and a steaming mug in his hands. His smile held only a trace of its former brilliance, and she noticed that his eyes were sad. "Your son possesses an insatiable curiosity," he went on, taking sudden interest in stirring the contents of the cup, "which, at times, can be a bit trying for my mother."

He sighed. "We agreed that it might be better for Robert to become acquainted with you once you've regained your health." Hesitantly he looked up, seeking her gaze.

Mrs. Golden had no doubt put her foot down about allowing Bobby to see his mother. Closing her eyes, Elena nodded, the pain of thinking . . . of living . . . of being . . . simply too much to bear.

Once she had feared death, but now she discovered she feared living all that much more.

Chapter 4

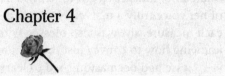

"Thank you for coming so promptly, Doctor. You've given us a great deal of hope for Ellie's recovery." Standing before the front door, Jesse shook the physician's hand. A cold autumn wind buffeted the house, rattling the windowpanes.

"Yes, it's good you found her when you did. A day or two hence could well have been too late." The older man buttoned his coat and pushed his hat firmly upon his balding head. His blue eyes regarded Jesse with compassion. "I'll stop by in a few days and see how things are coming. If you follow my directions, chances are that in two weeks' time you'll have a whole different woman on your hands."

After the door closed behind Dr. Schrantz, Jesse allowed himself to wonder just what kind of woman he *did* have on his hands. Once he'd believed he'd known everything about Elena Breen, but later events had proven that supposition false. Who was this woman to whom he'd promised his life . . . and with whom he'd created a child?

Was it wrong to hope that the vibrant, dazzling singer with whom he had fallen in love awaited him beneath the cloak of illness and deprivation? Ellie's mischievous grin and effervescent personality had captivated him from the moment he'd glimpsed her at his first audition. Being cast opposite Elena in *If Not for*

You had been an incredible experience in many respects, and he'd promptly fallen for the delicate-featured leading lady who possessed a voice like none he'd ever heard.

Whether singing a light and airy composition, a soulful ballad, or a piece of great technical complexity, Elena had always offered her music as a gift to her listeners, the richness and ring of her voice truly a marvel. Not only did a part of herself go into each measure, she was also blessed with the innate ability of knowing how to convey just the right mood and tone.

Jesse had been astonished to learn that the first Elena had studied music was while making a name for herself onstage. Her manager had been a music teacher when Ellie had left home to seek her fortune. By chance, Stephen Villard had heard her sing and promptly recognized a diamond in the rough. As the tale went, Villard went from being her vocal instructor to her manager in one afternoon, and over the following years had skillfully developed Elena into a notable singer of the American stage.

Personally, Jesse never found much to like about the intense, dark-haired man, but he couldn't deny what success Elena's manager had wrought. At first he'd wondered if there was anything romantic between the two, for Villard seemed to act somewhat possessive about Ellie. When Jesse had met Elena, however, Villard was taken with a redheaded actress. And Elena had certainly seemed to reciprocate Jesse's infatuation with her, falling headlong with him into a passionate affair.

Once he and Ellie had wed, however, Jesse's misgivings about his wife's manager increased. With relentless intensity, the dark-haired man pushed Elena to rehearse and perform, disregarding the stress of pregnancy, then motherhood, upon her body. Trying to reason with the man was like talking to a brick wall, and tensions between Villard and himself grew enormously.

At first, Jesse had no plans to influence Elena's career one way or another. But when he realized the toll her occupation—and Villard's demands—was exacting upon their little family, he tried everything in his power to slow her pace. At the same time, he had come full circle in his season of spiritual rebellion, realizing it was time to return to his faith, leave the stage, and settle down with his wife and son.

Had Elena ever truly wished to join him? It was a question to which he'd never had a definitive answer. At times, it seemed as if she had wanted nothing more, though she had always been honest about not sharing his belief in God. At others, she had been vague and aloof, even brittle toward him.

Losing her had shattered his heart, never mind the difficulties of returning to Detroit with their one-year-old son and no wife. In dark moments, it had been easy to believe that Elena had never loved him at all, yet on occasion he was painfully bewildered by the tenderness, devotion, and commitment they had once shared. What had happened? Were these simply the consequences for a backslidden man who had married an unbeliever?

The rattle and clanking of pans from the kitchen drew his attention, and he sighed. After sending Robert to school, his mother had withdrawn to the kitchen in high dudgeon. It sounded as if she was giving every cupboard, nook, and cranny a vigorous cleaning. After their unpleasant exchange this morning, she had not sought his company.

Poor Robert appeared utterly confused by the goings-on in his heretofore peaceful home. Frances had been quick to identify Elena as their "visitor," flashing a warning glance in Jesse's direction as she spoke the word. *Don't you dare call that woman his mother*, her snapping gaze had conveyed. *How dare you bring her here!*

How could a man's heart be tugged in so many directions at once? His wife . . . his son . . . his mother. Glancing around the sitting room, Jesse knew he would soon have to approach the kitchen. Throughout the morning Elena had consumed small bits of the gruel, but she needed to be fed again, and bathed. He hoped his mother hadn't used all the hot water in her cleaning frenzy, but even more fervently he hoped she would never learn about the parasites Dr. Schrantz had found in Ellie's hair.

Pushing open the swinging door to the kitchen, he found his mother on her knees, reaching deep inside a lower cupboard. Various items of bakeware were strewn about, and beside her was the scrub bucket. It appeared as if the cabinet had been emptied with no particular care and was now getting the scouring of its life.

"Mother?" Jesse called, watching her movements cease and her spine stiffen. "The doctor has just left, and he's given me a list of foods that will be good for Ellie. I also need some warm water to give her a bath." *And kerosene to take care of the other problem, but I trust what you don't know won't hurt you.*

A long silence ensued, during which Jesse went to the stove and checked the water in the reservoir. It was warm, so he set about filling the bath bucket. A covered plate on the small side table caught his attention, and he lifted the mixing bowl to find a whole boiled chicken and some cooked vegetables carefully arranged on the serving platter.

"I'll be making soup directly," came his mother's tight voice. She'd backed out of the cupboard, but did not turn to look at him. "The broth is settling out on the back porch."

"Thank you very much," he said, his relief no doubt apparent in the sigh he released. Sidestepping the array of pots and pans, he went to her side and knelt beside her. "Beef and chicken broth were two of the things the doctor suggested for Elena."

"I didn't need a medical doctor to tell me *that*," Frances Golden retorted, finally turning her head but keeping her gaze directed toward the floor. "She'll need to be nourished with small, frequent feedings if she's to recover."

Jesse nodded, saddened by his mother's swollen eyes. If there had been time to prepare her for Elena's arrival he certainly would have done so, but things had happened so quickly. No matter how much water had passed beneath the bridge, there had been no question of leaving Robert's mother behind at that poverty-stricken hospital. Though his mother might disagree, Ellie was his wife, and her rightful place was with him.

Wasn't it?

He had not taken lightly the matrimonial vows he'd made, believing marriage to be a permanent and indissoluble state. As long as Elena drew breath, she was his wife, and he remained her husband. Though having her in their home was causing discord, he believed that he could have made no other choice and continued to live with himself.

The weight of self-recrimination already bore down heavily upon him. After receiving Sister Evangeline's summons and rushing to the hospital, he couldn't help but wonder what more he could have done to prevent this heartrending situation. Yet during his restless and uncomfortable night, he'd spent much time gazing at the emaciated, run-down woman in the bed, wondering if he'd once again rushed ahead of God's will by recklessly bringing Elena home. Toward dawn, a thought had come to his heart, giving him a measure of peace, reassuring him that he had taken care of what was set before him.

That's why committing Elena, her healing, and their marriage to almighty God had been a matter of such urgency this morning. He'd known Ellie was wary and ill at ease while he'd knelt and prayed aloud, but there was no other way to begin again.

Surely his mother, a faithful and generous Christian woman, would come to recognize that he was trying to serve God by being a good and faithful husband. *Sooner, Lord, rather than later,* he prayed, recognizing the stubborn angle of Frances Golden's chin. Most often her resolution—even obstinacy— manifested itself regarding matters of faith and morality. The elder Mrs. Golden wasn't one to give in or mince words when she witnessed a compromise of righteousness. On the occasions she was in error, spoke without love, or judged without complete knowledge of the facts, however, she could be downright unpleasant to live with.

A wave of exhaustion rolled over Jesse as he contemplated

the long journey before him: Elena's ill health . . . her lack of faith in Christ . . . their uncertain marriage . . . his mother's animosity toward her daughter-in-law . . . Robert's desire to know his mother. Added to that were his worries of their financial future. If he did not soon have a play produced, his savings would reach an alarming level of depletion.

One thing at a time, his subconscious spoke, focusing him on the tasks at hand—washing and delousing his wife.

"I'll come for the soup once Elena is cleaned up," he said, stifling another sigh and injecting brightness into his tone. "She's feeling a little better," he added, seeing no change in his mother's expression.

Not knowing what to do or say, he rose from his position and took up Elena's wash water. As he exited the kitchen, the sound of a scrub brush attacking the wooden shelf drew a veil of despair over his heart.

His soul was further distressed when he approached Elena to accomplish the duties that lay before him. Despite Dr. Schrantz's hopeful prognosis, Jesse wondered how a person in Ellie's condition could even be alive. The covers barely moved up and down with the rhythm of her shallow breathing. With her closed eyes and gaunt cheeks, she looked the same as any other dearly departed for whom a stream of mourners would come to pay their final respects.

Should he let her rest? She must be exhausted by the activity of the morning.

"Jesse . . . I wish you didn't have to do this," she said weakly without opening her eyes, having sensed his presence. "See me like this."

He silenced a long sigh before dipping the cloth into the basin of water. "You're my wife, Elena," he said as he tenderly drew the washcloth over her face. He prayed his words spoke reassurance of his commitment to her while he reeled with fresh shock at the wastage wrought by her starvation.

As gently and quickly as possible he completed the majority of the bath, deciding to leave the delousing for later, until after his mother had left for her Ladies' Aide meeting. For some reason, he lingered at her feet, nearly in tears while he observed their deterioration as well. These feet had once run to him with joy, danced upon stages across the country, and borne the additional weight of her pregnancy as she carried their son in her womb.

Oh, Ellie.

In silence he grieved as he washed her feet, overcome by sadness and guilt that his wife was in the state she was. For how much of her condition was he responsible? Some of it? All of it? He was her husband, and he had failed to protect her. Why hadn't he tried harder? He could have.

With infinite care, he blotted the water from her feet, his heart filled with misery while he contemplated all the ways that things could have been different between them.

꙳

Though Elena wasn't sure how many days she'd been at Jesse's now—three? four?—she could tell her brain was clearing. She felt a little stronger and was aware that her body no longer ached as badly as it once did. A kind-eyed doctor had come twice to see her, announcing yesterday that he believed she would live.

Though she had been in great pain at the hospital, the muddled state of her mind had made her existence less difficult to bear than her current circumstances. There she had been resigned to her fate, wondering only how long it would take for her body to cease functioning. Now she knew not what the future held, just that her heart could scarcely bear its present suffering.

She still smarted—physically and emotionally—from the kerosene scrubbing of her scalp at the hands of her husband. It had been necessary to rid her of vermin, she understood, yet it had been one of the most humiliating experiences of her life. Jesse had been her husband, her lover, a dashing man of the stage. How could he bathe, feed, and nurse her as a mother would tend a little child?

43

You mean like a proper mother would tend to her little child.

Suffocating guilt pressed down upon her as she thought of Bobby and wondered how many times he had been ill. How often had he yearned for his mother, having to settle instead for his dour grandmother? Jesse's mother had come to the bedroom door several times but had never set foot across the threshold. Her voice sounded tight and mean, and her footsteps clacked up and down the hallway like the keys of a typewriter.

In dismissing Jesse and little Bobby from her life, what events had she set in motion? She often heard Bobby in the hall, but he did not try to enter, no doubt terrified of the consequences his grandmother would wreak. What kind of woman could treat people the way Frances Golden did? she asked herself, wiping tears from the corners of her eyes.

Indeed, Elena, what kind of woman?

Jesse, at least, unlike his mother, didn't seem disposed toward bitterness. He served her with gentleness, patiently enduring her refusals and cynicism and despair. Did he regret having brought her to his home? she wondered. What would happen between them if she got better, as the physician seemed to believe? Each day he prayed—aloud!—that God would restore their marriage, yet he did not act like the Jesse she remembered.

The debonair blond tenor with the devil-may-care grin was gone, replaced by a resolute man whose burdens seemed to wear heavily upon him. She was not blind to the toll her presence here was taking. Dark circles marred the skin beneath his eyes, and she saw the heaviness of spirit he tried to disguise, particularly after he had talked with his mother.

How could he help but regret his decision? she lamented. She was ugly and sick, no longer of any value whatsoever. Not only were her looks a thing of the past, but so was her singing voice. After her last miserable performance on stage, Stephen had rejected her in a fury, telling her that her career was over. "I never want to hear from you again," he'd threatened, "about anything."

By then she'd been so ill, so tired, so numb. If she looked

at things honestly, she had been in decline ever since the day she'd sent Jesse and Bobby away. Over the past four years her name and popularity had plummeted, gaining her exposure in only third-rate theaters toward the end. She had begged Stephen for another chance, for more time for her voice to heal, but he'd refused, informing her that she had been replaced by a youthful, starry-eyed sensation from the middle of Kansas. Just like that, their years of association were over.

Lord, have mercy on the girl from Kansas, she thought, wondering why she should invoke God's name when she wasn't sure he gave a fig about poor young women, if he even existed. Still, the memory of Stephen Villard's dark eyes smoldering with a malevolent intensity she'd dared not challenge made her shiver instinctively. Even now she feared him and what he might do.

Somehow she'd scraped together enough money to buy passage from Chicago to Detroit, wanting to be near Jesse and Bobby, even if she was no longer a part of their lives. The thought that they were somewhere in this great, bustling city brought her a measure of comfort, of rightness, even in her despair. In all these thousands of people, what was the likelihood that he should find her? Through a determined little nun, no less?

A sound at the door made her look up. Jesse had left not long ago to do some errands, assuring her he would be back in less than two hours' time. It hadn't been long since his departure, and he always opened the door after politely knocking.

Again came a knocking, different from Jesse's but too strong for that of a little boy. Mrs. Golden? Elena swallowed a sudden fluttering feeling and called, "Come in."

Never having fully seen Jesse's mother, she took advantage of the daylight to study the older woman as she came in the door with a steaming bowl in her hand. Fair, silvered hair swept gracefully away from her oval face, captured in a well-pinned knot. Her strong, attractive features would have made her quite beautiful if not for the stiffness upon her countenance. Unlike

Jesse's dark eyes, hers were blue, but the resemblance between mother and son was unmistakable.

"I brought you some mash." Her mother-in-law spoke in clipped tones, keeping her gaze fixed at a spot on the wall above the bed.

"Thank you," Elena replied automatically.

"Can you manage it by yourself?" Shoes clicking against the hardwood floor, Jesse's mother walked forward and set the bowl on the bedside table.

Nodding slightly, Elena impulsively asked, "Is Bobby home right now?"

In the act of bending over and setting the dish on the table, Frances Golden stiffened like an overstarched shirt. "Master *Robert* is at school this morning," she said in a voice laden with meaning.

"When can I see him?"

"Never, if I have anything to do with it," pronounced the silver-haired matron, straightening her spine in a slow graceful motion. The blue gaze turned toward her, pinning Elena with its intensity. "You gave him up."

"I . . . I . . ." Not expecting such directness from the woman who had avoided her since her arrival, Elena found herself at a loss for words.

"Neither will I allow you to flounce back into Jesse's life and tear his heart apart again. Once you're well enough to be out the door, you'll be on your way."

At the older woman's condescending words, mutiny rose inside Elena's breast. "What if I don't want to leave?"

"If you know what's good for you, you'll go."

"And you presume to know what's good for me?"

"It isn't my son." Arms akimbo, Frances Golden stood her ground. "You're nothing but a cheap . . ." Crimson flags of color spread across the older woman's cheeks as she checked her words. A second later, an outraged gasp escaped from her lips, and she bent to look beneath the bed.

"What's this? My missing can of kerosene?" Straightening,

she held the evidence aloft, her eyes narrowing. "I thought it smelled in here. You *do* carry vermin, don't you?"

Anger and defensiveness coalesced inside Elena as Jesse's mother regarded her with contempt.

"Out of bed."

"What?"

"I want you out of bed and in this chair." Frances Golden's snappish tone brooked no argument. In the next second, the covers were whisked off her, the sudden loss of warmth raising gooseflesh all over Elena's body.

With great effort, Elena swung her feet over the side of the bed. Only last evening, with Jesse's assistance, had she begun sitting up, but she would not allow this woman a chance to lay a hand on her. She would get into the chair, salvaging whatever dignity she could, or die trying.

"The bed's got to be washed down with brine, sheets scalded, and you could probably stand another scrubbing yourself." Elena felt the scorching heat of her mother-in-law's blue eyes as they flicked over her, assessing her appearance. "Heaven above," she disparaged, "you're nothing but a living skeleton. What did Jesse ever see in you?"

The nightgown in which Jesse had dressed her was no protection against the room's chill, and her feet were bare. Trying not to shiver, not to cry, and not to feel, Elena laboriously crossed the short distance to the chair and sat down, while the older woman ripped apart the bed with a vengeance.

❧

"What—have—you—done?"

The tone in Jesse's voice was like nothing Frances Golden had ever heard, and trepidation rolled through her insides at the crashing sound of his footfalls. Giving the sheets in the copper wash-boiler another stir, she felt her palms go wet—not because of the steam—and her mouth go dry.

But what had she to be ashamed of? She had only meant to do a good deed by bringing Elena some mash.

A good deed? That isn't entirely true, her conscience accused. *You knew Jesse was out of the house, and you wanted to get a good look at her . . . and warn her away.*

Because of the younger woman's insolent manner, one thing had led to another. Then Frances had discovered the kerosene and Jesse's secretive, inexpert attempt to sanitize Elena and the bed. Didn't he know there was no sense killing vermin if a person remained in an infested bed?

After stripping the bed, she had scalded every surface with boiling water, then filled the crevices with salt and washed the bedstead again with a strong brine. She'd also taken the kerosene once more to Elena's head, trying to remain impersonal as she regarded the irritated, pink scalp and the woman's obvious weakness.

Finally, she'd made a pallet on the floor for the girl to rest on, for it appeared that she might soon faint . . . not that the chit would give her the courtesy of warning her. Frances could see the effort it had cost Elena to remain upright in the chair, but Elena had uttered not a word. It was as if her son's wife were made of stone, possessing no feelings whatsoever. How could Jesse ever have gotten involved with such a horrid woman? It was clear that she was as far from being a fit mother as north was from south, and Frances felt completely justified in keeping Robert from her.

She didn't sound indifferent when she asked about seeing Robert. It was only after you hauled her over the coals that she showed antagonism.

"This time you've gone too far." The swinging door flew open, banging the wall, as Jesse stalked into the kitchen. "Elena has done *nothing* to you, yet the treatment she received at your hands this morning was reprehensible."

"She was carrying vermin!"

"You don't know that. For your information, Dr. Schrantz examined her scalp yesterday and pronounced her free of lice."

"How could she be if you didn't change the sheets?"

"I *did* change the sheets, and I boiled them while you were at your Ladies' Aide meeting. I also turned the mattress, got her a fresh pillow, and touched the cracks in the headboard with a feather dipped in kerosene. Your manual on practical house-keeping was most explicit in its instructions for treating bedbugs. But this isn't really the heart of the matter, is it?"

Guilt stabbed at Frances's conscience as she regarded her sensitive, impassioned son. He had always been one to cham-pion the underdog, showing compassion to a fault. Yet where Elena was concerned, he had an unfailing blind spot . . . or else the wicked girl had bewitched him with a manner of charms that Frances failed to find apparent. No amount of talking would make him see reason. Countless times she had tried—and failed—to reflect what poor choices he had made, yet he refused to receive her wise counsel.

Another thought followed on the heels of these, a realiza-tion that made her eyes narrow with sudden suspicion. No doubt the girl had seen an opportunity and was trying to take advantage of her position.

"So she's a tattletale besides? What did she tell you? No doubt she's making a mountain of a molehill."

Jesse's eyes widened, and he took a step closer, placing his hands on his hips. "For your information, Elena said nothing except that you had been in to change the bed. What she *didn't* say was obvious, and I'll have you know your sharp tongue and rough handling doubtlessly set her back some days." Turning, he walked from the kitchen.

Guilt and righteous indignation warred inside Frances as she mentally formulated her defense. Though Elena was ill, there were no two ways about it: she had to go. Already Jesse's sensi-bilities and loyalties were crumbling, and heaven only knew what would happen if dear Robert were to be exposed to that rough, shameful, emaciated creature.

At the same time, Frances was aware that she had behaved badly. Rather than filling her with remorse, however, the knowledge elicited self-aggravation. She was not as sorry for sinning as she was angry that she had fallen. Many times her husband had cautioned her, "Watch your pride, Frannie, else the devil make merry with you."

But this wasn't about pride; it was about saving their family. A God-fearing Christian woman she was, whose temper had temporarily carried her away in her concern for righteousness. Speak of the devil, Jesse obviously didn't realize he had carried the enemy right through the door with him the other night. Having Elena in the house was unleashing all sorts of evil inside these four walls. Frances hastened from the kitchen to catch her son before he returned upstairs.

"Jesse," she called, watching his broad-shouldered form stop at the foot of the stairs. With a deep sigh, he turned to face her.

"I only want what's best for our family," she appealed, holding her hands out before her.

Jesse's gaze, so like her husband's, pinned her. "Doesn't it bother you that you may have harmed my wife?"

"Can't you see what having that woman here is doing to you . . . to us?" she went on, her voice growing louder. At the same time she prayed for him to see reason. "She's tearing us apart, and for what? Do you really believe she's going to become a proper wife and mother? Are you really so foolish to believe you'll live happily ever after?"

"Regardless of your opinions, Mother, these are the facts: Elena is my *wife*. I married her, for better or worse, till death do us part. Because she is my lawful-wedded wife, you will treat her with courtesy and respect. If you cannot manage that, then perhaps this house is too small for all of us."

"Jesse! No!" Terror struck Frances's heart. "You can't take Robert away!"

"If it's the only way to prevent his young mind from being poisoned against his mother, then it's what I must do."

"But I haven't said anything to him about her."

"Who keeps wanting to tell him his mother is dead?"

"She might have been!"

"But she's not." His expression was grim, his words emphatic. "And when he comes home from school this afternoon, he will meet her. I also insist you ask Elena's forgiveness for your behavior."

Had her son taken complete leave of his senses? "Think about what you're doing," she implored. "What if she deserts you again?"

"I've committed our marriage to God Almighty, and I believe he can do anything. When I married Elena, I made a promise to love and honor her all the days of her life, and that's what I intend to do."

"You can't still imagine yourself *in love* with her! And how can you honor such a—" At her son's thunderous expression, she paused, trying a different tack. "You told me she doesn't even believe in God! What happens when she doesn't reciprocate your love? What happens when she leaves you again?"

"That doesn't change my responsibility. Now do I have your word that Elena will receive your apology by the end of the day?"

❧

Upstairs, Elena wiped her hand across her eyes. Frances's reply to her son's demand was low and muffled, and Elena was unable to hear it.

The idea of living as a family filled her with absurd longing, but she knew better than to believe it could ever happen. Life had shown her that hope was a luxury she could not afford. The price was too high, the pain too great.

Downstairs, Frances wept loudly about the terrible mess Jesse was making of their lives, though Mrs. Golden obviously had no idea what making a mess of one's life was all about. Elena did, and the pain of the years past came crashing down upon her.

Burying her head in the pillow, she wished Jesse had closed the door when he'd stormed out.

Chapter 5

After several days of blustery fall weather, the sun shone over southeastern Michigan. High cirrus clouds unfurled across the blue sky, their edges fading into feathery smudges of white. Elena sat in the bedroom chair having breakfast, while Jesse sat opposite her on the end of the bed. Sunshine spilled into the bedchamber, making the oaken floor shine golden.

"You have to come out of this room sometime, Ellie," he reasoned gently. "You've been here more than a fortnight, and I believe you're well enough to join us at the table."

"I don't have anything to wear," she disputed, making a gesture toward her nightgown. "Not even this is mine."

"You know my sister sent you a boxful of clothing. She's coming from Ann Arbor for a visit, and she very much wants to meet you."

"Does she favor your mother's side of the family?"

"Now, Elena," he reproved, his sternness softened by a wry smile. "I don't pretend to make excuses for my mother's behavior, but you have to trust me when I say that underneath, her heart wants only what's right."

As long as she's *right*, Elena refrained from speaking aloud. She realized Jesse watched her curiously as she brought a small

bit of toast to her mouth, birdlike, concentrating on the sensation of having food in her mouth . . . food in her belly.

She had gained back some weight and was feeling stronger.
Having gone with little food for so long, then none, it was
strange to reorient herself to the concept that tasty, nourishing
foods were so readily available. If nothing else, she had to admit
that Frances Golden was an excellent cook.

Lifting his plate, Jesse forked the remainder of his eggs into
his mouth, then wiped his lips with his napkin and set aside his
dish. "You should finish your eggs before they get cold," he
encouraged. "They'll help you get your strength back."

Strength for what? Sparring with your mother? Despite the
woman's wooden-faced apology last week, nothing had changed
in her eyes. If Jesse was not at home as much as he was, Elena
was certain the woman would have whisked her unwanted
daughter-in-law out the door with a broom and dustpan.

"Shall I help you get into your dress this morning, or do
you think you can manage?"

Now that she had regained a modicum of vigor, Elena was
even more conscious of her unbeautiful state. The thought of
Jesse looking upon her face and form made her want to weep
with shame. She had taken over washing herself and brushing
her hair, beginning to fully realize what sad effects her sickness
and starvation had wrought. After seeing her jaundiced eyes,
coarse hair, and skin like burlap, she had sent out the hand
mirror he'd brought in. The bones of her face were prominent;
her cheeks a pair of hollow caverns. Never did she want to gaze
upon her appearance again.

Even though Jesse continued speaking to God every morning about restoring their marriage, he related to Elena in the
manner of brother to sister. His mother's words—*"What did Jesse
ever see in you?"*—rang over and over in Elena's head. She wanted
to cringe very time her husband's eyes lingered upon her. Once
his gaze had been warm and appreciative; now it merely reflected
pity. What else could he be thinking?

Now that she was better, he explained that he must return

in earnest to writing his plays. Sometimes he wrote elsewhere in the house, but often he sat in the chair in the bedroom while she lay resting. She had been sadly surprised to find he was no longer singing, for his voice was one of the finest she'd ever heard.

A little knock came at the door, and hope fluttered in Elena's breast. As Jesse had directed, Bobby had indeed been introduced to his mother last week. She had steeled herself for indifference, or even a negative reaction, not daring to hope for a joyful reconciliation. Bobby's response had been somewhere between both ends of the spectrum: polite caution.

Each morning Bobby came to greet her, and each evening he came to say good night. He was unfailingly well mannered, but he maintained his distance, frightened, no doubt, by the sight of her.

"Good morning, Mama," Bobby addressed her, entering the room. "And Papa. How were your eggs? Nana made mine just right."

"My breakfast is very good, thank you." Elena drank in the sight of her son, knowing she could never tire of seeing him. How she longed to hold him in her arms again and kiss his soft cheeks!

"Today my cousins are coming to play," Bobby announced. "Pearl and Benjamin."

"How old are your cousins?" Elena inquired.

"I don't know. Pearl's big and Benjamin is six, I think."

"Pearl is nine and Benjamin is six," Jesse confirmed. "With the nice weather today, perhaps the three of you can play outdoors."

"Pearl runs faster than anyone." Bobby's eyes shone in obvious admiration as he took a step closer. "And she's not afraid to hold a snake."

Jesse laughed. "Her mother was the very same way."

"Aunt Sara? Do you think she'll bring a snake with her today?"

"No, Robert, I doubt she carries reptiles with her. But I

know she is very brave and not afraid of them. She taught me many things."

"She was your big sister."

"She still is, Son. And I love her very much."

"Then I wish I could have a big sister too!"

Jesse's and Elena's gazes crashed together awkwardly. While Jesse hastened to explain how such a thing was not possible, Elena gripped the arms of the chair, unnerved by her son's artless declaration.

"Perhaps one day you might be a big brother," Jesse concluded, his gaze sliding toward Elena for the briefest of moments. Was there a meaningful glint in his deep brown eyes . . . or was he merely gauging her reaction to his words?

Perspiration broke out between Elena's shoulder blades, and the breakfast she had so carefully eaten threatened to come up. "I need to lie down . . . tired," she managed to mumble, holding her plate out for Jesse to take.

She was surprised when Bobby came forward and offered her his hand, for he had not yet come so close to her. At her young son's kind offer, a dam of tears broke loose and streamed down her face as she allowed him to lead her the few steps to the bed. Jesse and Bobby looked at one another in alarm as she lay down and wept.

Could a child forgive a mother's abandonment? Could even God himself pardon such a thing? Despair echoed in the emptiness of her heart as her past deeds and choices mocked her desire that her little boy should love her. What *was* love? In being with Jesse she had known love, for she'd felt such magnificent things with him—things she had never before known. And when she'd held Bobby in her arms and gazed into Jesse's dark eyes, those feelings and emotions had multiplied, growing into something she could not put into words.

Back then she had dreamed that they could live together as a family. Those hopes, long dormant, now stirred inside her at the same time something soft was pressed into her palm.

"Mama? Take my handkerchief. It's clean, I promise."

Her son's generous action made Elena sob all the harder, and she buried her face in the cloth, grieving her past.

"Papa, why is she crying?" Bobby sounded near tears himself, his voice quavering. "I don't want my mama to cry. I want her to be happy."

"Your mama has been very ill, Robert, but once she regains her health, she will be as happy and robust as your aunt Sara. Run along for now, remembering to offer up a prayer for your mother."

"I *will* pray for you, Mama," came a loud, husky whisper in her ear, followed by an impetuous kiss against her cheek.

After he left, Jesse sat on the edge of the bed and took Elena's hands in his. "What is it? You can tell me."

Could she tell him? *What* could she tell him?

"Was it what I said about another baby?" he went on tenderly. "We won't rush into anything, Ellie, so if that's what's bothering you, set your mind to rest. There is much to be accomplished before we . . ."

Elena felt her face color as her husband's words trail off. The past few days she had been afraid to think of resuming that part of their marriage, yet she was also fearful he wouldn't want to.

"No, it's—" She started to speak, then broke off. There was too much, simply too much between them. His mother was right; she did not belong here, nor did she and Jesse belong together. They were from two different worlds.

"Ellie, I hardly know what happened to you since . . . well, since we separated. I followed you in the newspapers for a time, and I even came to see you once. I took the train to Akron."

"You did?" At that, a thrill swooped through her stomach. If she'd only known he was in the audience, she might have left of her own accord, Stephen Villard and his threats be blasted.

"I used to sing for you," she whispered, scarcely daring to open her eyes, yet she had to . . . had to see his face. "You and Bobby."

"How much time did we waste, Ellie?" His voice was hoarse

as he gripped her hands with feeling. "I suspect more was going on than I knew about, and I hope you will trust me one day with your secrets."

What did he know? What did he suspect? A sudden urge to unburden herself came over her, but quickly she quelled the absurdity of such a notion.

There were things that must never be told.

"I love you, Elena," he said slowly. "I wonder if you ever truly believed that. I pray one day you will believe that you are worthy of receiving love, whether it be mine, Robert's, or the heavenly Father's. Especially God's, for there is no more kind nor loving father than our Father in heaven." After a long pause, he added, "What little you told me about your father led me to believe he wasn't an outstanding model of paternity."

"My father was a mean drunk." Elena wiped her eyes and nose, sniffled, and wiped again. "I suppose your father was like Romy's."

"Romy . . . Romy and Olivia were your two friends from Missouri, weren't they?"

Elena nodded.

"I don't know about Romy's father, but mine was kind and fair. His eyes twinkled and he always had a good sense of humor. He made my mother laugh."

Elena thought of the sour smell of her father's breath, his curses, his cruelty toward his wife and children. Kindness had no place in his life, nor did laughter—unless one counted the unholy glee he took in performing spiteful acts.

"My father laughed when he tore the head off my doll," Elena found herself saying, remembering an experience she hadn't thought of in years. What she didn't add was that he'd also told her to stop crying unless she wanted the same thing to happen to her.

"No wonder you left," Jesse said in a low voice, his expression revealing outrage. "If I were your brother, I would have protected you."

"No, if you were my brother, you would have—" With

bitterness, Elena broke off her words, the heat of her anger drying her tears.

"I would have what?" Jesse asked, his dark gaze snapping with intensity. "What would I have done if I were one of your brothers?"

"Nothing."

"Don't tell me 'nothing.' Just now I learned more about your family than I ever have, and I find what you tell me very troubling."

"If you find it so troubling, then maybe you shouldn't have married me. Poor Jesse Golden stuck with such a low girl like Elena Breen."

Why did she lash out at Jesse? She wasn't angry with *him*, yet the fury inside her seemed determined to have its way. Her sense of helplessness, of powerlessness, only added fuel to its raging fire.

"Elena, you're ill, and right now you're obviously over-wrought." Though Jesse appeared the picture of composure, she saw that his shoulders appeared as rigid as if hewn from granite. He took a deep breath, then released it slowly. "For as long as I've known you, you've sidestepped talking about the things of your past. If we're to live as man and wife, there must be trust between us. I pray, Ellie, that you will find me a man worthy of your trust."

His penetrating gaze did not leave her face.

"No one can be trusted" she spat, turning her head toward the wall. The expression in Jesse's eyes was too terrible to receive. Sympathy. Seeking. Understanding. If ever there had been a person in life to trust, it was Jesse. *What about Olivia? Romy? Their families?* her subconscious added.

"God can be trusted," came the soft reply.

"*God?*" Enraged, she spun her head back to face her husband. "God doesn't care about anyone."

"I take heart that you didn't qualify your remark with 'if he exists,'" Jesse remarked, quirking one eyebrow. "What you can't accept, I think, is that God loves you . . . or that anyone loves you."

"What is love?" Her words were as blistering as her thoughts. "All those songs we sang about love were meaningless. No—they were lies. *I'd* like to write a song about love and tell the truth; it's better not to love. That way people can't hurt you."

"Maybe not as much."

"What?"

"Not as much, but people can still hurt you. Even though you try living with a shield around your heart, Ellie, people *have* hurt you. I know that."

"You don't know what you're talking about."

"I would challenge you with the same, dear wife."

"Go away," she demanded, even more furious to find tears in her eyes again. She had never been one to cry, yet it was all she had done these past many days.

"I'll be downstairs if you need me." Without another word, Jesse rose and left the room, leaving Elena feeling surprisingly bereft in the midst of her anger.

⁂

"Uncle Jesse! Uncle Jesse!" cried Pearl and Benjamin as they tumbled in the front door with haste and excitement. "Is our new aunt here? Is she going to meet us today?"

"Goodness, children!" Jesse's sister Sara exclaimed, hastening in behind her daughter and son. The telltale cut of her dress revealed that she was again in the family way. Though Jesse hadn't known, the sight made him unaccountably pleased. And at the same time wistful.

"Hello, Brother," Sara greeted him with a kiss on the cheek, reserving her next words for his ear alone. "I thought it was time for some reinforcements. Since Scott is away on business, I decided to come to Detroit for a few days. I have been praying that Mother hasn't made these past weeks too difficult for you."

"Thank you," he whispered, his throat thick.

"Hello, Mama. And Robert—I think you've grown another few inches!" Sara sang out brightly over Jesse's shoulder, pressing her cheek against his for a long moment before stepping free and greeting her mother and nephew. "The children have been so excited to visit."

"We want to meet our aunt Elena!" cried Benjamin as the driver carried in their bags.

"She's resting right now," Robert answered solemnly. "My mother has been sick, and she gets very tired."

"I've just baked some cookies," announced Frances, her face and voice tight with tension. "Shall we have some in the kitchen?"

With cries of delight, Sara's children shed their coats and followed Robert and their grandmother from the room.

"Oh my," Sara commented in a low voice, her deep brown eyes filled with compassion. "When I received Mama's letter last week, I had a feeling it was going poorly for you . . . and Elena."

Jesse made no reply, thinking of what had transpired with Ellie this morning. Though he had tried to maintain a façade of calm, he was both troubled and shaken by their exchange.

"Jess? I asked if I might go up and see her," Sara was saying, touching his elbow. "You look as if you're a million miles away."

"Enter at your own risk," he said with a shrug. "None of the women of this household seem to be in a very fine humor today."

"Well, I am," Sara averred, flashing a determined smile. "And I brought some things that might make Elena feel better." Extracting a large, brocade satchel from the pile of bags inside the front door, his sister strode confidently up the staircase, leaving Jesse to wonder what her reception would be.

Taking up the sheaf of papers that constituted the first two-thirds of the play he was currently writing, he retired to his chair in the sitting room to read. To his surprise, he was disturbed by neither the merry party in the kitchen nor by any disturbance from his wife and sister.

Sometime later, just as his curiosity threatened to get the

better of him, he heard footfalls on the stairs. As he rose from his chair and set the papers aside, he was surprised to see both Sara and Elena descending. Ellie moved slowly, her great effort evident.

"I convinced your lovely wife to come down and meet her niece and nephew." Sara's face beamed at him, and if Jesse wasn't mistaken, her right brow arched in a slightly superior manner.

"Ellie, it's so good to see you up!" Jesse complimented quite sincerely, going to her side and offering his arm. "May I?"

With a nod and downcast gaze, Elena accepted his assistance. As his palm closed around her small hand, a fierce, protective feeling rose within him, and he vowed he would never again let Ellie go. No matter what lay in her past, he had to somehow prove to her that a future with hope—with God—could prevail over the greatest evil.

A delicate fragrance rose to his nostrils, and he looked down, belatedly noticing the artful arrangement of his wife's hair. Sara had obviously been armed with a bagful of beauty-begetting items as she had marched up the stairs, and she had employed them admirably.

The lifelessness of Elena's hair was gone, replaced by a smooth, elegant style that bespoke of its former glory. In the afternoon sunshine illuminating the room, golden highlights glinted enchantingly. How had Sara managed such a feat in less than an hour's time?

An unfamiliar day dress of teal and buttermilk hung loose upon Elena's form, but the colors enhanced the soft strength of her coloring, making her wan face burst with surprising vibrancy. Of course Sara had not been able to do anything about her sister-in-law's gauntness, but Jesse would not be surprised if a few pots of cosmetics had been smuggled into the house, their contents skillfully applied to Elena's face. At the very least, it seemed as though Ellie's dry, coarse skin had been nourished with a rich emollient.

The overall effect was remarkable. Stunning. He felt his

heart quicken within his chest as he considered what he might say to this woman with whom he had once flirted most outrageously. Yet no inspiration came, leaving him with the desperate feeling of being tongue-tied.

A look of amusement crossed Sara's face as he looked at her; then his saucy sister had the audacity to wink. Thank goodness Elena was not looking in Sara's direction, or he might well have colored. Leading his wife to her chair, he kept hold of her arm until she had taken her seat in the sitting room. A deep sigh came from her, and he noticed the rapid flutter of her heartbeat in the bit of throat exposed at her collar.

"Can I get you something to drink?" he asked, kneeling at her side. The air between them had not yet been cleared since their words this morning, and he wondered how much ferocity remained in her eyes.

Instead, if he wasn't mistaken, he saw softness. Their gazes met, and the beginnings of a shy smile curved her lips before she looked away. "Yes, thank you."

Ridiculous, he told himself as he went to the kitchen for a glass, trying to temper the giddy, jubilant feeling in his heart with reason. His emotions were behaving as if he were thirteen years old and Betsy Black had just asked him to carry her books. Elena was already his wife, the mother of his child, and he had known her for more than six years.

Yes, but do you really know her?

His thoughts abruptly broke off when he entered the kitchen and caught sight of his mother. "Is there more eggnog?" he asked, taking a glass out of the cupboard.

"Enough for you," she replied, peeling potatoes.

"It's for Elena," he corrected. "She came downstairs."

"She did?" The expression on Robert's face was incredulous and joyful at once, and he pushed back his chair from the small, rectangular table. His cousins hastily followed suit, and all three children scampered from the kitchen, leaving behind cookie crumbs and empty glasses of milk.

"You have no idea what you're doing," Frances Golden

spoke with a shaking voice, removing potato skin with uneven movements. "If you think your heart was broken before, just wait till she leaves again and breaks Robert's heart along with yours. On Judgment Day, you won't like answering to God for that."

"I wouldn't like to answer to him about leaving my wife to die in poverty, either," Jesse replied with more calmness than he felt, pouring the remainder of the eggnog into the glass. *Lord, is there no way this can work?* he cried from his soul while a leaden feeling overtook his mind and limbs. *I don't know how much longer I can stand things the way they are between Elena and my mother.*

A moment later he thought of the brightness and gaiety Sara had brought to their home this very afternoon and of the beauty she had coaxed from his ailing wife. He doubted he could have gotten Elena downstairs as quickly as Sara had, and he certainly wouldn't have had the first idea of how to beautify her the way his sister had.

Instead of allowing his hope to flag, he ought to be thankful for Sara's involvement today. If not for her visit, the inflammation between Elena and him would still be unresolved, and the friction from Mother even greater. Sara's good humor was not only hard to resist but infectious. Benjamin and Pearl had a way of bringing out their grandmother's best as well. Already God was about, answering his desperate prayers even before he had prayed them.

Upon returning to the sitting room, he found all three children before Elena's chair and Sara just finishing introductions. "Benjamin's middle name, Gerald, is after his grandfather, who died ten years ago, but you probably already knew that."

"It's very good to meet you," Elena replied, a girlish smile lighting her features. Her gaze took in her niece and nephew, then shone upon her son. "You were right, Bobby. You have very nice cousins."

"*Bobby?*" commented Benjamin quizzically. "We call him Robert."

"I've always called him Bobby," Elena said softly, a series of emotions dancing across her countenance.

"*Bobby* is his mama's special name for him," Jesse interjected in a jovial tone, fearful of what further questions the boy might ask his fragile aunt.

"My mother is the finest soprano in the country," boasted Robert, looking between his cousins.

"Our mother sings too," countered Benjamin.

"I know that, but *my* mother sang on the stage. Papa said she is the best singer of all, even better than Aunt Sara." Looking toward Jesse for confirmation, Robert did not notice the pain suffusing Elena's face.

One glance at Sara's face showed Jesse that his sister was as taken aback as he was by the children's unexpected one-upmanship. But before he could formulate a disarmament, Pearl entreated, "Will you sing us a song, Aunt Elena?"

Mute, Elena shook her head, dropping her gaze toward her lap. What faint color she'd had seemed to leave her face all at once.

"Why not?" wailed Robert, dull red rising in his cheeks.

"I can't sing." The admission was hoarse and filled with pain.

"Yes you can! Papa said—"

"Your mama has been quite ill, Robert." Sara, as usual, was the first to recover her wits. "You must allow her time to heal. In the meantime, I wonder if my little brother remembers the harmony for 'Pop! Goes the Weasel.'"

Benjamin clapped his hands. "Will you play the piano, Mama, too? Please?"

"I believe I can manage that," Sara replied with a bright smile, walking to the instrument. After taking her seat and opening the lid, she ran through a few scales before playing the first line of the melody in a lighthearted, staccato manner. "I'm ready. Jesse?"

"Ready," he said, taking his place at her side. Three measures into the verse, he became aware that his mother stood just inside the doorway. Robert, too, noticed her, and with a reproachful look at the bowed head of his mother, left her side to go to his grandmother.

Like a protective shield, Frances's arms went around his shoulders, and she drew him firmly against her. Robert's chin quivered with the effort of holding back his tears, while Frances shot an expression of censure toward Jesse, then one of outright hatred at Elena.

What to do? Finish or stop? Jesse was in agony. With her back to the proceedings, Sara did not see any of the goings-on. Her lithe voice soared to high E while his harmonized in C-sharp. All of his training and experience told him to go on, to finish, yet at the same time he longed to shout for everyone's attention, then exorcise—once and for all—the legion of heart-rending behaviors and emotions filling this household. He looked again at his wife.

As he and Sara sang on, Elena seemed to shrink further into herself. Her head drooped even farther downward, and if he wasn't mistaken, her shoulders shook slightly. Pearl and Benjamin continued standing next to their aunt, appearing bewildered by her strange reaction to what ought to be a joyful event. Catching Jesse's eye, Pearl cast him a glance that begged explanation.

Finally, mercifully, the song came to its end, and Jesse tore his gaze from the trio at the chair back toward the doorway, which was now empty. Robert and his grandmother were no longer there.

Noticing Elena's distress, Sara hastened with compunction from the piano bench to her sister-in-law's side, insisting Jesse carry Elena upstairs immediately. Aloud, she chided herself for failing to see Elena's exhaustion, not realizing there was more to the situation than what met the eye.

"Jesse, right this second!" Sara's command startled him out of his nightmarish reverie, and he sprang into action.

Ellie seemed to weigh no more than a feather as he took

her in his arms. Her face was the color of chalk, and her eyes, though squeezed tightly shut, leaked tears.

Oh, Ellie.

"I'm sorry," he whispered near her ear as he approached the stairs. "Please forgive me for letting you be hurt."

For just a second, the chocolate-colored eyes opened and focused on him; then an expression of misery too terrible to describe distorted her face. She began to weep then, no longer silently, but loudly, as a soul in great pain.

She wept for a very long time.

Chapter 6

Emerging from her grief felt like being washed up, waterlogged, on the edge of some uncertain shore. Where was she? *Who* was she? Why was she here? What was the meaning of this existence called life?

Opening her swollen eyes, Elena found that the bright afternoon had given way to dusk. In the bedchamber's semi-darkness, she glanced down at the cheerful dress of blue and cream she had donned with such hope, its pattern now drab gray against darker gray.

Why had she allowed Sara to primp and preen her like a china doll? Jesse's sister had burst into this room with such an air of disarming joy and warmth that Elena's defenses had immediately faltered. Or had the companionship and instant camaraderie she had felt with Jesse's sister taken her back to more carefree days, reminding her of the times she had spent with Romy and Olivia? They had often done one another's hair and mixed up concoctions to smooth their complexions and bleach their freckles.

But day always turned to night, laughter to sorrow, anticipation to misery. She should have known better than to believe any good could have come from Sara's enthusiastic attempts to renovate her appearance and disposition.

If she looked into her heart, she also had to admit to her secret yearning for Jesse to look upon her with something more than sympathy in his eyes. Had Sara instinctively known this, or was it just in her nature to visit the sick and spread cheer?

"Elena?" Sara's soft voice at the door preceded a gentle rapping. "Elena, may I come in?"

Making no reply, Elena dimly recalled Jesse carrying her back upstairs, both he and Sara trying to console her, their efforts to no avail. Perhaps Jesse had some inkling of the cause of her despair, but Sara, a loving wife and mother, could not possibly comprehend what it was like to be a failure in her children's eyes. When Elena had admitted to Bobby that she could no longer sing—and had seen the hopeful light in his trusting eyes extinguished—the weight in her soul became unbearable.

Sara slipped into the room and quietly closed the door behind her. Her skirts swished as she walked to the bed and settled herself on the edge of the mattress. "I thought you might be all cried out, so I came to sit with you for a spell. Sometimes that helps."

"There's no help for me."

"Oh no? There's help for everyone, just for the asking."

A cynical sound left Elena's lips. "If you're talking about God, I've asked him for help in every way I know how. He's either deaf, uncaring, or not there."

A long pause ensued before Sara spoke again. "I spoke with Robert this afternoon, and he understands now that you weren't up to singing today. I believe he also realizes that his motivation for wanting to show off your talent wasn't right or godly, either. Although it wouldn't take much to show me up—Jesse was endowed with most of the musical talent in this family." Sara's gentle, comfortable laugh spoke to her peace at being who she was. "Maybe one day you could teach me a few things."

"Your voice is beautiful the way it is. Don't let anyone try and change it."

"I thank you for your compliment, but I'm a bit bewildered by the bitterness I hear in your words."

Elena sighed and rubbed her hands over her face. "When I said I can't sing, I meant I *can't* sing anymore. My manager . . . he . . ." Pausing, she finished in a whisper. "My voice is ruined. My name is ruined. What future can there be for me?"

"What future? What about your husband and son? The other children that may one day be? Today I rejoiced at meeting my brother's wife—my new sister—and I thought she rejoiced at meeting me. There is always a future, Elena, and God holds yours in the palm of his hand."

"Sara, you don't underst—"

"Will you let me say some things to you? Think on them, and perhaps even pray about them." Her sister-in-law's warm fingers sought hers, squeezing her hand with firmness.

"I'll listen, but I doubt I'll do any praying."

"I suspect your life has been very difficult, but that doesn't mean God has abandoned you. He has loved you from all eternity, Elena. At the chosen time, he formed you in your mother's womb and called you into being. He knows everything about you and is familiar with all your ways. You are his precious, unique, and irreplaceable daughter."

"That all sounds lovely, but—" A sob ruined the deliberate sarcasm of Elena's words.

"But what?"

"Where was he when . . ." A smothering, choking feeling gripped her chest. Panic? "Where is he when evil is done? Why didn't he help me?"

"Shh, now," Sara soothed, moving forward and easing Elena's head and shoulders into her lap. "The wisest theologians of all time could not answer your question. Only God himself knows the unfolding of your life, each page and chapter. 'For I know the thoughts that I think toward you, saith the Lord, thoughts of peace, and not of evil, to give you an expected end. Then shall ye call upon me, and ye shall go and pray unto me, and I will hearken unto you.'"

"Does that come from the Bible?"

"From the prophet Jeremiah."

"I've prayed, for all the good it's done me."

"Listen to just a little more: 'Ye shall seek me, and find me, when ye shall search for me with all your heart. And I will be found of you, saith the Lord.'"

"If I ever find him, I'm going to have some questions for him!"

"You aren't the only one who feels that way."

Elena heard a tender smile in Sara's reply as warm fingers stroked her hair, freeing the pins and smoothing the coils. Gradually, the pounding of her heart eased.

"But in all your questions and reasoning, you must remember that God *loves* you. He loves you so much that he sent his only begotten son to the cross so that you might have eternal life."

The urge to continue fighting Sara's gentle words was stealthily overcome by a languor Elena could not fight. How long had it been since anyone had ministered to her in such a fashion? *The little nun had.* Yes, Sister Evangeline had no doubt rescued her from death, but she was a woman dedicated to serving God her whole life. It was expected that one who took Jesus Christ for a spouse and tended to the poor would be of a kindly, unselfish nature.

Unexpectedly, Granny Esmond came to mind. Though the older woman could be tart-tongued and painfully candid, her life had been one of devotion to the Lord . . . and selfless service to people. Olivia and Romy had trusted in a loving God, but if they had known how many desperate prayers Elena had poured out—prayers that had gone unanswered—would their opinion of him be different? she wondered.

What did it mean to live a life of faith, excepting those who were pastors and priests, sisters and monks? The expectations of the various types of religious life were clear and well defined, she decided, not like trying to navigate in a world of instability and uncertainty. Adeline Esmond had managed to live a life of faithfulness, but there were not many Granny Esmonds in the world.

Jesse had been at a crossroad of faith and life when he and Elena had met, ultimately swinging back toward fidelity to the unseen God. Her new sister-in-law obviously strove to speak well of the Almighty and conduct herself in a loving fashion, yet Frances Golden, a supposed godly woman, behaved in a manner resembling a many-horned devil more than one resembling Jesus Christ, in Elena's opinion. Where was the sense in Christianity? the reason? Except for a few notable examples, it seemed to be nothing more than a practice fraught with hypocrisy, populated by hypocrites.

"You may feel God has forgotten you, Elena, yet do you think your being here is the result of mere coincidence? You were near death, and your husband was sent to rescue you. If I were you, I'd be trembling with anticipation, awaiting what else God has in store!"

How *had* she gotten here? Obviously, she had traveled to Detroit of her own accord. Was God responsible for the chain of events after that? A troubling thought came on the heels of that, making her wonder if he could have had anything to do with the persistent, unrelenting urge she'd had to come to this city. Wasn't that allowing her imagination to take things too far? Surely her reasons for coming to Detroit were only to be near Jesse and Bobby; she'd had no intention of seeking contact with them.

Though Elena's body was tranquil, her brain was occupied with thoughts and concepts unfamiliar to her. The experiences of her life did not lend themselves to the heavenly-minded optimism her sister-in-law espoused, but at the same time she could almost accept the words Sara spoke as being a possibility. How else *had* she ended up in her husband's home?

"Sleep, dear one," Sara urged. "Your head has grown heavy and tired, and you still have a long journey to travel toward wellness. I will help you every way I can, and I promise to honor and love you as the sister I never had. I have prayed faithfully for you all these years you have been lost to us, and I give thanks to God that you have been found. Elena, if you trust in him, even a little, he will work to increase your faith and bring healing and marvels that you never dreamed possible."

Elena did not know where Sara's words left off and her sleep began. She dreamed of a long-ago summer night beneath the stars with Olivia and Romy, giggling over girlish dreams and aspirations. Their laughter warmed her, and she basked in the embrace of loyal companionship, enthusiasm, and zest for life. All the future lay before them, filled with one exciting possibility after another. All agreed that they were best friends and nothing could ever separate them.

Yet before she knew what was happening, Stephen Villard intruded on their gathering. Romy, Olivia, and the August-perfumed Missouri countryside vanished in an instant. Villard's promises were as sweet as spun honey, and so was his attention. Where were they going? Where was he taking her? In a whirlwind, she tasted the headiness of power and plenty. How had she gone from having nothing to having everything she wanted, all she had ever dreamed of having?

Or had she?

With steely determination glittering in his deep blue gaze, Stephen Villard bound her with cords that could never be severed by anyone but himself. His handsome, smiling face took on a sinister cast, mocking her distress. *I own you,* his eyes boasted.

Shame and desperation stole her breath, made her bile rise. What was happening? To what had she agreed? With Jesse she thought she had found her escape, but in the end, she discovered there was no such thing as freedom. Villard was too strong, his invisible cords too tight. He reveled in that knowledge, reminding her often that there was no salvation for her.

Yet in the midst of this maelstrom of defeat and hopelessness strode Jesse once again, like a white knight bent on rescuing a princess. "I want to help you," he pledged, coming to her side. "Let me help you, Ellie."

With silent menace, Villard stood behind her, his long, lean fingers holding fast to his cords. She reached toward Jesse, aching for the sanctuary of his arms, yet as she tried to move, her bonds seized more tightly, choking . . . suffocating her.

Fearful, murky shadows fell over the landscape of her dream, swelling and distending her world into a hopeless sepulcher of black. *You're mine, Elena,* a familiar voice jeered. *You'll do as I say.*

"Ellie," Jesse's voice came as from far away. "I won't let anything hurt you. You're safe with me."

"I'm not!" she cried.

"Yes, you are," her white knight soothed so convincingly that she almost believed him. For just a moment, the bonds loosened and she could breathe. She couldn't see anything, but she imagined herself lying in his arms, resting her head against his strong chest. His fingers stroked her hair, and beneath her cheek she felt the reassuring thudding of his heart. She was so tired . . . so very tired.

The darkness parted then, revealing scenes that could never be forgotten. Pain clutched her heart with the fierce grip of talons, causing her involuntary cry, "No!" Writhing and thrashing, she tried to escape, but she was caught too cleverly for that.

"No!" she wailed again, "Don't show me that. I want . . . I just want . . ."

"What do you want?" came Jesse's voice, as from a distance. "You can tell me what you want, Ellie."

She almost said, "I want to be free," but the combination of forces against her was too great. Down she went against the onslaught . . . down . . . down . . . down. Mercifully, this time, the darkness closed all around her.

"Elena," came Jesse's voice, nearer, almost in her ear. "What is it that you want?"

Confused, she wondered how Jesse could be in the darkness with her. How did he get here? Didn't he ever give up? Didn't he know that he would end up the same as her if he persisted?

"Wake up, Ellie." A hand shook her shoulder.

It took her a long moment to realize the hand was attached to an arm, and that the arm encircled her. The side of her face lay against soft cotton cloth, warmed by the solid flesh and bone of the man beneath it. In fact, their bodies were in contact from head to toe, and she belatedly became aware that her arm lay boldly across a chest that rose and fell in measured cadence. The velvet darkness of night pressed in on all sides.

"Are you awake now?" Though Jesse's words were calm, she heard the skein of worry in his question.

"I think so," she replied, still enmeshed in the lingering effects—fear, hopelessness, confusion—of her dream state. "Where am I?"

"Safe in bed, dearest. You fell asleep when Sara came to sit with you, and you've been at it ever since."

"What time is it?"

"A little after three. The clock struck just a short while ago."

"Oh." Tensing, she lifted her head.

"Don't feel as though you have to move on my account," her husband remarked wryly. "I've rather enjoyed holding you again. Do you remember how often we used to lie like this?"

"I remember." Her acknowledgment was nothing more than a whisper as his fingers urged her head back down. His touch was light, yet infinitely reassuring. How could she ever have believed that leaving this man was the best thing to do? Wasn't there some way she could have made things work?

Awakening in his arms was a memory she'd stricken from her mind these four years they'd been apart. In the living misery her life had become, it was just too painful to remember the fleeting happiness she'd enjoyed. Now . . . tonight, finding herself in a position she'd never dared hope she'd be in again, she realized that much of the unease she'd felt with her husband had melted away.

"You're safe as safe can be, Ellie," he said, his arms tightening around her for a heavenly moment. "You're my wife, and I would never let anything happen to you."

"Oh, Jess," she sighed, curving into him. The remaining vestiges of her nightmare fled as their lips met, parted, and met again. Had four years truly passed since their last embrace?

"Tell me what you were dreaming," he said finally, nuzzling her cheek.

"It was nothing."

"It was more than nothing."

"A bad dream, then," she replied lightly, her hand cupping his face. "Oh, Jess, I've missed you so much."

"I've missed you too, Ellie, and I need you to believe my love for you is stronger than any obstacle that stands between us."

"I believe you."

"Tell me what haunts you." After pressing a whisper-soft kiss against her cheek, he stroked her forehead.

"There's nothing," she spoke quickly, smoothly, seeking the sweetness of his lips. To her surprise, he pulled away.

"Your kisses are more than tempting, my love, but there must be trust between us before there can be anything else."

Elena stiffened, stung by his rebuff. Again he spoke of trust, but perhaps what he really meant was that he no longer found her desirable.

"Someone was trying to cause you harm. Who was it . . . and why?" he persisted, causing anger to ignite inside her. "If it was just a dream, you can certainly tell me."

"I don't remember it anymore," she lied, her voice sounding clipped. Turning away, she sought to distance herself from him.

"Not so fast." His arms tightened, preventing her escape. "You'll pardon me if I don't find your words convincing. I've been praying that God would give us the opportunity to draw close in ways we never did before, and I believe this is one of those moments. I don't know what made me lie down beside you tonight when I came to check on you, but it felt so right to be next to you again. And when you began thrashing and talking in your sleep, I put my arms around you, held you close, and prayed for the healing of whatever plagues your soul."

"This isn't going to work." Her voice was tense with unshed tears.

"What isn't?"

"We aren't. Us."

"What makes you believe such a thing?"

"Because . . . your mother hates me." She seized upon the first thing she could think of and was satisfied to hear a long sigh leave her husband.

"We don't have to live here," he replied after a moment. "When you're well, we'll find another home."

"How will we live?" she shot back, having sensed a tension in Jesse about his livelihood. "You're not singing anymore."

"I'm hoping to have some plays produced in the near future. I've written several now."

"You know as well as I the lot of the common playwright. There's no money in that."

"And you know as well as I the dubious morality of today's theater. Elena, I have something *un*common in mind: the beauty of God's truth, principles, and precepts wrapped inside engaging entertainment. It's the vision he's placed on my heart."

"Who, God?"

"Yes."

"How can you know something like that?" she scoffed.

"Through much time and prayer. Perhaps it's a way to atone for my sin of wandering far from him and failing to glorify him with the gifts he gave me."

"Guilt, then."

"Maybe that was mixed in at one time, but not anymore."

"Is that why you found me? Out of guilt? Am I yet another reminder of that 'sinful' time of your life that you need to atone for? Is Bobby? We conceived him out of wedlock, if you recall."

Another sigh. "Elena, you're being as inflammatory as you were four years ago. It was against my every wish that you separated yourself from Robert and me. No matter how we started our marriage, I never wanted you *not* to be my wife. I love you and want us to be together. Let me ask you this: Have you spent any time dwelling on the fact that while, yes, a few weeks ago I found you and brought you home, I wasn't actively looking for you? How did that happen? Mere coincidence?"

"It could have been—"

"It could have been many things, I suppose, but I choose to believe it was the hand of God. He does not wish for husbands and wives to be parted, and I have not stopped praying for our reconciliation. Do you remember the vows we made on our wedding day?"

She made no answer.

"We made a covenant before the almighty Lord, Ellie. To God Most High I swore to love, protect, and provide for you all the days of my life. He doesn't take those promises lightly, and neither do I. Because of this, and because I love and serve him, I trust that he will supply every grace needed to make our marriage work."

"I don't," she said flatly.

"I know you don't trust anyone. Probably not even God."

"Tell me why I should."

"Better yet, why don't you tell me why you shouldn't? Help me understand what makes up Elena Golden."

You wouldn't want to know.

"What was your mother like?" he asked gently. "I don't know anything about Robert's other grandmother."

"Her name was Katherine. She was sick for many years; then she died." Her words were toneless, devoid of emotion.

"Yes, I believe you told me that much. Did your father remarry?"

"No."

"What did your mother's hands look like?"

"My mother's *hands*? What kind of question is that?" Her anger flared, burning hotter, at his unexpected query. At the same time, however, an unbidden image flickered in her mind's eye of long, tapered fingers with oval-rounded nails. She remembered those fingers reaching for hers, caressing her face and brushing back her hair, expressing love in a thousand different ways. Next they lay cold and lifeless, crossed over a silent chest that no longer flailed for breath.

Oh, Mama. Why did you have to die? No one will ever love me the way you did. I used to tell myself you were better off dead than living sick the way you did for so long, but I wish you weren't gone. I miss you . . . I miss you touching me.

Elena failed to stifle the sob that welled up and spilled noisily from her throat. It hurt too much to think of her mother, hurt too much to be here with Jesse. She had to leave . . . had to get away. Blindly, wildly, she tried to extricate herself from the arms of the man who held her, but he was too strong, his methods ruthless and overpowering.

"'Flow gently, sweet Afton, among thy green braes,'" he sang with tenderness, holding her close to his chest. "'Flow gently, I'll sing thee a song in thy praise.'"

"No! Stop it!"

"'My Mary's asleep by the murmuring stream . . . flow gently, sweet Afton, disturb not her dream.'"

"Nooo," she wailed, falling limp against him. She was too weak, too tired to fight anymore. How could Jesse ever have known that "Flow Gently, Sweet Afton" had been one of her mother's favorite songs? In her mind's eye, she saw a younger, healthier Katherine Breen, her apron filled with fresh green pea pods, sitting on the porch stair. As her mother shelled the peas and tossed them into a pot, she sang Robert Burns's ode of love in her pure, clear voice. Sunlight drenched the western side of the house, and a chorus of martins complimented the graceful melody.

"'Thou stock dove, whose echo resounds from the hill,'" Jesse continued softly, his voice every bit as magnificent as she remembered, "'ye wild whistling blackbirds in yon thorny dell . . .'"

How old had she been on that day? Five? Six? Elena remembered playing with her doll in the grass beyond the foot of the stairs, looking up often at her beautiful, doting mother.

Not long after that, Katherine Breen had taken ill, beginning the slow decline that had eventually claimed her life.

Perhaps sensing that the fight had gone out of her, Jesse's arms loosened as he began the second verse. The tears slid silently from Elena's eyes now, dampening her husband's shirt. This weeping was different than the hopeless agony that had engulfed her earlier—in some ways more painful, and in a curious way less.

Sudden drowsiness overtook her, and she returned to the land of dreams, this time accompanied by a sure, strong voice that sang of sleep and sweetly flowing rivers.

Chapter 7

With sadness in her heart, Frances observed the growing pile of bags in the front entry throughout the morning. After spending a week in Detroit, Sara, Pearl, and Benjamin were going back to Ann Arbor this afternoon. Sara's husband, Scott, a businessman, was due home from Philadelphia tomorrow.

Coming from the kitchen with an armload of freshly ironed table linens, Frances saw Sara and Elena in the sitting room, deep in conversation. To her dismay, the two young women had hit it off immediately. She'd warned Sara against becoming involved with Elena and what she hoped was merely a temporary situation, but her too-generous-hearted daughter would hear none of what she had to say.

"Mama, Elena is Jesse's wife—and little Robert's own mother," she'd sweetly contended. "You certainly can't mean that I ought not care about her. The poor woman has been so dreadfully ill and deprived . . . and hasn't our Lord Jesus commanded us to do unto others as we would have them do unto us?"

"That doesn't mean you have to be her friend!"

"Oh, Mama," she'd pronounced with a graceful smile, and Frances had not known if disregard, pity, or perhaps even a mild reproof was behind Sara's words.

After the dreadful musical debacle that had occurred the day of their arrival—not to mention Robert's wounded feelings and Elena's endless, frightful weeping—things had settled down somewhat. Sara was determined to integrate everyone in this household, and in her charming way she had accomplished much. It was hard not to think of her daughter as a traitor, however, with all the kindness and attention she had shown the worldly woman whose presence continued to darken their home.

Their visitor now came downstairs for every meal. Her emaciated features were beginning to fill in, and Frances could see traces of the former loveliness about which Jesse had spoken. Thanks to Sara, Elena was neat and clean, and her blonde hair was well tended. In Frances's opinion, however, the girl was sullen, for she did not speak unless spoken to, and invisible shutters guarded a pair of eyes that made Frances think of ripe black cherries.

What was most disturbing of all to Frances was that she suspected Jesse and Elena had spent a night together. When the girl was first here and in grave health, she understood that Jesse had a legitimate reason to be near her. But now propriety dictated that the pair ought to exercise prudence.

Propriety, Frances? Prudence? They're man and wife!

Though Gerald had been gone more than ten years, sometimes it seemed as if she could still hear his voice gently chiding her. His manner with her had never been harsh, and because of that she was sometimes able to see where she was lacking. "Some folks will rub you like silk, Frannie, and others like sandpaper. I've always tried to be the silk." She understood what had been left unsaid, but Gerald had not been the kind of man to rub a person's nose in his or her failings.

Well, if she was sandpaper, Elena was . . . something much worse. The girl had scarcely said two words to her, but Frances could read an abrasive personality just as well as she could read the newspaper. Would someone kind and gentle abandon her husband and son, being more willing to face death than meet up with the consequences of her past? Worse yet, Jesse had yoked himself to an unbeliever. When invited to this past Sunday service, Elena had actually grimaced before saying she didn't feel up to it.

There was no doubt about it: Jesse and Robert must be protected from this perilous person at any cost. Jesse had to be shown the folly of believing something good might be salvaged out of a relationship so fundamentally flawed.

A burst of laughter came from the sitting room, causing Frances's unpleasant humor to grow. In one respect it had been a relief to have Sara and the children here, for their happy presence acted as a buffer state. What would happen when they left? she wondered. Would she be expected to speak to Elena? Would Elena speak to her?

Many times throughout the past week she had caught Jesse's gaze upon the blonde-haired woman, and it grieved her to see the affection in his eyes. And even though Robert had suffered Elena's rebuff by merely asking her to sing, Frances knew her grandson well enough to discern the intense curiosity and attraction he continued to hold for the mother he had never known.

A knock at the door took Frances by surprise. The children were upstairs playing, and Jesse had gone out to meet with a man about producing one of his plays.

"I'll get it, Mama," Sara bubbled, moving toward the door in a most unladylike hurry. Didn't she know what kind of danger such movement posed for her unborn child?

After placing the starched and folded table linens in the center drawer of the sideboard, Frances straightened. As a black-coated gentleman was admitted, she hurriedly smoothed her apron and tucked an errant wisp of hair behind her ear.

"Why, Dr. Suffington, how good to see you," greeted Sara, as if finding one of Detroit's most eminent professors of music at their door was not one bit out of the ordinary.

"Good morning, young lady," he responded with a courtly bow, doffing his hat. "And to you, Mrs. Golden," he added, catching sight of Frances beside the dining-room table as he resumed his elegant, upright bearing.

"Good morning," Frances replied faintly, wondering why on earth her children's former voice teacher had chosen to call. Fifteen years ago Dr. Suffington had been a popular teacher of music, but in the ensuing years his status had soared. After studying abroad, he had returned to the city and now gave private lessons to the musical elite as well as directing an internationally renowned chorus.

The last time she'd seen him was when Jesse was under his tutelage, perhaps seven years ago. Since then his grizzled hair had been transformed completely to silver. A matching mustache and goatee completed his august appearance.

"How can we ever thank you for coming?" Sara said effusively, making Frances wonder what impetuousness her daughter was up to now.

The doctor's reply confirmed her worst thoughts.

"After receiving your urgent and most intriguing message, madam, I could no more stay away than deny myself the very air I breathe."

"My sister-in-law, Elena, is right here. Please follow me." With a light step, Sara led Dr. Suffington around the corner from the entry to the sitting room.

Dare she join them? Should she remain where she was? Frances suffered intense curiosity and painful indecision about what she ought to do next. The professor's ringing voice was easy to hear as Sara made introductions, but she was forced to take a few steps forward to make out the words of Elena's low response, praying at the same time the girl would not bring shame upon their family.

"Elena tells me her singing voice has been ruined," Sara was saying, "and I just can't accept that such a tragedy is so. That's why I sent for you."

"Mmm-hmm," was Dr. Suffington's enigmatic reply. "Tell me more."

"Well, she says . . . Elena, dear, why don't you just relate your symptoms? That would be simpler all around."

After a pause of excruciating length, Frances heard her daughter-in-law begin to speak. Her voice did not carry as well as the others', making it necessary for Frances to edge a bit closer yet to the doorway of the sitting room.

"What, if any, medical evaluations have been made of your condition?" Dr. Suffington queried.

"My manager called a doctor a few times."

Even without seeing Elena, Frances could imagine the shrug of the girl's too-thin shoulders as she related as little as she possibly could. Combined with her closed expression and averted gaze, Dr. Suffington would no doubt take umbrage at his wasted trip. Yet to Frances's surprise, the professor continued in his investigation, sounding not the least bit unruffled.

"What did he advise?"

"A gargle and some lozenges, but they did not help."

"I see. Was rest prescribed?"

"Rest?" A short, wry laugh ensued. "They say there is none for the wicked."

"Nonsense, Elena," Sara loyally interjected. "You are most certainly not a wicked woman."

It took every bit of willpower to refrain from marching around the corner into the sitting room, agreeing wholeheartedly with Elena's self-assessment, and putting an end to the interview. Poor Dr. Suffington had more important things to do than waste his time on a common woman of the stage.

"How long has it been since you have sung?"

"Almost two months." Again came the hard little laugh. "But what I was doing before that could hardly be called singing."

"Mmm-hmm. What was your type of training, madam, and how long did you remain under your teachers?"

"I never . . . I mean, my manager had been a vocal teacher—"

An unmistakable sound of masculine disdain rang out.
"Say no more. I am acquainted with that type of parasite. He will wring every bit of talent and profit possible from those of whom

he takes advantage. Once his victims are no longer of any use to him, he casts off their empty husks and finds others to exploit."

Silence came from the next room, then a sniffle.

Warmth and compassion were evident as the authoritative voice went on. "Ah yes, I've seen this tragedy time and time again. There, now. Take my handkerchief. It is my business to know a great deal about music, the good and the bad. Unfortunately, nothing is done to stop these most base predators. You might be surprised to know that I did hear you sing once in Kansas. I attended Crawford's Opera House to see my former student—Mr. Golden—perform in *If Not for You*. I recall that your music was done quite well, but sung rather by assault. I also remember thinking that if you continued to abuse your voice in such a fashion, it would be to your ruin."

"Oh no! Is it too late?" Sara asked breathlessly. "Isn't there anything that can be done?"

"Perhaps," came the slow reply. "Too few realize that the vocal mechanism is really a musical instrument, of far more value than any violin or flute. Simple physiological laws govern its operation, yet so often this precious instrument is destroyed by precepts in direct opposition to its function. It is not enough to merely sing well. Every singer ought to have an intelligent knowledge of music and the voice itself. Sadly, this is not the case, and irreparable damage often results from poor vocal hygiene. This is never the case with *my* students," he added with obvious pride.

"Will you take Elena as your student, Dr. Suffington?" Sara blurted out. "If anyone can help her, I know it's you!"

"Yes, that's probably true," he discreetly agreed, "but first a thorough evaluation of her condition must be made."

Frances could keep silent no longer. Her arms gesticulated with a life of their own as she hied around the corner and began to protest this ridiculous travesty.

"Dr. Suffington, you must excuse my daughter's flight of fancy," she began, not disguising her displeasure toward the two younger women. "She has presumed upon our previous relationship with you, and for that I beg your forgiveness. You are obviously an extremely busy man, and we realize your clientele is now very limited—and elite." With a scorching expression, she looked first at Sara, then at Elena.

Sara's eyes were wide with hurt and shock as she looked at her mother, then directed an expression of pained apology toward Elena. As for her daughter-in-law, Frances had been surprised to find, upon bursting into the room, a look of softness upon Elena's countenance. As Frances continued with her harangue, however, a subtle expression of mutiny replaced that openness as quickly as boiling syrup went through the hard-crack stage.

"My dear Mrs. Golden," Dr. Suffington interjected silkily, "I do not believe I have given any indication of having been put out by this consultation." Turning to Elena, he went on. "Please come to the conservatory a week from tomorrow at ten o'clock in the morning. I would like to spend some time with you and have one of my colleagues do a laryngoscopic examination of your vocal apparatus. That procedure may be a bit uncomfortable, but the information we gain as a result will be invaluable in your recovery, if there is to be any."

Joy broke through the distress on Sara's face, and she impulsively hugged the slight shoulders of the blonde woman beside her. "Oh, Elena! What do you say, my dear new sister? I know your grief at losing your musical voice. Will you allow Dr. Suffington to help you sing again?"

"I don't—" Elena began, her face wooden.

"Oh, I know nothing is for certain," Sara went on, "but if there's even the smallest chance your voice can be healed, wouldn't you want to take it?"

With the patience of a saint, Dr. Suffington gazed indulgently at the young women as they spoke, then turned toward Frances. "How is it that time has so graciously preserved your appearance, Mrs. Golden, while taking its toll upon mine? In the years that have passed since our last meeting, you have not changed a bit. Are the secrets of the Fountain of Youth to be found on Adelaide Street?"

"Dr. Suffington . . . y-you're too kind." Self-consciously, Frances dropped her eyes and smoothed her already smooth apron, almost forgetting her indignation as a flush of heat rose in her cheeks.

"I am serious when I say that making an assessment of your new daughter would be my privilege. If she can be helped, it would be my honor to do so."

"But I don't know if Sara realizes that y-your fee . . ." Frances trailed off, ill at ease with the discussion of payment. Sara's and Jesse's voice lessons had not been inexpensive, and that was years ago, before Dr. Suffington's rise to prominence. They were by no means poor, but the household finances were budgeted carefully. Jesse was writing away on his plays, earning hardly . . .

"Let's not put the cart before the horse, Mrs. Golden. A discussion of my fee will come later, once we have discerned the degree of damage that has been done. I will see you a week from tomorrow, ten o'clock," he repeated, turning toward Elena.

"You most certainly will," Sara hastily supplied, "if I have to bring her myself! But I am sure Jesse will be delighted to do the honors."

"Ah yes. I look forward to seeing your brother again."

Appearing hesitant, Elena looked to Sara's beaming face, then to Dr. Suffington. Quickly her dark eyes flicked toward Frances, after which all uncertainty fled her features.

Speaking clearly and with eloquence, Elena addressed their visitor. "I am most grateful for this opportunity, Doctor, and I will ask my husband to bring me to you at the appointed time. Thank you," she concluded simply, engaging Dr. Suffington with a tilt of her head and an accompanying smile of transforming beauty. "And thank you, too, Sara."

"I declare, there is altogether too much loveliness in this house for one man to bear," said the old gentleman with a pleased nod. "I must be going before my physician puts me on another pill for my heart."

"Oh my! Do you have a heart ailment, Dr. Suffington?" Frances inquired with alarm, her hand fluttering to her chest.

"My good woman," replied the professor with an enigmatic smile, "where beautiful women are concerned, a man always suspects his heart is ailing. I can't tell you what a pleasure it's been to see you again." He bowed toward her, then made his farewells to Sara and Elena.

"Mama!" exclaimed Sara in a loud whisper after the door had shut behind him. "He was acting sweet on you! What do you think, Elena? Dr. Suffington is a widower, after all."

"What nonsense," disagreed Frances swiftly, feeling her anger rise along with another unwanted flush. "I have been away too long from my work." As she withdrew to the kitchen, excited chatter resumed in the sitting room.

Only a few items remained to be pressed; then the noon meal must be started. Frances glanced around the kitchen, not really seeing anything, while she put the iron back on the stove to heat.

Why did it seem that every time her world grew calm and ordered, the applecart had to be upset? Life was always full of surprises, of course, but her own widowhood had been sprung upon her without any warning whatsoever. Thank goodness for the arrival of little Pearl six months after Gerald's death; being a new grandmother had been just the remedy to help her go on.

Then, just as she was settling into contentment once again, Jesse began his period of rebellion. After an unpleasant season, he struck out on his own and joined the theater, leaving her all alone and in a state of unceasing worry for his soul. When he came back, wreathed in sorrow and repentance, he brought with him a very active one-year-old son.

After months of upheaval—not to mention learning how to blend the roles of mother and grandmother in order to help Jesse raise little Robert as best she possibly could—the three of them were finally enjoying a peaceful domestic existence. And now Jesse had to go and bring *her* here.

Elena.

Why did everyone rush about, catering to every wish and whim of the wayward woman he'd carelessly wed? Didn't they realize it was Frances who had to prepare the prescribed diet and desired foods? comfort the confused, distressed young boy? fend off the solicitous queries and outright curious remarks of neighbors and parishioners?

What next, Lord? she asked rather ungraciously while sprinkling the next item to be ironed. *I don't understand what you're asking of me, and I certainly don't understand what you've asked of Jesse—if you've asked anything at all. I've done my share to nurse Elena back to health, yet it seems my children show her more loyalty than they do to their own mother.*

She paused, realizing her prayer was far from reverent. Setting down the sprinkling jar, she sighed and began again, this time folding her hands and bowing her head. But try as she might, no words came.

Only more tears.

✿

Jesse entered the house with his portfolio tucked under his arm. The aroma of his mother's fried chicken was something that would hearten any man, but he felt too dispirited to be revived even by its tantalizing fragrance.

His interview at White's Grand Theater had started on a cautiously optimistic note but ended the same way all his recent such appointments had—with Jesse being shown the door. The reasons had begun to blend together in a smudge pot of sayings that he now knew by heart:

The subject matter isn't exactly right for our patrons. . . . Your work shows promise, but unfortunately the timing is wrong. . . . Come back and see us when you've gotten yourself established.

"Papa!" Robert called as Jesse removed his coat and hat. "You're almost late for dinner! Nana just told us to wash our hands and sit down. Don't you remember? Pearl and Benjamin and Auntie Sara are going home straight afterward."

Indeed, the table was set, and already there were dishes of steaming food upon its center. Sara walked from the kitchen with a basket of bread and gave him a brilliant smile.

"I'll be right there," he called, walking to his desk in the study. Setting down his portfolio, he sighed heavily and rubbed his hands over his face. What was he doing with his life? Had God truly intended for him to be a playwright? How could he hope to provide for his family if his work was politely refused by every theater in town?

Another sigh left his chest. What would Sara's departure do to the dynamics in this home? What was going to happen with Elena? In the physical sense she was healing, but the tentacles of her past had a stranglehold upon her interior self. Would there ever come a day when she could trust in anyone or anything? in him? Could she ever believe that Christ was the solution to all her problems and pain?

Do you *believe I am the solution for all* your *problems and pain, Jesse?* came a quiet voice from inside his heart. *Do you trust me?*

"Jess?" came Elena's soft query, causing him to start. He hadn't known she was in the room, but there she sat in the blue chair beside the window, her blonde hair upswept in a soft style. The sunlight played with the golden lights, forming a brilliant corona about her head. Her dark eyes reflected concern, making him recall her attentiveness in the early days of their marriage. "Come talk to me. What's put such an expression on your face?"

He almost went to her and poured everything out, yearning to move the open book on her knee and rest his head in its place, feeling her fingers weave random patterns through his hair. But how could he do such a thing when he had assured her that she could rely on him for anything and everything she needed? He couldn't admit he wasn't able to make a living. He felt like a fraud, an utter failure.

"Dinner's on the table," called Sara from the dining room. "And wait till you hear what happened to Elena this morning, Jesse!"

Arranging his features into what he hoped was a smile, Jesse walked to the chair and offered Elena his arm. "You had some excitement today?"

"Your sister is quite a busy woman," she began with a slow curving of her lips, accepting his assistance.

"You mean a busy*body*," he replied, his melancholy mood eased by the sensation of her hand in his, her warmth and sweet fragrance against his side.

"I heard that," Sara said from the doorway, her eyes sparkling, "but I don't care. You can call me whatever you like, for I am the one, after all, who arranged for Dr. Suffington to meet with Elena about recovering her voice."

"You did?" exclaimed Jesse, looking back and forth between the two women. "Dr. Suffington?"

"Yes, indeedy," came his sister's saucy reply. "He would like Elena to come to the conservatory a week from tomorrow."

With concern, Jesse turned back to Elena. "Are you feeling up to singing yet?" Though a slight weight gain was visible, she still tired easily and remained more frail than robust.

"I'd like to try," she said softly, an expression of hope and longing on her features. He recalled how she used to gaze at him like that, back when she'd believed in him with her whole heart . . . before nameless reasons had caused her to conclude she was better off on her own.

"Then how can I refuse you such an opportunity?" he asked, laying his other hand over hers. "I dare say Dr. Suffington is one of the best in the world."

Elena offered him another smile. "I heard he was your vocal teacher."

"He was," Jesse replied, recalling the tension of his last meeting with the esteemed professor of music. After he'd returned to Detroit with Robert, Suffington had contacted him, wanting him to sing in his exclusive chorale, which frequently toured throughout the United States and Europe. With the responsibility of sole parenthood on his shoulders, however, Jesse didn't have to think twice about turning down the offer. Robert needed the steady presence of his father in the home, period.

He'd also tried explaining the calling he felt toward writing plays, but Suffington had been quite put out by his refusal, telling him that today's theater would never accept such overtly religious material as Jesse hoped to produce. People could go to church on Sundays and receive their helpings of virtues and morals and hymns, the older man had said; when they went to the theater, they came to see progressive, sophisticated entertainment. In parting, Suffington had given him a sound lecture on allowing his God-given vocal talents to sit idle.

Neither Sara nor his mother knew of this meeting with his former teacher of voice, and in light of that, he was frankly surprised that Suffington was willing to help Elena. Most likely the wily and determined professor had an ulterior motive in mind and saw this as a way to achieve his end. Jesse also knew that Suffington's expert teaching did not come cheap. How would he be able to meet those expenses?

Another look into Elena's melting dark eyes made his heart roll heavily, and he told himself he'd do whatever he could to help her. Her voice lifted in song was one of the most beautiful sounds on earth, and he longed to hear her sing again.

If Villard had caused permanent ruin to Ellie's ability to sing, the man would have to answer to him for such brutal treatment. He also suspected Elena's former manager of far more than that. After years of successful and well-attended performances, how was it that his wife had not so much as a penny to her name? Villard had always assured Elena, and then him, that the bulk of her money had been wisely invested.

"Goodness, Jesse, I sincerely hope your face doesn't freeze in such a sour position. You must be hungry. Our meal is getting cold; let's sit down." Sara's words were light, but her eyes probed his with concern. He knew she would seek out a private moment to speak with him before she departed.

Weariness coursed through him, making him wish that he could lie down, sleep, and awaken to a life of no problems. *Do you believe I am the solution for all your problems and pain, Jesse?* echoed the quiet voice within his heart. *Do you trust me?*

He wished he could.

Chapter 8

The first snow flurries of the season were falling as Jesse drove Elena to the Detroit Conservatory of Music. Fluffy flakes fell from the sky with the softness of spun sugar, dusting the horses' backs and collecting lightly on the carriage.

Bundled in a warm cloak, Elena savored being out of the house. The chill air felt refreshing against her face, and with a shy glance at the handsome figure of a man beside her, she snuggled more deeply within the wool folds. A spark of excitement burned within her, something she'd never believed would happen in her life again.

"Are you cold?" asked Jesse, turning his head at her movement. "I have another blanket behind the seat if you need it."

"I'm fine," she said, feeling her heart quicken as their gazes met.

"Nervous?" he asked, waggling his brows just as he'd done before they used to go onstage.

"Yes," she answered truthfully. "I want to hope that my voice can be healed but . . ."

"But what?"

"You don't realize how ugly it became. That's why I wouldn't sing for you . . . or for Bobby that day."

"Ellie," he said with such gentleness and intimacy that her

stomach swooped, "it doesn't matter to me if you never recover your voice. Hearing you sing again would fill me with pleasure, but waking up beside you every morning for the rest of my life means far more than that. It's *you* I care about, not whether or not you can sing."

Her eyes misted over as he laid his hand over hers for a long moment. She couldn't help but contrast his sentiments with the last words she'd heard from Stephen Villard's lips. In the end, her manager had been clear about her value to him: Without a voice, she was of no significance.

"We're almost there," Jesse said, pointing toward the conservatory.

Recalling Dr. Suffington's fine dress and cultured air, it occurred to Elena that she was most likely about to enter a very different world of music than the one to which she had been accustomed. The American musical stage, while popular with many people, was a far cry from the Italian and German operas frequented by the well-to-do.

"Maybe we shouldn't have come," she said nervously as Jesse parked the carriage and helped her dismount. What if Jesse's mother was right about this being a waste of the professor's time? she asked herself, feeling her heart thrum in her chest. Perhaps the grand Dr. Suffington would find her so sadly lacking in musical ability that he would regret making his offer to her. She didn't wish to bring shame to Jesse, nor to his family, before his former teacher.

"My dear, we're already at the doorstep. Let's at least find out what the doctor thinks." Jesse's words did little to reassure her as they walked through the door and were greeted by the receptionist. After a short wait, they were shown into a grand office of polished wood. A thick, expensive carpet swathed the floor, and the walls were covered with photographs, official-looking diplomas and certificates, seemingly as numerous as shingles on a roof. A shiny grand piano sat in the corner, its lid raised.

After only a few minutes, Dr. Suffington entered his office

by a side door. His coat was a four-button cutaway, and he wore a matching plaid vest of fine kersey. "Good morning to both of you," he said, smiling widely, looking back and forth between them.

"It's good to see you again, sir." Jesse shook the older man's hand.

"Yes, yes. It was my great pleasure to finally meet your wife. How are you this morning, Mrs. Golden?"

"I feel as though I have a case of first-night nerves," she admitted.

"Ah, but that won't do." The bearded gentleman waved his hand, dismissing her concerns. "You must relax in order for my evaluation of your voice to be properly made. After you sing for me, we will go to Dr. Dudley's examination room to have a look with the mirrors." Shuffling through some papers on his desk, he extracted a small book, opened it to a particular page, and handed it to Elena before taking a seat at the piano.

"We will begin with some scales and other exercises. When I instruct you to do so, begin on the top of page twenty-three. Stand here so I can see you," he added, pointing to an area beside the piano. "Relax your shoulders and neck. They are tensed already."

As Elena took her place, she glanced at the book, relieved to see that the vocalises did not appear too difficult. Jesse seated himself in one of the padded chairs before Dr. Suffington's desk and gave her an encouraging smile.

Playing a chord, the music professor demonstrated the pattern of the scale he wished sung. When he played the chord again, Elena followed his example, aghast at how weak she sounded. Each new chord introduced was a half step higher than the last. As they climbed upward, her voice began to fail at a point far lower than the range she had been previously capable of singing.

"Stop! Never brace yourself to get a note out! Down now," directed Suffington, leading her in descending scales. After that came a test of her tonal memory, with the doctor playing arbitrary sequences of notes and requesting that she sing them back to him.

"Now from the book." Striking the piano's middle C, Suffington gave her a reference from which to begin, then removed his hands from the instrument. Though his eyes were alert, his expression was inscrutable.

Slowly, Elena began singing the music before her. To her ears, the once-sleek sound of her voice had been replaced with harshness. Too, she was lacking in her former steadiness and power.

"Enough," commanded the older man before she had finished the page. Sorting through the pile of music beside him on the bench, he extracted a folder and held it toward her. "Sing this."

Elena's heart plummeted as she viewed a piece called "Sacrifizio d'Abraham." "I don't know Italian," she confessed.

"Just the melody, then, with whatever sound you choose."

Licking her lips, Elena began the first measure, only to be interrupted by the professor. "Stop. Sing a G-sharp."

In her middle register, this note sounded purer than the higher ones she had just been singing.

"D below."

Somewhat confused, Elena looked away from the music and followed Dr. Suffington's rather odd directions.

"B-flat below. F above. Now middle C."

Glancing at Jesse, she was surprised to see his lips curved in a faintly satisfied smile. "The good doctor has just confirmed your absolute pitch, Ellie," he said of her ability to recognize and sing any given, isolated note without benefit of instrumental accompaniment.

"Mmm-hmm," was the official reply. "Before you and your voice suffer further fatigue, Mrs. Golden, we will now proceed to Dr. Dudley's office to take a look at what mischief has been wrought to your instrument."

"What is your opinion?" Elena impulsively asked as the doctor took his feet, wondering if there was hope for recovery.

"He is still formulating that," Jesse supplied, rising, "and will not give it to you until all pieces of evidence are in his possession."

"Ah yes, Mr. Golden was always one of my brightest pupils," said the professor with a wink, offering Elena his arm.

The next thirty minutes were uncomfortable though not unbearable. After establishing that there was no imperfection in her speaking voice, Dr. Dudley took a history of her health and made a careful examination of her ears, neck, nose, and throat. Then came the insertion of the laryngeal mirrors to view her vocal cords. Running up and down the notes of the scale with this warmed metal device in her throat was difficult, especially with the serious-looking physician—wearing a shiny reflector over his left eye—peering so intently into her oral cavity. Dr. Suffington stood nearby, making copious notes on a tablet of paper. Afterward, she was directed to return to the grand office while the two specialists conferred with one another.

"How was it?" Jesse asked, appearing anxious. Quickly, he walked toward her and drew her into his embrace, pressing a kiss against her forehead.

"It was nothing I'd want to do every day, but I survived," she said lightly, though her heart waited in dread for the professor's findings.

Jesse's arms tensed around her, his voice coming as a growl in her ear. "Stephen Villard ought to be in prison for what he did to your voice. Your upper range . . ." he trailed off, obviously fighting against saying more.

Oh, Jess, you'd murder him with your bare hands if you knew what he was guilty of. And me along with him. An icy shudder passed through her as she considered the awful possibility of the two men meeting again. At the time she and Jesse had separated, the tension between him and Villard was at the breaking point.

What would her old manager do if he knew she was under Jesse's protection once again? Had he truly washed his hands of her, as he'd said, or would he try to destroy them? destroy her? As much as Elena wished she could banish Stephen Villard's name from her mind forevermore, she could not forget he held the keys to her undoing.

It was dangerous to allow herself to care any more deeply for Jesse . . . for Bobby. Already she had become too attached. Too vulnerable. Yet her husband's nearness drew her heart, tempting her to believe that perhaps all *could* be well. He was convinced that she, Jesse, and Bobby could live happily ever after, but he had no idea of the obstacles standing against such a thing. Though she wished she could trust Jesse with everything, the lessons of life had taught her that nothing was permanent, that good things never lasted.

"You're cold," Jesse said solicitously, drawing her toward the chair and removing his coat. "Take this. You've had quite a morning."

Drawing warmth from Jesse's jacket, she strove to eject all thoughts of Stephen Villard from her mind. "Tell me what Dr. Suffington was like when you were his student," she asked, trying to change the stream of her thoughts.

"Stern, rigorous, exacting—"

"And I haven't changed a bit," the older man proclaimed, entering again through the side door. "Do you think you can put up with that, madam? My traveling schedule is light through the winter; therefore I will be able to monitor you quite closely. I am not an easy taskmaster, as your husband has already attested."

"Are you saying you can help me?" she burst out, clasping her hands over her breast.

"Yes. I have studied in London under the incomparable master Manuel Garcia, not to mention Dr. Lennox Browne, who is surgeon to the Royal Society of Musicians, among other things. From these men I learned a great deal about treating acantophonia, which is the impairment of singing voice you suffer, in your case evidenced by the failure of the higher notes."

"What do you propose?" asked Jesse, a furrow marring his smooth forehead.

"Short sessions of basic scales at home for the remainder of the week, with an emphasis on proper breathing and muscular relaxation, followed by a lesson here with me on Monday at two o'clock. Then the real work begins."

"About your fee, Professor," Jesse began.

Raising his right hand, Dr. Suffington shook his head. "We needn't trouble your lovely wife with such matters. You and I will meet to discuss my compensation, but rest assured that I have every confidence we will come to a satisfactory agreement. My first priority is to restore this woman's sorely abused voice."

Sensing Jesse's hesitation, Elena spoke up. "If this is going to cause any kind of hardship, Jess, I don't have to—"

"I want it for you, Ellie," her husband replied, giving her a smile that didn't quite reach his eyes.

"Do not worry, Mr. Golden," the older man reassured.

Jesse nodded. "I'll come by tomorrow then."

"Lunch at the Russell House. Noon. My treat."

Elena sensed Jesse's restlessness as Dr. Suffington then proceeded to lecture her on correct breathing, singing her scales without the influence or involvement of any other parts of her body, and many other aspects of vocal hygiene. Finally, the appointment was over, and she and Jesse left the conservatory.

During the ride home, her husband was faraway in thought. He had seemed sincere in his desire for her to recover her powers of singing, but she sensed there was something troubling him. Also, she had noticed a subtle tension between him and the professor.

"Jess, can we talk?" she asked, laying her hand upon his arm.

"What would you like to talk about?" His dark eyes turned to her in question.

"Is something the . . . matter?" she faltered, feeling suddenly self-conscious.

His sigh mingled with the sifting snowflakes. Another carriage passed, and he turned his attention back to the reins. "I'm starting to lose hope, Ellie," he finally said, still looking forward.

"Hope for what?"

He shrugged. "Hope for everything. Anything."

"Oh, Jess," she breathed, compunction stabbing at her heart. "If only you hadn't found me, then everything would be—"

"You'd be dead, Elena," he interrupted her with blunt language. "Or is that your preference?"

"Of course not! It just . . . it just grieves me to know what a burden I am to you."

"Why don't you forget about being a burden?" He spat the word *burden* as if it were a curse. "I want you to be my wife."

"I *am* your wife."

"Are you? Were you ever, really? Did you ever give me your heart?"

"Y-yes, I did, I—"

"I'll grant that you gave me a part of it, but then you took it back. I want to know about Stephen Villard." His voice grew harsh as he asked, "Why did you choose him over me?"

"I . . . I didn't."

"Yes, you did."

"Do you still love him?"

"*No!*" she said with all the vehemence she could muster, tears stinging her eyes. "I don't love him. I hate him."

"But you loved him once, didn't you?"

"I . . ." Feeling cornered, she couldn't think quickly enough to formulate a reply. How had the conversation taken such a turn? She couldn't believe any of this was happening.

"Why did you let him ruin your voice? your health? All these years I've stifled my suspicions about him. He was 'just your manager . . . just your manager,' both of you kept insisting, and I was foolish enough to believe it. Well, I don't believe it anymore, Elena, and I want to know why—if he was just your manager—*you nearly let him kill you!*"

To Elena, the world seemed to be moving in slow motion.

"If you want to be my wife," he went on slowly, with pain in his voice, "you will answer these questions."

After a seemingly interminable silence, she admitted, "I . . . when I was young . . . I thought I was in love." Her words came out in choppy bursts, and her chest felt as if it were on fire. "I'm sorry, Jess. I'm so sorry."

A long silence ensued from him as well, before he went on. "You were what . . . fifteen?"

"I had just turned sixteen." Tears tumbled down her cheeks. "He said he could make me famous. I was . . . starving," she admitted shamefully.

"Let's see . . . you were starving because you had run away from home, from your father who drank too much and terrorized you." He had stopped the carriage at the end of a lightly traveled street. The Detroit River ran slowly before them, its dark waters greedily lapping up the white snowflakes. "Now we're getting somewhere."

Elena made no reply as a deep, tearing pain rent through her heart.

"You can tell me about your family another time," he said grimly, though with a trace of compassion. "Right now I want to know what Stephen Villard means to you."

"Nothing," she whispered. "He is every bit as cruel and uncaring as my father."

"Four years ago, why did you leave me for him?" he persisted. "For love? Money? To stay on the stage? Or was it because you preferred him to me in other ways?"

"No!" she gasped. "After we were married I *never*—"

"But you did before." He didn't allow her to answer as he continued speaking, punctuating his words with a short, humorless laugh. "I suspected as much, but I told myself it didn't matter because I wanted you so badly. I shocked everyone by defying my upbringing and becoming a common musical actor—not to mention taking up with an uncommonly beautiful actress. You were the most incredible woman I had ever met, Elena, and I was determined to make you mine."

Elena looked downward into her lap. Tears fell on her mittened hands, pooling for a moment before soaking into the soft wool. Even when they had lived together as man and wife, Jesse had not bared so much of his heart to her.

"I was elated when you became pregnant, because then I could marry you. You see, I thought once you were my wife, nothing could ever take you from me. Of course then I didn't know my reasoning was a poor foundation upon which to build a lifelong union, indeed even poorer because my decisions were made by my flesh, in my own wisdom."

A low formation of geese flew overhead, honking loudly.

"I repented of all that—not of loving you, because I never stopped loving you, but of the wrong choices I made in response to that love—and now God has brought you back into my life. When I found you at that hospital, I was in awe of what a miracle he had performed in leading me to you. I was certain something magnificent was going to happen, but I don't know how it can when you keep Robert and me at arm's length. Lately I've been wondering how long it will be before you say good-bye again. Until you're well and have sufficiently recovered your voice?"

"Is that what you think of me?" she asked, knowing full well she deserved his low opinion.

Instead of answering, he ground out, "After I came to Detroit with our son, I offered up every part of my life to the Lord. I was utterly convinced that God wanted me to write plays, so I closed the door to music and have been writing plays. I happen to believe some of them are very good! Two have been sold and adapted. But can I get any produced on my own? How am I supposed to support my family? And now here comes my wife again, with a closetful of secrets she holds on to for dear life. What kind of cruel joke is God playing on me?"

"God's not like that!" she burst out, shocked that he had said such a thing against the Lord to whom he so earnestly prayed. "He isn't responsible for as much of this as people are . . ." Hesitantly, she touched his arm. "As *I* am. The fault lies with me."

After a long moment, he asked, "Why can't you trust me, Elena? Don't you know I would do anything for you?" His voice was hoarse, his eyes red-rimmed. "I would give my life for you. Why do you persist in believing otherwise?"

"Because I'm not worth it. You don't understand what kind—"

"Elena, I understand that I love *you*. There's nothing you can tell me that will make me love you any less."

Yes, there is. And you must never know.

"And in a sad, flawed way," he continued, sighing, "my love is a mere reflection of God's perfect love for you. I'm sorry, Ellie. I lost my hope and my head just now. Please forgive me for pressing you the way I did." Taking her hands in his, he looked her full in the face. "You may not think you're worth anything, but just the opposite is true. You're of more value than you could ever possibly realize."

"I do love you, Jesse," she wept, pierced by the tender, fierce love she saw reflected in his dark eyes. "I never wanted to hurt you. I love you and Bobby so very much."

"Then let's build from this moment. Do you want to do that?"

She nodded, unable to speak.

A shadow came over his face as he went on. "No doubt I sounded like the weakest of all Christians when you had to remind me of God's character a short while ago. And you were absolutely correct. The Lord does not play cruel jokes on his people. He loves us. Sometimes I become impatient because my prayers aren't answered as quickly as I want, or in the way I think they ought to be. Ellie, I realize faith can't be forced upon anyone, but I beg you to pray that God will reveal himself to you. As much as I want to be the one to heal all your hurts, it is only he who can do so."

"I suppose I can do that much," she assented, efficiently forcing her fears back into hiding.

"If you think about it, you cannot deny his involvement in your life."

A small smile quirked at the corners of her mouth. "Your

sister said the same thing while she was visiting. Quite frequently, as I recall."

"Ah, she's an intelligent woman. You should listen to her." With his hand, he tilted her chin, raising her face toward his. "We have many obstacles to face, Elena, but with God's help, there can be nothing too difficult."

A part of her heart yearned to accept that his words were true, but her memories and experiences disputed the validity of his simple, unadorned statement. Knowing that Jesse still cared for her the way he did—though she was completely undeserving—undid some of the bitterness and self-defensiveness shielding her heart.

The touch of his lips against hers brought back a bouquet of sweet memories of the too-brief time in her life when she had believed that love was enough to conquer all.

"Ellie," he murmured, "shall we go home?"

Could she believe in a lifetime of love with this man? Was it possible to nurture hope for the future once again? to dream? to dare think of happiness? Was she willing to bear his children and pray to his God?

Yes, she wanted to cry with all her heart. *I want what Jesse offers. I don't want to wake up every morning expecting the worst, waiting all day for it to happen. I want to live with hope in my heart. I want to be . . . free.*

"Yes," she said aloud, feeling her heart pound crazily against her ribs. The old arguments rose immediately in her mind, telling her such freedom was unattainable.

"Elena?"

"Let's go home," she said quickly, before she said something to extinguish the sudden happiness that shone forth from her husband's face.

Chapter 9

What did Dr. Suffington have up his sleeve? Jesse continued to wonder some days after their meeting, uncertain of the older man's motives. The figure he had named for Elena's music lessons was well below the standard fee. Why his generosity?

Jesse had been wary about sharing lunch with the professor, suspecting that he would want to revisit Jesse's refusal to tour with Suffington's chorale. To his surprise, the silver-haired man did not even bring the matter up. Their conversation was pleasant, centered on Suffington's optimism for Elena to make a musical recovery. He'd also asked about Jesse's plays, seeming genuinely disappointed to hear that no major productions were forthcoming. A smattering of local happenings, talk about their families, and prognostications for the coming winter rounded out the remainder of their discussion.

"Papa?" came Robert's piping voice, interrupting Jesse's thoughts. Setting his pen in its marble rest, he turned his attention toward his son, who had approached the desk without his notice. "Do you think Mama will play another game of draughts with me tonight?" the boy asked, his dark eyes hopeful.

"I'm sure she will, Robert." Pushing back his chair, Jesse welcomed his son into his lap.

"Are you writing another play, Papa?" Leaning forward,

Robert examined the sheaf of papers on the desk. "What does it say?"

"Probably a whole bunch of nothing."

Robert eyed the pages. "You used a lot of paper to say nothing."

Jesse laughed, filling the room with a rich, warm sound. "Son, you are wise beyond your years." Wrapping both arms around the boy, he held Robert tight for a long moment.

Nestled against his breast, Robert asked softly, "Papa, are you happy that Mama is here?"

"I am indeed. Are you?"

The blond head nodded against his chest. "I was scared at first."

"Scared of what?"

"That Mama would die. She was very sick." After a moment's pause, he added, "Where has she been? Why didn't she want to live here with us before?"

Jesse's heart was pierced by the candor of his son's questions, and he swallowed hard against the thick lump in his throat. Though Robert's movements had stilled, tension radiated from his young body.

"Your mother loved you more than you could ever imagine," Jesse said with conviction, recalling the days after Robert's birth. "She tended you with such care, and all day long she sang you the most beautiful lullabies. When she gave you a bath, she used to kiss your little toes and make you laugh."

Robert's voice quavered as he asked, "Does she still love me that much?"

"Robert," Jesse replied in a voice husky with unshed tears, "I'm sure she loves you even more than that. Her love for you never stopped . . . it just kept growing."

"Then why did she . . ." Robert began, then stopped. "Will she go away again?" he asked anxiously.

Reflecting on the past hopeful days with Elena, he replied carefully, "I believe your Mama wants to live here with us."

"Nana isn't happy."

Jesse sighed and nodded. "I know."

"Her face looks mad a lot."

"Nana is still adjusting. Do you know what that means?"

"Getting settled?"

"That's right." Jesse gently tousled his son's blond hair. "The past several weeks have been topsy-turvy with your mother's arrival and her sickness. It sometimes takes a while for things to become settled."

"I am adjusted to having Mama here now." Robert's face was bright as he turned toward him. "Are you?"

"Oh yes. I want your mama to live with us forever so we can be the family that God intended us to be."

"Papa . . . are you and Mama going to sleep together every night now?"

Jesse cleared his throat, trying to think best how to answer such a question. "Mothers and fathers like to lie close to each other at night," he began slowly, "so now that your mama is not so sick anymore, I can be near her. It was good of you to share your room with me after she first arrived."

Robert nodded, seemingly accepting of the new nighttime arrangements. "Is Nana angry because Mama didn't live with us before?" he asked, his young brow furrowed.

"I think that is part of your grandmother's unhappiness."

"After she gets home from her ladies' meeting, Nana should play draughts with Mama. Then she would see how nice and funny and pretty she is."

Jesse's laughter was mingled with sadness as he thought of all the ways his mother distanced herself from Elena. If Elena was in a room, Frances did not enter. If Elena entered a room, Frances quietly exited. Mealtimes were the exception to that, when his mother ate her food with swift efficiency.

Last Sunday, Elena had expressed willingness to go to church with them, but instead of being happy, Frances sat all through the service as if she were holding a slice of lemon on her tongue. It was safe to say that Frances Golden had always been a complex woman, but generosity and a godly nature were usually her foremost attributes. Would her heart ever thaw toward Elena? Jesse wondered. If so . . . when?

"Mama's up from her nap. Here she comes!" Robert announced, bounding off Jesse's lap. "Do you think there is time for a game of draughts before supper, Mama?" wheedled their son as Elena entered the study.

With a sweet, indulgent smile, Elena nodded.

"I'll set up the board!" Robert cried, hastening to do just that.

"My mother prepared a macaroni before she left for her meeting," Jesse said, his eyes drinking in the kittenish appearance of his just-awakened wife. "It should be done baking soon."

"I could have made us something," said Elena, a shadow passing over her face. She finished in a whisper, her voice intended for Jesse's ears alone. "But I believe your mother would rather drink rat poison than have me in her kitchen."

"Be patient, Ellie. She'll come around," he replied, unable to refute her words. Nonetheless, he was glad for the respite this evening while his mother was at her ladies' meeting. Whenever Frances was away, the atmosphere of the home lost its strain. A short while ago he had laid a fire in the hearth, and now it crackled warmly. The sun was setting, and the aroma of the dish in the oven tugged at his appetite.

"Ready, Mama," called Robert from the small, rectangular table on the other side of the room.

"Oh, dear," Elena sighed with theatrical flair, her skirt flowing gracefully as she walked to the chair. "I wonder if I will ever be able to win at this game."

"Don't feel too sorry for yourself. I can scarcely beat him myself anymore," volunteered Jesse, feeling contentment well up in his heart as his wife and son faced each other across the small table and made their opening moves.

Though the thought of Elena in Stephen Villard's arms tightened his neck and made his blood run hot, at the same time it was an incredible relief to have his worst suspicion out in the open. So much more made sense now. When he'd begun talking about leaving the theater and taking Elena and Robert home to Michigan, no doubt Villard had bullied Elena into staying, threatening to reveal their past. Also, without her talent and drawing power, Villard's earnings would have quickly ceased.

The man was worse than a criminal. He was a—it was with difficulty that Jesse curbed the curse word that came to his mind, thinking it must have been invented for men like Villard. How could anyone treat someone the way Elena's manager had treated her?

His talk with Elena after their first visit to the conservatory had been filled with pain for both of them, but he could not deny that much good had come out of it. Her confession about her previous association with Villard told him that she was willing to trust him in ways she never had before. In the midst of that snowy afternoon, they encountered a turning point, and Jesse was filled with hope for the future.

He suspected there was a lifetime of suffering hidden in Elena's past, particularly with her family, but he chose to believe that time and love would enable her to trust him enough to open up and share those hurts. The injustice of her upbringing and later exploitation made him feel powerless and angry. How was it that he and Sara had grown up in a household of love and Christian stability while Elena had had to endure the circumstances she had? Where was the fairness in life?

On a large scale he trusted in God's goodness, but he was left with disturbing questions as he pondered such things. Of course he knew that bad things happened the world over and had been happening since the beginning of time. Many times his heart was wrenched by reading the newspapers or listening to prayer requests at church. Was putting his beloved Ellie's face to the appalling things she had revealed what was bothering him so much?

Yet despite her woebegone upbringing, God had provided Elena with her two girlhood friends Romy and Olivia. From what she had told him, they sounded like God-fearing girls who had come from pious homes and families . . . her sanctuary amidst a childhood of distress. Over the past years she had allowed those relationships to lapse, but perhaps she might be persuaded to renew them.

Laughter came from the draught board as Robert announced he was double jumping his mother. "You clever boy! Why don't I ever see that coming?" Elena cried, allowing a beaming Robert to remove two of her pieces. Her gaze tugged at Jesse's and lingered for a few seconds, communicating her pleasure.

Elena was beginning to sparkle again.

The singing actress with whom he had fallen in love had been a bright, vibrant creature who radiated energy and life. From the first moment he had laid eyes upon Elena Breen, he'd been captivated by her sauciness and appeal. She was—

Mentally, he stopped short, realizing the dichotomy of his thoughts. How was it logical to think of Elena in the contradictory ways he just had? Was she a child of misfortune, or was she one of the world's brightest, most beautiful lights? Could she be both? There was much, much more he wanted to learn about this woman he had wed. Would he ever know her? understand her? How many layers would be peeled away before he was able to truly enter her heart?

Would she ever allow God to enter her heart?

By virtue of the fact that she had willingly gone to church last Sunday, he had hope for her conversion. Neither did he get the sense she was any longer bucking his daily, vocal prayers for their marriage. The closeness of their early days was returning, but it was different, tempered by time, responsibilities, and maturity. No longer were they young and hot-blooded, living the exciting, carefree life of the stage. They had both been changed by the past four years.

"I won!" Robert exulted, clapping his hands together. After arising, Elena went to his chair and congratulated him. He welcomed her embrace, and as she enfolded him in her arms she closed her eyes, an expression of maternal bliss spreading across her face.

"The winner sets the table," Jesse called with a smile, looking forward to the dinner the three of them would soon share.

"The winner *and* the winner's mother will set the table," Elena replied saucily, opening her eyes and arching one brow. "Come on, Bobby."

As Jesse followed his family to the dining room, he began believing that things were really going to work out after all.

❧

The days became shorter as autumn marched relentlessly toward winter. Today was cold but clear, the sky a brilliant shade of cobalt. Deciding this might be the last halfway nice day before spring, Frances was intent on making the most of her fall cleaning.

With a soft cloth dipped in her homemade mixture of alcohol, linseed oil, balsam fir, and acetic ether, she carefully polished the oak sideboard. Already she had hung out the rugs and beat them, run a cloth-covered broom into every corner of the house, and was now nearly finished with the woodwork. Corned beef and vegetables simmered on the back burner of the kitchen stove.

Though she had always taken pride in maintaining a clean and orderly home, these days she performed her household duties with grim determination. Her movements slowed, then intensified as a cascade of lovely notes reached her ears. Elena was upstairs practicing her music.

In the weeks since Dr. Suffington had begun his work with Elena, the sullen, uncommunicative, eye-averting girl was beginning to come out of herself. Or did the reason have more to do with Jesse, who behaved toward his wife in the same manner he might as if he were courting a princess? And just as she had feared, little Robert was becoming painfully attached to their fair-haired visitor.

That's how Frances chose to continue thinking of Elena—as their visitor. She had no doubt that one day the girl would pack up and disappear, and when that day came, it was Frances's greatest worry that there would be more children involved. Jesse no longer bunked with Robert, but had reclaimed his room.

Again came the voice, causing an unpleasant mixture of feelings inside her. The sound made her think of days long ago, when their lives had been filled with lessons, scales, recitals, and performances. Jesse had been blessed with remarkable talent, following after Gerald, his father. She and Sara had sung, though not with the same natural ability as the men of their family. Wistfulness filled Frances as she recalled those busy, beautiful years, and she recognized that she missed them.

Even though she despised Elena, she could not deny that the younger woman was endowed with an incredible voice. Even with its present impairment, her talent was obvious. It was not a great leap to imagine her daughter-in-law before an audience, evoking sighs and tears with her music.

In addition to Elena's twice-weekly lessons at the conservatory, Dr. Suffington had begun stopping by at least that often to check on his pupil and to work with her on some of the finer points of his instructions. The first time he had knocked at the door, he had accepted Frances's invitation for a slice of prune coffee cake before meeting with Elena. Since that day, Frances had made a point of having something tasty on hand for his visits. He didn't linger overlong at the dining-room table, but they talked and laughed as he ate, reminiscing about days gone by. His appreciation of her cooking was flagrant, making her wonder if she shouldn't invite him for Sunday dinner one day soon. He was a widower, after all, and she had the idea he took most of his meals alone in restaurants. That was simply no way to live.

A long sigh left her, and she set aside her musings about the silver-haired—and silver-tongued—professor. She was at an age where one must be careful not to lose her head. She had watched Sheila Hunt become an absolute ninny over George Morse, and then it turned out he was making time with three other widows in the church all at once.

Straightening, she felt her body protest. Her shoulders ached from all her labors, and so did her low back. At breakfast this morning Elena had asked if she could help with anything, but Frances couldn't see the sense in working someone so scrawny and recently ill. Besides, what would a theater woman know about properly keeping a house?

You could teach her, came that irritatingly reasonable voice from deep within her mind. *She seems to be tidy by nature. There is never anything out of order in Jesse's room, and she never leaves a mess behind her.*

When Jesse was out and Robert at school, Elena stayed upstairs so as to keep out of her way, Frances supposed. Well, that was fine with her. Again came the lovely voice, rising upward, this time breaking off abruptly. A long silence ensued. What was she doing up there? Weeping, Frances wondered, or was she angry? Did she want to give up?

More than once Frances had overheard Elena's despair over the failure of her upper register. Dr. Suffington seemed unruffled as he calmed his pupil's discouragement with matter-of-fact counsel about patience, time, and hard work. Jesse gave spirited encouragement, and while he was honest with his wife, he was also lavish in his praise.

The voice began again, low, slowly working upward. Realizing she had stopped her work, Frances began polishing the sideboard again, acknowledging that if nothing else, the girl was tenacious. Determined. Gritty.

Lord, have mercy on this home and this family, she prayed, wondering how much longer it would take the Almighty to rectify this situation that had already gone on far too long. *When are you going to get rid of her?* she asked, endeavoring to make her petition as polite as possible. Truth be told, she looked forward to her Ladies' Aide meeting tonight, if only to escape the walls of her home that, since Elena's arrival, pressed in like the bars of a prison cell.

❧

Taking a sip of water, Elena warred against her desire to throw herself across the bed and give up. Her voice was ugly. Despite her instruction from Dr. Suffington, it remained ugly. Ugly, ugly, ugly.

Its weakness and broken sound made her heartsick. Once it had taken no effort at all to project a brilliant note to the highest corners of a theater, and now she sounded worse than a sick crow.

She looked at the papers and pages of music on the dresser. All these exercises to do, some of them so silly. Stephen had never permitted the slightest bit of breathiness to detract from the purity of her voice, yet the unrelenting Professor Suffington insisted she do just the opposite. *For now you will sing forward,* he insisted, *and allow your voice to be carried on a slight breeze.*

She supposed she sounded better than she did when Stephen had dismissed her, but perhaps that was merely the result of her improved health. Since then she had regained weight and strength, but as she regarded herself in the mirror, a slender woman with too-sharp angles stared back at her. Who was she? she wondered with composed bewilderment. Why was she here? Who was she supposed to be?

She put her hand to her cheek, then allowed it to drift upward to touch her hair. Would it ever return to its former glory? Sara had given her half a dozen suggestions for softening treatments; before leaving for Ann Arbor she had trimmed away several strawlike inches. Sighing, Elena allowed her hand to fall to her side as the questions once again tugged at her mind: *Who am I? Why am I here? What am I supposed to be?*

Something banged downstairs, reminding her that Jesse's mother was in another one of her fanatical cleaning moods. Because of that, Jesse had gone out to the library to do his writing. He had invited Elena to accompany him, but she could not imagine sitting for the greater part of the day in such a stifling environment.

As opposed to what? she asked herself. She was a virtual prisoner in Jesse's room while the house beneath her was scrubbed, beaten, whisked, and oiled. More than once she had offered to assist Mrs. Golden with the household duties, but each of her offers was brusquely declined by her iron-jawed mother-in-law. *This is my territory,* the older woman seemed to be saying behind her words, *and let's not forget that, missy.*

However, something curious had been occurring lately when Professor Suffington came by. Frances's sour manner seemed to dissolve as quickly as sugar in hot tea. Now that Elena thought about it, tea was quickly and regularly served when the professor paid call. Before Elena's lesson Jesse's mother and Suffington would sit at the dining-room table, talking and laughing, while the widow plied the stylish gentleman with pastry or cake. More than once Jesse had muttered that he wished he knew what the old man was up to, but to Elena it was no mystery. Charles Suffington had his sights set on Frances Golden. She had read all the signs the day Sara had first greeted him at the door.

She wouldn't be surprised if the older woman was sweet on Suffington, too. Why else the purring and simpering, the elaborate desserts, the conspicuous absence of the ever-present apron whenever the man was here? Elena waited out their time together either upstairs or in the study, shaking her head at the astonishing alteration in her mother-in-law. The good thing about those days was that a little of Frances's niceness seemed to wear on even after the professor's departure.

Elena took another sip of water and resisted the urge to clear her throat. Back to Suffington's exercises. As she sang through them again, she could hear his instructions in her mind: *"Your neck and shoulders are as stiff as old leather. Relax your jaw more. Not so much. You didn't have a double chin when you came in here! Use your resonators, Mrs. Golden!"* She could almost hear the sound of his humming as he demonstrated his technique; then she would repeat back what she had heard. *"There, that's more like it.* Tsk, tsk. *What did I say about bracing yourself to get out a note?"*

Jesse had been correct—his former teacher was uncompromising to a fault. How was it possible she had managed to make a name for herself in musical theater if she couldn't even warm up to suit this stickler for perfection? Yet in the midst of his corrections and admonishments, quiet encouragement emanated from Suffington, as well as the self-assurance of a man who knows exactly what he is doing. Despite her frustration, she found herself wanting to please the old martinet.

Reaching the high end of her vocal exercise, Elena paid attention to all the objectives the professor had given her and was surprised to hear something almost pleasant leave her throat. Nothing like the old days, of course, but the sound gave her just enough incentive to pick up the next page and begin the next exercise.

A quarter hour later she was finished, just as Jesse came in. His dark eyes were warm with compliment. "I hear a big improvement already, Ellie."

Closing her eyes, she shook her head. "Oh, Jess. I wonder if this is doing any good at all. I sound so . . . bad."

"You sound like someone whose voice has been damaged," he said grimly, making a visible effort to lighten his next words. "If my opinion counts for anything, I think you've come a long way since you started with Dr. Suffington. You will sing again, and you will sing beautifully."

"How can you know that?"

"Because that's what Suffington says, and he wouldn't say something like that unless he was certain it would be so."

Coming near, Jesse put his arms around her and pressed a tender kiss against her cheek. Still holding her, he looked into her eyes. "Ellie, I want you to think of how far you've come since I found you at that hospital."

Elena nodded, feeling tears well up.

"Think of how far *we've* come since then. I love you, Elena." Though his voice was low, the intensity of his words communicated a depth of feeling that left her slightly off balance.

"I . . . I love you too, Jess," she admitted freely, helplessly, for the first time since he had found her. She surrendered herself against his strong chest. "I've never stopped loving you." Tears coursed down her cheeks. "I'm just so afraid—"

"Shh . . . Ellie, there's nothing to be afraid of anymore. I treasure you, dear one, and I won't let anyone or anything hurt you ever again."

How could she begin to explain to him the things that she feared? He couldn't protect her from her past nor from the razor-sharp memories that clawed at her heart. If he were to ever find out . . .

He would leave her. He wouldn't love her anymore.

Yet at the same time she craved the love and acceptance he offered, the shelter and security. All along she'd known she didn't deserve a man like Jesse Golden. He wanted her trust, she knew, and she was willing to give more to him than ever before. Would it be enough? she wondered. Could she live out the remainder of her life with part of her heart in exile?

"How was your writing today?" she asked, her last word interrupted by a hiccupping sigh.

"Better than some I've had lately," he replied thoughtfully, still holding her.

"Will you let me read some of your plays?" she asked, overwhelmed with tenderness at all the energy and devotion he poured into his passion.

"I don't know if you'll like them. They have a lot to do with faith and God."

"I want to read them," she repeated sincerely, finding that her resistance against things of religion had waned considerably during the past few weeks.

"Careful . . . it's my prayer that my work will move people toward God."

"Would that be so bad?"

"Oh, Ellie." His sigh was filled with emotion and laughter as he held her even tighter. "No, that wouldn't be bad, not at all."

Chapter 10

"I'm grateful for Thanksgiving because it means Christmas is coming!" announced Bobby at the holiday banquet table his grandmother had prepared, evoking laughter. After grace, Sara had suggested they go around the table and each tell what he was most thankful for.

The house was brimming with life and activity since Sara and her husband, Scott, and their children had arrived last evening. Bobby was delighted to have Pearl and Benjamin with him once again, and everyone was enlivened by Sara's warm presence. Elena also liked Scott, a prosperous-looking but kind man who appeared unfazed by his wife's vivacity.

"Family," stressed Jesse when it came to his turn. "I'm most grateful for family." He looked around the table before allowing his gaze to rest meaningfully on Elena, then on Bobby. Through the fan of her lashes, Elena observed that her mother-in-law stiffened as if stung by a bee.

Seated beside her husband, Elena was next. She echoed Jesse's declaration of being most thankful for family, a shiver running through her as his fingers sought hers beneath the table. As her eyes gazed upon Bobby, their son, she felt joy and grief mingle in her heart, and just briefly she allowed herself to wonder about the remainder of her family. *Not today,* she told herself, blinking back sudden, stinging tears. *Not today.*

Scott spoke after her, voicing his thanks for God's gracious provision for them. As he concluded with appreciation for the fine meal Frances had prepared, Elena pushed aside her bleak thoughts and realized another thing for which she was grateful— that Frances Golden's perennial bad humor had been diluted today by all the people and commotion.

The older woman had put a feast on the table to rival that for any emperor. For two days she had been engaged in a solitary flurry of cleaning, dusting, and baking that would have put an entire domestic staff to shame. The result was a sparkling home and a table laden with brown-crackled roast turkey, cranberry sauce, mashed potatoes and turnips, gravy, biscuits and rye bread, slaw, apple sweet pickles, an assortment of fresh and cooked vegetables, doughnuts and ginger cakes, plum pudding, and pumpkin pie.

Elena could never remember seeing so much food all at once, not to mention its beautiful presentation. Today the table was dressed in a lacy white cloth, and a low centerpiece of flowers graced its center. A set of blue-and-white china she had never before seen had been laid out, and the silver gleamed from yesterday's polishing. As the dishes were passed and conversation ensued, Elena realized she was having the type of Thanksgiving dinner that, as a girl, she'd always dreamed of.

During the years she was able, Katherine Breen had done her best to make holidays special with a rich pudding or an iced layer cake. Before serving the Thanksgiving meal, she would carefully place a vase of flowers from her indoor plants amidst the chipped and mismatched plates. If nothing was abloom, she might arrange some greens or dried weeds prettily in a saucer. All this was lost on Elena's father and brothers, who would descend upon the table like a plague of locusts, chewing noisily and belching without any thought to discretion. When finished, they left just as abruptly as they had come, without so much as a thank-you, leaving their chairs pushed away from the table helter-skelter.

The Goldens weren't rich, but they lived in a modest, well-cared-for home and had the privilege of enjoying good food. Well before her mother's passing, Elena had been solely responsible for the Breens' cooking, housework, and laundry. After her mother's death, her father and older brothers did more drinking than farming, which sometimes turned out to be a blessing for Elena, because they wouldn't come in to eat at all. Those were the days she was free to spend with Olivia and Romy.

Her friends' homes were far from palatial, but they were warm and orderly and clean, infused with love. How she'd always longed to live in such a house. After she'd run away and begun the ascent to success on the stage, she had stayed at hotels of increasing affluence, seeking comfort in surrounding herself with the trappings of material wealth. As she sat here at this table today, she realized with clarity that the trappings of wealth were not what she really sought. She had really never wanted anything more than a good home and a loving family.

Despite Mrs. Golden's rancor toward her, Elena knew the woman had provided a snug and loving home for her family. She had initially misread her mother-in-law's protectiveness toward Bobby as cruelty, but it hadn't taken long for Elena to recognize that the older woman was behaving as a mother bear might if her cub was threatened. Frances Golden was a *grand*-mother bear who loved her grandson fiercely. Unfortunately, she continued to view Elena as the enemy.

Taking a bite of moist turkey, Elena allowed her gaze to drift about the room as she chewed. The overhead molding gleamed, framing the dining room and its subtle caramel-colored print wallpaper. Crisp white curtains framed windows so clean as to appear they did not exist at all, and the perfect number of pictures and knickknacks adorned the walls and shelves.

How did a woman learn to keep house in this way? At the time Elena had left Missouri, the Breen dwelling was practically falling down around their ears. It did little good to sweep or wash or dust, because the menfolk had no regard for cleanliness. Hats and boots were worn indoors, and some days Elena believed more mud and manure existed indoors than out. They thought nothing of spitting or blowing out their nose whenever and wherever the humor happened to strike them.

In that house more things were broken than not, and neither her father nor brothers made repairs. The day the back door had rotted off its hinges, she'd had to drag it out of the way. It wouldn't surprise her to know that whatever was left of the door was still lying in the yard—

"Elena?" asked Sara. "I asked how you think your lessons with Dr. Suffington have been. Jesse tells us you're doing very well."

"I don't know about that," she demurred. "He asks me to sing in ways that I find difficult."

"The professor is pleased with her progress," put in Jesse with obvious pride, turning his head and catching her gaze. "Whether you know it or not, Ellie, you're starting to make lovely music again."

"Maybe today, Mama, you could sing something for us." Bobby's words were polite, his dark eyes glinting with hope. "If you feel well enough."

"I am fit," she replied warmly, "and after we have allowed this delicious meal to digest, I will sing." Again she felt Jesse's touch, although she did not know whether it was in appreciation for her willingness to sing or giving his mother a public compliment.

She tasted the cranberry sauce, finding it ideally sweetened. The potatoes were as fluffy as clouds, and the gravy the best she'd ever enjoyed. How ironic it was that she was living in the type of home her heart had always desired, wife of a good man and mother of an adorable son, yet she did not really have a place here. This was not her house, and each day her mother-in-law saw to it that she did not contribute anything that would make her feel more a part.

Why is there always some deterrent to prevent me from fully belonging anywhere? she asked herself, thinking back on her life. The house in St. Louis had become so unbearable that she had seen no other choice but to run away. Life in the theater was nomadic, with few performers maintaining permanent homes. She had stayed first in the most inexpensive boardinghouses she could find, then later, when she had attained success, in luxurious hotels. As her health and voice had worsened, the process had reversed itself until she was subsisting on the streets . . . and then not even that.

Due to a series of coincidences—or not, according to Sara—she now resided in a comfortable home on Adelaide Street in Detroit, Michigan. But was it home? Did she belong here? Would she ever fit in anywhere?

She thought of one of Jesse's plays, *Season of Grace.* She had read several now, finding them very well written. He'd been accurate when he'd said his work had much to do with faith and God. As his characters struggled against the difficulties of life, they did so within the structure of Christian thinking. She found the concept at the same time familiar and alien, pleasing and uncomfortable. Aside from Olivia and Romy and their families, and Jesse and Sara, she was not well acquainted with Christians who lived out their religious convictions.

The theme of *Season of Grace* was that the meaning of happiness and home wasn't found in physical, earthly things, but instead in the state of a person's heart. Of all Jesse's plays she had read, this one continued tugging at her thoughts. When she'd asked him about it, he'd explained the work as a modern-day allegory of the conversion of Saint Augustine, a fourth-century sinner whose search for truth had led him to Christianity.

"Our hearts are restless, O God, until they rest in thee."

A single sentence of Augustine's writings had been the inspiration for the entire play, Jesse had told her, trying to explain his sense of inner dispossession during the few years he was in the theater. Like his character Arthur, he'd searched for happiness in the world, ultimately realizing that he would never be at peace without faith in Christ.

She remembered the other thing Jesse had said about his writing: *"Careful . . . it's my prayer that my work will move people toward God."* Was that what *Season of Grace* was doing to her? She wasn't *trying* to think about the play she had read a few weeks previously, but nonetheless she found her thoughts on it several times throughout the day. Also, without really knowing how, she also found herself thinking about Jesus more than she would have ever believed possible.

Her coy remark back to Jesse—*"Would that be so bad?"*—had come back to haunt her. She'd only wanted to share more of her husband's heart. By reading his work, she'd hoped to gain a deeper understanding of the things that stirred him. Yet it was she who found herself strangely and unpleasantly stirred.

She had been attending church, hoping the preaching might propel her toward comprehending this faith of her husband's . . . her sister-in-law's . . . her girlhood friends'. Elena could tell Frances was embarrassed by her presence amongst all their pious church friends, and to be truthful, it gave Elena a dash of satisfaction to watch her mother-in-law's discomfort as she was forced to make introductions.

Standing in sharp contrast to that was the unconditional caring of the little hospital nun, Evangeline. Elena's memories of the blackened-ceiling infirmary were hazy, at best, but she knew she would never forget Sister Evangeline's pure face. Most clearly she recalled the sister's staunch conviction of God's existence, and her tender insistence that the Almighty cared for her. *"He wants you—every bit of you. . . . He loves you in a way you do not understand. . . . You live to display the glory of God!"*

Lately she had been awakening during the night with these things turning over and over in her mind. Beside the warmth of her sleeping husband, she wondered how she, Elena, could possibly live to display the glory of God. And if God loved her as much as Sister Evangeline said, why had he allowed her life to take the course it had?

"What do you want from me?" she had whispered into the darkness one night. "Do you know I'm here?"

"Aren't you hungry, Ellie?" Jesse touched her arm, pulling her thoughts back to the present. "You've hardly done more than taste your food."

"It's all wonderful," she replied, obediently spearing another piece of turkey. What would Jesse say if she were to tell him of the thoughts that constantly vied for place in her mind? Would he think her mental state unbalanced? Perhaps Sara might be sympathetic. Before the close of the weekend, maybe Elena could find some time to talk with her in confidence.

Just then, her sister-in-law exclaimed, "Oof!" and giggled.

"Heavens, Sara, what is it?" Frances asked with concern marring her elegant features.

"She just received a good, swift kick," Scott explained dryly while his wife rubbed her belly, her face wreathed with a beautiful smile. "The little tyke seems wont to behave this way at mealtimes."

"He's a smart boy. He likes Nana's cooking!" Benjamin immediately put in.

"You mean *she* likes Nana's cooking," countered Pearl.

Jesse grinned with mischief. "Maybe *they* like their grandmother's cooking."

"Such a topic for the dinner table!" Frances reproached, though Elena wondered if she detected just a trace of softening about the older woman's lips.

While Pearl and Benjamin argued about the possibility of their mother having twins, Elena felt Bobby's eyes on her and read the unspoken question in his young eyes. *Will you ever have another baby, Mama?*

Fortunately, once the uproar from Jesse's impish comment died down, the meal concluded smoothly, without further incident. All the same, Elena continued feeling unsettled. Here she was sharing a lovely Thanksgiving dinner in the type of home she'd always longed for. Her marriage to Jesse gave her legal and relational rights to be amongst this family, yet deep down she knew she still didn't belong anywhere.

Would she ever?

✵

"Try that section again," Dr. Suffington said, a frown marring his features. He touched the music with his pointer. "From this measure."

Jesse read the not-so-subtle signs of stress on Elena's lovely face as she suppressed a sigh and gave a slight nod. This was the sixth or seventh time Suffington had asked her to sing this particular passage. On the way to the conservatory this morning, she had expressed her frustration with what she viewed as a slow and dismal recovery of her voice.

"What about Thanksgiving?" he'd asked. "You made Robert the proudest boy in the whole country by singing for him that day."

"He's a boy of *five*," she had countered, her eyes darkening. "What does he know about music?"

"Ellie, everyone thought you did wonderfully. Your singing was a highlight of the holiday."

"Oh yes. 'The Arkansas Traveler' is such a demanding piece."

"You're being far too critical. In fact, you were the one who taught me that making music involves far more than singing the notes. Because of your incredible talent, you make even simple songs into something wonderful by bringing the words to life. None of that is contrived, and it comes through with such spontaneity and effortlessness."

To his gingerly spoken reasoning that she had made an astonishing resurgence since he'd taken her home from the hospital, she maintained that her singing was of the poorest quality. Dreadful. Appalling. For some minutes she had gone on, releasing her dissatisfaction and disappointment regarding her affliction.

He'd offered to sit in the room during her lesson today, promising to give her an honest assessment, later, of his observations.

"I quit!"

Jesse was startled from his thoughts by his wife's abrupt declaration, and he straightened in his chair. She had finished the passage, her voice having dissipated once again on the two highest notes. "I mean it—I quit!" she repeated emphatically. "Don't tell me you couldn't hear that. My voice will never be normal again." Her gaze flew to him, daring him to disagree, then to Suffington. "I beg your pardon, but this is nothing but a waste of time."

"Now, now," Professor Suffington tsked. "We all heard something, but I daresay it might mean something different to each of us."

"And what is *that* supposed to mean?" she shot back, her hands going to her hips in a defensive posture. How well Jesse remembered the fiery Elena Breen, whose desire for beautiful music sometimes drove her to passionate outbursts during rehearsals.

"And while I'm at it, let me say something else." With pink cheeks and heaving chest she continued addressing Suffington. "I have no intention of ever singing Italian opera. Stop making me sing these wretched songs I can't even understand. *Ebben, m'aspetta, ti seguiro sea te compagno in vita non mi vol—le.* Yes, you've told me what the words mean, but how am I supposed to put any emotion into the music when I have to think so hard about what I'm singing?"

"Madam, how can I make you sing anything if you have already quit?" replied the unruffled professor, dusting an imaginary piece of lint from his vest.

"Ooh . . . I don't . . . ooh!"

Had she stamped her foot? Jesse rose from his chair, uncertain if approaching Elena would bring her comfort or cause more distress.

"Some of the world's greatest singers have felt just the way you do right now," Suffington went on, his voice rich with compassion, "and many of them have suffered with various ailments of health and voice. To tell you the truth, madam, I am pleased by your eruption today. It tells me that you are coming along quite nicely . . . and that you are ready to begin putting yourself back into your music."

"But my *voice*—"

"Patience, madam. The voice is coming. It is your expression I wish to talk about right now. Your feelings. You—*Elena.*"

"What about me?" Wariness laced her question.

"You, woman, the night I saw you perform in Kansas, you captivated an entire theater. People were afraid to breathe for missing your slightest line. Was it because you were the best singer on both continents? No. I can think of several sopranos possessing greater technical ability, yet I cannot think of very many whose very soul saturates their music so thoroughly. Madam, in that simple musical play you were light and fire, passion and fury, sweetness and purity."

Jesse watched the uncertainty on his wife's face, thinking just how perfectly Suffington had expressed his own experience of Elena. There was simply no one like her.

The professor continued, his speaking voice a compelling instrument. "In the ensuing years I know you have suffered many tribulations. Though you are presently safe and sound and well on the road to regathering your health, I sense something remains out of order. I venture to say you are afraid of . . . what? I wonder."

Elena's eyes widened, watered up, then her gaze dropped down to her hands. Her chin jutted out in that defiant way of hers Jesse remembered so well, as her shoulders stiffened. "Thank you for your assistance, Dr. Suffington," she responded stiffly. "I will be going now."

"But Ellie—" Jesse began, glancing helplessly at the silver-haired professor, "your lesson is only half over. Maybe a drink of water and some fresh air would—"

"Please take me home, Jesse," she repeated without raising

her eyes. Her graceful hands gathered the music into a neat pile on the stand before she walked toward the coatrack, leaving the sheets behind.

Suffington nodded to him, appearing not the least bit disturbed by Elena's behavior. The silence in the music room pressed heavily against Jesse's ears while he and Elena donned their coats and departed. In only a few minutes, they were back in the carriage, heading up Woodward Avenue.

"Talk to me, Ellie," he initiated, glancing at her scarf-wrapped, unyielding profile. "How about we stop for lunch somewhere?"

"I'm not hungry," came the muffled reply from behind her scarf.

At the next intersection he was forced to pull the horses to a halt as a large wagon passed on the cross street. "What's got you more upset, your voice or what Suffington said to you?"

"Does it matter?"

"Yes."

"Sometimes I wonder if anything matters," she said so softly he almost missed her words.

"Everything matters, my dearest," he said, leaning close. "Especially to God."

"Your character Arthur said that in your play," she snapped, suddenly turning to face him. Her eyes appeared to have no bottom.

"Do you mean *Season of Grace?*" A shout from the driver behind him made him realize the oversized wagon had cleared the intersection. He shook the reins and spoke to the team. "Giddap."

"How did he *know* that?" she quizzed as their carriage moved forward, her brows drawing downward. "How do *you* know that?"

Sensing there was a great deal going on beneath his wife's hard-boiled exterior, he took advantage of the opportunity to turn at the next intersection toward the tearoom he knew lay ahead.

"Let's not go home yet," he suggested, bracing for more disagreement. "There's a place ahead where we can stop and talk."

To his surprise, she made no protest. A parking spot in front of the little café became available as they approached, and soon they were seated at a small round table in the front corner of the shop. Gathered, cheery curtains hung on the window beside their table, each one drawn to the side to leave a center opening and view of the street. A sweet, delicious fragrance wafted from the kitchen, making Jesse's stomach growl.

Once their orders had been taken by a young woman in a blue dress, he reached across the table for Elena's hands. They were cold, and as he felt their smallness within his grasp, protectiveness welled up inside him. Though his warmer, larger hands quickly absorbed their cold, he knew the pain inside her could not be managed so simply. *Help me to help her, Lord,* he prayed. *Give me the words.*

He thought of his writing and of how long it often took to make a single line of dialogue flow smoothly, expressing the precise meaning he intended. His tongue was not so skilled, nor was there the opportunity in speech to cross something out and rewrite it. Something badly spoken remained badly spoken . . . and remembered.

"Are you certain you want to quit singing with Dr. Suffington? Your voice really has come a long way."

The dark eyes flashed toward him. "For what purpose? To polish my drawing-room performances for young children who think I sing 'Sweet Betsy from Pike' wonderfully? I don't plan a return to the stage, Jess. And for all your years of training, I notice you don't sing anymore either." She sighed, her expression and voice becoming shadowy. "These lessons are costing you money that I know is dear to you. That's not right."

"Don't you dare feel guilty about your lessons," he said firmly. "They've been an important part of your recovery, and besides, Suffington is giving me a remarkable break on his fee."

"Is there another reason *you* aren't singing, besides your

belief that God is calling you to write plays?" she asked suddenly, perceptively.

"I couldn't leave Robert," he said as gently as he could, not wishing to add to her misery. "Dr. Suffington tried to persuade me to tour with this chorale a few years back, but I turned him down."

"Do you regret it?" Her voice caught slightly on her question.

"Not a bit," he reassured, giving her hands a gentle squeeze. "I don't know what the Lord's plans are for all these plays I've written, but I am certain I did the right thing by saying no to touring."

"Unlike me."

"Ellie . . . I know these years have been difficult," he said slowly. "But you also need to know that I forgive you for leaving our marriage. The words *I forgive you* mean I hold nothing against you."

Tears filled her eyes, and she dropped her head.

"I can think of two things that might help you right now," he continued, "if you want to hear them."

As he saw her head nod ever so slightly, he gathered his courage and spoke.

Chapter 11

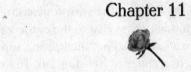

Jesse's voice was filled with tenderness, the warmth of his hands preserving Elena from being enveloped by the desolation inside her. At the conservatory this morning her frustration had gotten the better of her, spilling from her in cold, hard waves of anger.

What she normally did next was pack her feelings into ice, then stow them deeply away. Right now she wanted to do that, to feel numb, but somehow she couldn't. She felt sad and lost, like a little child, and this frightened her.

The wait girl came then, bearing a tray with a steaming teapot, two cups and saucers, a bowl of sugar and a creamer, and a plate of scones. After she had efficiently served them, she retreated with a little bow.

Jesse had let go of Elena's hands while the young woman set the dishes on the table, but once she stepped away, he took them again. Her heart thumped against her ribs at the serious expression on his face. As she watched him swallow, she wondered if he was feeling nervous as well.

A short breath, not quite a sigh, left him. "The first thing I want to say is this: If you haven't asked God's forgiveness for your sins, Ellie, I promise that you will feel a great sense of relief at doing so," he began, allowing a long pause. She said nothing, waiting for him to continue, her heart pounding like a set of timpani.

"I know you know many things *about* God, but do you realize he is waiting to welcome you into his arms and forgive your every sin? You only have to ask him."

Not trusting her voice, she remained silent.

"The other thing that will bring you freedom is forgiving yourself, Elena. What's done is done, and what's in the past lies in the past." His voice and eyes were afire with conviction. "Do you remember our talk after your first visit to the conservatory?"

That was the day she'd confessed her illicit association with Stephen Villard. A sick feeling clutched her stomach. To her surprise, Jesse's next words had nothing to do with that or her former manager.

"We agreed to build from that moment. . . . Do you remember?"

Again she nodded, tears blurring her eyes.

"I haven't stopped praying that the Lord would reveal himself to you somehow . . . somewhere . . . through someone."

"Jesse, I don't know what that means." She breathed out a tearful sigh, experiencing a helpless mixture of ignorance and frustration. Looking down at her husband's strong hands, she whispered, "How am I supposed to know God is revealing himself to me? And how . . . h-how am I supposed to forgive myself? I can't erase my past or any of my memories. I try not to think about them, but sometimes I can't help it."

"Ellie, there's no way you can do all that yourself. If you invite Jesus Christ into your heart—if you ask him to be Lord of all your life—his supernatural grace will give you victory over the pain of your past."

After bending and kissing each of her hands, Jesse straightened and took a sip of his tea. Elena did not feel that he had withdrawn, but rather that he was trying very hard not to force her into anything. Plead his case, yes, but not twist her arm.

Even so, she felt as if she were treading along the edge of a deep abyss. To remain where she was was dangerous, yet at least she could feel her feet against the ground. To do what Jesse asked—to ask Jesus to be the Lord of her life—meant casting her fate into the hands of an unknowable and untrustworthy God. Where was the assurance that her life would be transformed? her sins forgiven?

Would anything even happen?

And how was her bitter Christian mother-in-law living a life of supernatural grace?

"I'm sorry . . . I can't do this right now," she replied to her husband in a low voice. "I know that must disappoint you, but I just can't."

He nodded, his eyes gentle and sad. "I respect your honesty. And you're right, Ellie, your heart has to be willing. But that doesn't mean I'll stop praying for your conversion."

"Oh, Jess," she whispered, touched beyond words by his sincerity.

As they drank their tea, she couldn't help but wonder, for all the shambles she had made of her life, how she had ended up here in this place with Jesse. She certainly didn't deserve a man like him or such a wonderful, trusting son. Again she pondered the possibility of a concerned and all-merciful God, as the pastor at church had described the Almighty last Sunday.

Thank you for Jesse and Bobby, she thought as she gazed across the table at her husband, belatedly realizing her expression of gratefulness was more than a pleasant sentiment. Who was she thanking? Had she just said a prayer?

Mentally shaking herself, she pushed these disturbing thoughts from her head and forced herself to drink her tea. Even so, she knew it wouldn't be long before they were back, like a flock of sparrows pecking at seeds.

❧

By lamplight, Frances darned a patch onto the knee of one of Robert's trousers, deciding she might as well let the hems down while she had her sewing basket out. He was growing like a weed again. Glancing over toward the table where her grandson and his mother were playing a game of draughts, she felt the familiar antagonism rise up inside her. Robert adored his fickle, fair-haired "Mama," who, a few weeks previously, had decided to turn up her nose at Dr. Suffington's voice treatments.

The girl was utterly ungrateful. Didn't she know the amount of sacrifice involved in Jesse's taking time away from his writing to drive her to the conservatory, or how precious was the money he paid for her lessons? What must the professor be thinking of them? And what was the matter with Jesse? He acted like none of this bothered him at all.

Perhaps it was because of the message that had come shortly afterward, from a theater in Ann Arbor, wanting to produce one of his plays. He was distracted. For nearly a week he'd been staying with Sara and Scott and the children, sending word that all was well and that he expected to be home in the next few days. Frances knew she should be happy for him, but the timing of this particular turn of events was wretched, leaving her to contend with Elena.

With the turning of the calendar page to December, Frances's thoughts usually turned pleasantly toward Christmas and all its associated events and celebrations. Her ladies' group was busier than usual this time of year due to their almsgiving to the city's poor. Also, the house would need another good cleaning, and she must begin making all her traditional puddings, candies, and cookies.

In her spare moments she'd sewn many items for Sara and the new baby, which was due at the end of January. Christmas gifts for her children and grandchildren were already wrapped and hidden carefully away.

She had yet to decide what she was going to do about their visitor.

She didn't want to give Elena a present. In fact, it seemed hypocritical to do so when Frances felt the way she did about her, but at the same time she knew Jesse would be upset if she failed to acknowledge his wife. In her opinion, the most suitable gift was a one-way train ticket out of town.

Oh, why wasn't she gone already? After all, running away

was the girl's style. Frances remembered Jesse's telling her that Elena had left home at fifteen or sixteen to make her way in the world. What scandalous behavior, especially since she had quickly fallen in with the improper type who acted and sang on stage, traveling from city to city with God only knew what kind of living accommodations. The fact that Elena had given birth to Robert just six months after a hasty, out-of-town wedding to Jesse bore out the truth that her son had married an indecent woman with shameful wiles.

So, Frances, how does that make Jesse blameless?

How was it that she could still imagine Gerald's voice speaking to her after all these years of widowhood? Nonetheless, she didn't like these arguing-type words that came to her as she was thinking things through. She was right; she knew she was right. Why was everyone else blind to the truth?

The next hour passed slowly for Frances while she patched and mended, her anger growing ever more ragged. Elena had not only run away from her home, she'd also run away from her marriage. A woman like that could not be counted on for anything. Finishing the last item, a blue apron, without saying a word, Frances bit the thread with her teeth, inwardly fuming at the way Elena simpered and fawned over her son. What a show the great actress was putting on, and poor, unsuspecting Robert was eating it up with a spoon.

Picking up her Bible, Frances tried concentrating on the account of the Annunciation, then on Mary's visit to her cousin Elizabeth. She allowed Elena to put Robert to bed, offering her cheek to her grandson for a good-night kiss on his way out of the room. Let his so-called mother tuck him in. Given Elena's character and past performance, it was just a matter of time until things would get difficult and she would flee. And again Frances would be there to pick up the pieces.

The ticking of the mantel clock, usually soothing, grated on her nerves. One good thing about the evenings was that, since Jesse's departure, Elena retired to her room once Robert was in bed. Taking a deep breath, Frances closed her eyes and tried to loosen her knotted shoulders.

At the sound of light footsteps on the stairs, her eyes snapped open and her muscles tensed. Couldn't she enjoy even a few relaxing moments in her own home?

"I thought I'd have tea," came Elena's voice a moment later. "Can I get you some too?"

"No, you can't," Frances snapped, taking in the sight of her still-too-skinny daughter-in-law framed in the doorway. Elena's dark eyes focused on her were shocked, suspicious, and hurt.

"Well, what are you staring at then?" she added for good measure, her anger too far gone to control.

"Nothing." A tight smile crossed the girl's face, wiping away any and all vulnerability. "I didn't think you'd changed your mind about me."

"And why should I?"

"Because of Jesse . . . or Bobby?"

Frances exploded, thumping the Bible on the table beside her chair. "When will you stop calling my grandson that dreadful name? His name is Robert, *not Bobby.*" In one motion she came to her feet, blood roaring in her ears, determined to have it out with this immoral creature. "I know what kind of woman you are," she sneered.

"What kind is that?"

"I've read plenty about women of the stage and the parties that go on. You probably drink alcohol and smoke cigars, and . . . and think nothing of gambling!"

Elena's jaw jutted forward slightly, giving her a defiant expression.

"What? No argument?"

The thin shoulders shrugged. "You already seem to know everything about me."

Infuriated, Frances took a step forward, hissing, "You are . . . loose and a seducer of men. I'm sure you were no virgin when you took up with my son."

Something glittered in those black-cherry eyes. "As a matter of fact, I wasn't."

"Y-You! You hideous creature! Lord, have mercy! You have all the morality of a she-cat roaming the alley! Do you know nothing of chastity? Does the godly virtue of virginity mean anything to you at all?"

Bracing her hands against her hips, Elena took a step forward also, meeting Frances's sputtering rage with icy detachment. "I'll give you the definition of virginity, Mrs. Golden. Where I come from, a virgin is a girl who can run faster than her father and brothers."

Incredulous, Frances shook her head. "What kind of filthy talk is that?"

"The filthy truth." The dark gaze dropped to the floor as Elena's next sentence escaped in a shadowy whisper, her bravado suddenly gone. "For all the good it did me, I ran."

A smart slap in the mouth could not have done more to silence Frances. Whether it was the words or how they were said, Frances instinctively knew Elena was speaking with candor. Unexpected pity rose inside her—and with it, pain. She did not know what to do next.

But before Frances could speak, Elena whirled and disappeared into the darkness. Should she follow her? A moment later, there were footsteps on the stairs, and then a door closed. Shame enfolded her, and not just the disgrace of having treated Jesse's wife with such offensiveness. A long-forgotten face rose in her mind, a face she'd successfully not recalled in years.

Uncle Clyde.

Hands and knees shaking, Frances sank to the carpet. Uncle Clyde. Her breath came in little gasps. Why, oh why, did she have to remember? *Oh, God, why are you letting this happen?*

Clyde Bastman had been the husband of her mother's sister, a boisterous, jolly fellow with a shining bald head and a thick, walrus mustache. He and Aunt Jennifer had been childless, forever inviting their nephews and nieces to come stay with them. Because they lived nearby, Frances and her younger sisters had been frequent visitors.

Uncle Clyde went to great lengths to entertain the children with stories, jokes, and little gifts. At first Frances had felt special when he'd begun paying extra attention to her, giving her coins or pretty hair ribbons. Then he'd sought her company, just hers, telling her how much he liked talking with her, making her feel important.

After that . . .

A shudder went through Frances. Her face was wet with tears, though she had no idea when she'd begun to cry. Uncle Clyde's touch had been gentle, persistent, invasive. Evil. Shame filled her as she recalled how many years she had silently submitted to his depraved desires. What was the matter with her? Why had she allowed it? Even a motherless girl like Elena had known better than to acquiesce to such sinful activity and had fled.

You're weak, Frances, and a fraud. How can you accuse Elena of impurity when you went to your marriage bed in the state you did, praying that Gerald would never know? What about the—

Her heart seemed to rend in two, and she slumped to the floor. Memories she had tried all her life to suppress gushed forth with the force of a spurting, open wound.

What about the baby? A girl, so tiny and white. She tried to breathe, but then she stopped. You wrapped her in an old blanket and buried her in the woods beneath the ferns. Then you went home, washed your hands, and ate supper.

Frances's constitution had been poor that summer, her fourteenth year, her belly sore and torpid. Believing she was suffering constipation, Mother had fed her wheat bran and vegetables and insisted she walk briskly for one hour every afternoon. It was on one of these walks that the cramping had begun. All through the night her belly had pulled and tightened from deep within, and she'd noticed some blood when she'd used the chamber pot, her mother's dietary treatments having a profound effect.

Mother had allowed her to rest from her chores the next morning, insisting Frances get out of doors in the afternoon for her fresh air. Though she felt terrible, Frances had meekly obeyed. Once she reached the woods, the drawing pain in her belly had finally forced her to the ground. Sudden wetness and pressure between her legs made her cry out.

Then a baby had come out of her.

Moaning with shock and fear, she had not known what to do. The baby's eyes were sealed, like a kitten's, and in the dappled sunlight Frances had noticed the fine, faintly dark hair covering her head. Ten fingers and ten toes, all perfectly formed, bore delicate nails no bigger than pearly white flower seeds. The translucent skin of the tiny baby's chest moved in time with the slow-thudding heart that lay beneath. A half dozen quavering sighs had shaken the infant; then she lay silent. Dying. Dead.

More pressure had tightened Frances's belly then, and a small, shiny afterbirth followed with a rush of red blood. Her undergarments were soaked, and red stains marred her shift and skirt. She had lain there for what seemed like hours, looking at her baby and not knowing what to do. Finally, it came to her that she had to do *something*. Tenderly, she wrapped the miniature white baby in the cleanest part of her shift and laid her against a tree.

Mother and her sisters were weeding the far part of the garden, their backs to her, when Frances emerged from the woods, and as quickly as she could, she sped to the house, undetected. With haste, she changed her clothes, bundling her soiled garments into a tight ball. She took them and the little quilt her grandmother had made her long ago out to the barn. Stowing her clothing behind a stack of hay bales, she took a shovel from the wall and returned to the woods, carrying shovel and blanket, to bury her daughter.

Laura. In the silence of her heart she'd named the baby Laura, and as she'd shoveled the earth over the blanketed bundle, then tenderly replaced the ferns, she'd asked God to take Laura to heaven to sing with the angels.

Uncle Clyde had not bothered her again, not after she told him about the baby. Years of guilt had devoured her as she wondered if he had turned instead to her sisters or her cousins. She was the oldest, and in her selfishness and fear she had failed to protect them.

Lord, I can't bear this. It hurts too much. Frances wept into the carpet and pounded her fists, trying to escape the physical pain that furrowed the hard-packed soil beneath her breast as effectively as her father's shiny, newly sharpened plow had broken up the earth. *Make it stop! Please, make it stop! There's no reason for this,* she cried, recalling the smell of damp earth and the white-velvet softness of her oldest daughter's skin. Again, blades of pain slashed at her heart.

"H-have mercy," she sobbed, her voice breaking free. "I don't think I killed my baby, b-but she's buried all alone in the woods. Please forgive me for all the wicked, shameful things I did with Uncle Clyde . . . and for letting the same things happen to the other girls. I pretend to be such a fine, upstanding woman . . . but I'm not. You know I'm not. I know I don't deserve your forgiveness, Jesus, but I'm asking for it."

Bleakness settled on her spirit as her sobs slowed and the clock ticked loudly into the night. An ironic thought struck her, twisting her face into a humorless smile. Elena might be a stage actress with a past, but at least she had the courage to speak the truth. Frances never had.

To anyone.

❧

In darkness, Elena lay across the bed, engulfed by memories and emotions she no longer had the power to elude. *Don't think . . . don't feel . . . keep moving.* The philosophy that had served her for the past twenty-seven years had collapsed like her voice . . . her career . . . her life.

She could no longer keep the past at bay—or pretend she didn't care. Worse still, rather than diminishing in intensity, the feelings accompanying each remembrance had fermented into a bubbling, overflowing mass. Sadness had become despair, regret anguish, and shame inwardly bowed her head till her neck was at its breaking point.

What had happened to the incredible energy she'd once possessed, her drive and desire? her strength? All her life there had been nothing she couldn't bear, couldn't do, couldn't overcome, yet now she was too limp and weak to fight any longer. Last fall she had tried ending her life because she had seen no hope, no reason to keep fighting.

No matter what she did or said, how she dressed or acted or amended her life, there would always be an invisible line between her—a woman of the stage—and people like Frances Golden. The righteous. The churchgoers. Yet wasn't it funny, how at the height of Elena Breen's success, it was decent folk who had always been first in line to buy tickets for her shows? Then after the curtain fell and the applause faded away, they would return to their nice families, their fine homes, and their pious places of worship while she retired to a rented hotel room.

Elena knew this boundary between her and Jesse's mother had never ceased to exist, and tonight the older woman had finally declared her feelings without restraint, calling her immoral. Loose. A seducer of men. While it was true that Elena had fallen prey to Stephen Villard's charms, then years later been swept away into a relationship with Jesse without benefit of matrimonial bonds, she had never set out to seduce any man.

With the impetuous retort she'd made to the older woman's accusations, she'd meant to strike back at Frances Golden's meanness in kind. The scene in the sitting room replayed itself in her head, making her cover her eyes in the dark room. She rolled from her back to her side, pulling her legs up in a belated gesture of self-defense. What had possessed her to go on the way she had, revealing her family's sordid, loathsome secrets to the woman who hated her so? If Frances Golden had wanted her out of the house before, she'd be doubly motivated to drive her detestable daughter-in-law away now. No doubt she was downstairs now, plotting how to get rid of her.

Why don't you leave?

The insidious thought beckoned her to dry her eyes, pack what few things she had, and slip out the door. Where she would go or what she would do were not utmost priorities. She only wanted to be away from Frances Golden and her critical, disapproving eyes. Jesse's mother hated her, and nothing was ever going to change that.

Yet how could she abandon Bobby—again? It would be worse than terrible to skulk out of the house in the middle of the night without so much as a good-bye, leaving her poor son to wonder why his mother didn't want him . . . when nothing could be further from the truth. Each day of the four years apart from her son, she had pined for him, bitterly regretting the decisions she'd made.

And Jesse. Pain engulfed her heart as she thought of the man who loved her far beyond her limited ability to understand such devotion and loyalty. Yes, she loved her husband and their son enough to gladly die for them, but she could not accept that there was anyone on earth who would do the same for her.

Jesus died for you.

Not again. Why wouldn't that play of Jesse's leave her alone? Pieces of dialogue and the main character, Arthur's, disturbing introspection continued coming to her at odd moments. The quote from Augustine—*"Our hearts are restless, O Lord, until they rest in thee"*—Jesse's inspiration for *Season of Grace*, chased itself in circles in her mind, like a playful puppy after its tail.

If there was a way her heart could rest, she wanted it. Yet the things Jesse had written in his play, just like the things the pastor had said in church on Sunday, were impossible to grasp. How was her heart supposed to rest in the Lord—or wasn't it that he was supposed to reside in her?—when that organ beat inside her breast, and God was far away in heaven? Why was it so important to believe that Jesus had died for her?

And what made Frances Golden such a good Christian woman when she loathed Elena the way she did? If nothing else, Elena had learned that Christianity was supposed to be about forgiveness. That had been the theme Jesse stressed the day they'd stopped at the tearoom.

"If you haven't asked God's forgiveness for your sins, Ellie, I promise you will feel a great sense of relief at doing so. . . . The other thing that will bring you freedom is forgiving yourself."

Her thoughts darted from forgiveness to frantically wondering what she could do. Where she could go. Yet while her mind roiled with these questions, she knew she could no more walk out the door tonight than cut off her right arm. Even though she wanted nothing more than to be as far from Jesse's mother as north was from south, she couldn't leave Bobby. She wouldn't leave Bobby.

"And I *will* call him Bobby," she whispered into the darkness. "I'm his mother, and he's my son."

Chapter 12

Jesse's pleasure at having a play in the initial stages of production paled once he arrived back home and experienced the strangely muffled moods of his wife and mother. What had happened while he was away? he puzzled, watching them move through mornings, afternoons, and evenings with quiet efficiency. Questioned separately, each woman denied anything was amiss, but both were withdrawn to the point of remoteness.

Toward one another they were exceedingly courteous, which was a mystifying change from the barely submerged tension that had festered between them before his departure. His intuition told him something was afoot, though he could not guess what it might be.

He wondered if his mother was sad that Dr. Suffington was no longer coming around regularly. Elena had seemed to think something was developing between the music professor and her mother-in-law, but if that was the case, wouldn't Suffington make an effort to see her even though he was no longer in charge of Elena's musical recovery?

About her music, Elena expressed resignation to what she viewed as the annihilation of her talent. "I must face the fact that my singing days are over," she had said with an impersonal sigh, "and none of Dr. Suffington's remedies are going to resurrect what's been destroyed." To Jesse's gentle arguments that her voice had indeed made great gains since she began work with Suffington, she tightened her lips and shook her head. Recalling her drive for perfection while in rehearsal and onstage, he suspected that any deficiencies in her tone and range were intolerable for her to bear. Now that her health was restored and she was no longer under the control of Villard, she would rather not sing than sing with the slightest fault.

It was a gloomy Sunday morning, and not even the dining room's gaslights chased the somberness from its corners. He and Robert had just seated themselves at the table for breakfast. Elena was upstairs doing some last-minute fussing with her hair. His apron-clad mother entered from the kitchen with a basket of warm, fresh-baked apple-and-cinnamon muffins, their tops clad with crumbly streusel.

"Those look good, Nana. Even better than flapjacks," Robert complimented. His young face was bright, and his blond curls had been damp-combed in preparation for church.

"Thank you," she said with a colorless smile, setting the muffins on the table and moving back to the kitchen.

Elena joined them a few minutes later, her appearance lovely but in some indefinable way hollow. The table's everyday dishes had the dull luster of bones against the red-and-blue plaid tablecloth, imparting contrived cheerfulness in this household of mysterious emotions. They began their meal when Frances returned and poured coffee for Jesse and herself, then took her chair.

After Jesse offered the mealtime prayer as was his customary duty, he spread butter across his muffin, feeling oppressed and uncomfortable in the room's perplexing atmosphere. The bitter anger that had consumed his mother since Elena's arrival was gone, but he was hard-pressed to identify what had replaced it. Instead of issuing cutting glances and suffering with pent-up antagonism toward her daughter-in-law, Frances Golden now spoke carefully and politely, her face and body gestures devoid of hostility.

Jesse was relieved when the all-but-silent meal was over and he could go out and hitch the team to the carriage. The wind struck his face when he cleared the back steps, carrying with it the fresh, damp scent of coming snow. Robert would be happy to have more than the thin dusting of white the season had thus far offered.

An hour later they were at church. The sonorous bells in the church tower began ringing as they ascended the steps and went to their pew. Frances entered the seat first, then Robert, then Elena, and finally himself. He had taken Elena's hand for part of the short drive, reassuring himself that whatever strange disposition had come over her in his absence would soon pass.

A shiver went through Jesse as he sat down, and he was glad for the warmth of his coat. The stove that heated the church did little more than keep the air temperature above freezing. Adding to the chilliness of the stone structure this morning was the absence of sunshine. In today's dreary light, the stained-glass windows along the side walls were dull liturgical replicas of the brilliant, breathtaking scenes they normally represented.

Once again he took Elena's gloved hand in his, feeling its smallness within his large palm. How he longed to take away every pain and problem in her life, to make her eyes glow with complete happiness. He couldn't be more happy that she was attending church with them, yet he ached for her to surmount the obstacles that kept her from experiencing the forgiveness and peace of Christ. *"How am I supposed to know God is revealing himself to me?"* she had asked that day at the tearoom. In her words were helplessness, frustration, vulnerability. The reply he had made was true, yet he knew his proffered remedy—acceptance of Christ—had only added to the muddle of her confusing thoughts.

A rustling and shuffling of feet echoed in the sanctuary as members of the choir filed into their places. As she had for the past twenty-some-odd years, Mrs. Pond, the organist, began the Sunday service using her capable fingers and feet. Jesse recalled the many years he had sung with this choir, especially during the time when the young-man restlessness inside him had built and crescendoed, making him question everything he had ever known to be true.

He supposed his time of self-imposed spiritual exile couldn't be accurately compared to what Elena was experiencing. Yet as God had faithfully pursued his lost lamb Jesse Golden and brought him back into the fold, he sought Elena as well. With thanksgiving, Jesse recognized the gentle, persistent, uncomfortable pressure the Lord was putting upon his wife, and he prayed that her heart would soon yield.

The service continued with hymns, Scripture readings, and finally Reverend Fordham's sermon. This morning their wizened, gray-haired spiritual leader spoke passionately on the Advent theme of preparing the heart to receive Jesus. Since Elena had been coming to church with them, Jesse had hoped Fordham's kind, assured manner would win her trust.

"There is a conversion of heart that occurs when a sinner accepts Christ," the robed man exhorted from his pulpit. "Yet there is an ongoing conversion of heart that must occur if we are to continue in our Christian walk. Our hearts must always be open to the Savior, to repent and sorrow over our sins, and to receive the forgiveness and grace he offers."

Upon the conclusion of the edifying message, the likes of which Jesse had heard dozens of times before, he happened to glance at Elena. Noticing that her cheek was wet with tears, he felt a shock run through him. Today? Now? Yet there was no time to whisper anything to her as Mrs. Pond held an opening chord, indicating that it was time for the congregation to stand. To his surprise, "Amazing Grace" commenced, not a Christmas carol as he expected. Many of those at worship joined the choir to fill the sanctuary with sound. Until this morning, Elena had not sung in church, but his nerves were further electrified to hear her voice lift in song.

The passion and purity she poured into the hymn was no performance; it was the unguarded response of a heart set free. Never had Jesse heard his wife sing more beautifully than she did at this moment. With her eyes closed, her lashes lying in delicate arcs against her tear-dampened cheeks, she did not notice the heads that turned to seek the source of the remarkable sound that ascended to the heights of the sanctuary . . . and beyond. His mother's gaze met his, her jaw slack for a moment before she blinked hard and turned back toward Reverend Fordham. What had he seen on her face? Sadness? Envy? Regret?

Robert gazed up at his mother with a mixture of pride and awe. She had sung for him, yes, but never with the full power of her God-given talent. *Son, if you could have seen her when . . .* Jesse's thoughts began before he belatedly realized he could detect no flaw in Elena's voice. She sang without ornamentation—in plain *canto spianato* style—her articulation steady, clear, and expressive, her tone as exceptional as he had ever heard.

"'How precious did that grace appear . . . the hour I first believed. Thru many . . .'"

Another current went through him as he realized that this was the first hour of Elena's belief—that he, and every other soul in the sanctuary, were living, breathing witnesses to the grace of God being poured out in abundance. His own face was wet with tears of joy and relief, and as he gently squeezed her hand he allowed his voice to fade away, noticing that many others, overcome, had fallen silent and were wiping their eyes.

A hush fell across the congregation, spreading even to the choir and Mrs. Pond, leaving Elena, her soul transported, worshiping before the throne of grace. At the hymn's conclusion, Elena blinked as if waking suddenly from a jumbled sleep, then self-consciously wiped her face as the gray-haired pastor huskily prayed the final benediction.

The reverent atmosphere inspired by Elena's singing prevailed as people filed silently out. Discreet, sidelong glances, filled with wonderment, appreciation, and frank curiosity, were cast toward her. On a typical Sunday, quiet comments and conversations would begin perhaps fifteen feet from the door, the volume increasing to a loud, buzzing cloud of chatter as people waited to funnel past Reverend Fordham's station in the church vestibule.

Only a few quiet murmurs were heard this morning, and even the pastor's normally booming voice was subdued. Taking Robert's hand, Frances politely excused herself as she stepped past Elena, her grandson in tow. "I expect you and she would like a few moments alone," she said in a low tone, her words like the rustling of dried cornhusks. Without waiting for a reply, she moved on, merging into the slow-moving queue in the aisle.

Jesse was at the same time grateful for his mother's consideration and concerned about her manner, but uppermost in his heart and mind was the transformation of the woman at his side. His wife. Elena. A breathless sensation gripped him as he gazed down at her lovely, tearstained face. Serenity and uncertainty mingled in her expression, as if she were pleased to have arrived at a long-awaited destination yet did not know which way to travel now that she was there.

"Jesse, I let my heart say yes," she whispered with a shaky release of breath.

I know, he wanted to say, but didn't. Putting his arm around her, he drew her tight against his side, not trusting himself to reply. There were no words to express his gratitude or the interior happiness he felt. They stood together as the sanctuary emptied, their gazes drawn by the large wooden cross at the rear of the altar.

"The presence of God is real, isn't it?" she presently mused, wiping at her cheeks yet again. "When I was a girl, I felt it in my friends and in their homes. I used to pray." Turning her head, she looked up at him. "But God never answered my prayers the way he did Romy's and Olivia's. One night—" Her deep brown eyes filled with fresh tears. "My father and brothers . . . I had to leave . . ."

His heart twisted with anguish at what she was hinting at, warring against a flare of protective, righteous anger. Muscles in his legs and arms trembled with the force of his powerlessness, and he hugged her tighter.

"I've been running for years," she went on with a slight shake of her head. "From my family, from God, from my dear friends, from you and Bobby, from everyone. I was angry. And proud. In fact, I think I still am. But I'm so tired of holding myself up on my own. I want the relief you told me about, the peace that Reverend Fordham preaches . . . and I want the restlessness of my heart to be calmed like Arthur's in *Season of Grace*. Despite her tears, a hint of mischief sparkled in her gaze. "Congratulations, Jess, on the premier goal you've already accomplished as a playwright."

He was momentarily confused, because the theater in Ann Arbor was producing *Ten Long Steps*, not *Season of Grace*.

To what must have been his blank expression, she added, "Don't you remember? When I asked if I could read your plays, you warned me that you prayed for your work to move people toward God."

He felt a dawning smile spread across his face as he once again thought of her coy response: *"Would that be so bad?"* He'd never dreamed that his prayers would be answered so swiftly nor in the life of the woman for whom he cared so deeply. His thankfulness was as wide and light as the sky, yet a weighty thought followed: *Does this mean that others might be similarly stirred?*

Something fearful stalked across his soul as he recognized the power of the written word, the influence of the stage. What responsibility had he undertaken in this work he'd begun? Was it really the calling he believed it to be, or was he just chasing after a vain ambition for which he was poorly suited? He had not been educated as a writer. Nor was he a theologian. What if his work accomplished the exact opposite he intended? What if—

"My children," spoke Reverend Fordham, having come up from behind them to stand at Jesse's side. "Unless I am mistaken, I believe we at worship this morning were blessed to witness an extremely important occurrence."

Elena's smile had the power of the new electric lighting going in on Woodward Avenue. Though her beaming expression said everything, she replied to the black-robed cleric, "Yes, Reverend, I have just accepted the gospel message."

"Do you understand to what you have assented?" Fordham's wise, gold-flecked eyes searched her face.

"I have offered my heart, soul, and body to the triune God and asked Jesus Christ to forgive my sins," she answered. "I came to realize there was no other choice for me to make."

"Ah, so you have been paying attention to my sermons," he quipped, his smile giving him the look of a kindly patriarch.

Elena's brow arched in a winsome manner. "Pardon me for saying so, Reverend, but it wasn't your message that affected my decision so much as this unbearable restiveness in me."

"Unbearable restiveness," he repeated thoughtfully, his eyes lighting with interest. "Tell me more."

Taking a breath, she appeared to be composing her thoughts. "I find, of late, my mind continually turning toward God. Morning, afternoon, bedtime, middle of the night. It doesn't matter. Thoughts of him crowd my head. I have wondered if I am going mad or if my brain is being overtaken by some disorder. For no matter how hard I try not to think of God, thoughts of him, my life, and eternity buzz like bees inside my skull."

The clergyman nodded. "The conversions of some souls are silently sublime. Others are not."

"Then you've heard of this before?" Elena's gaze fastened upon the face of the reverend, begging him to reveal more.

"Heard of it? My good woman, forty-some years ago I suffered through something similar. Back in those days I was an angry young man with an axe to grind. I believed the world was a cruel and unjust place, and that God, if he was there, was not doing anything about it."

"What happened?"

"I trampled over his gentle messages and signs of love in my quest to disprove his existence and right the wrongs of the world. After that, he rolled up his sleeves and revealed himself to me in much the way you described. Oh, I resisted. I fought. I argued. And for months and months, I thought I would go out of my mind."

Jesse regarded the pastor with curiosity. Though logic told him that beneath his robes Reverend Fordham was a living, breathing man, same as any other, he did not often stop to consider him in any light other than his present persona invited. Of course Fordham had once been a young man, and there had to have been a point in his life where he had decided which path he was going to walk.

A self-effacing smile made the older man's eyes twinkle. "One day I told the Lord, 'Fine! You win! Have your way with me!' Rather ungracious sounding, I realize, but a proud young man had just assented to the fact that God was God . . . and I was not." The gold-flecked eyes grew tender. "Mrs. Golden, today you have begun a journey. Yes, you have been given a new life, but that doesn't mean that you have ceased being yourself. From this day forward, the Lord will be sanctifying you. Do you know what that means?"

"Making me holy?" she asked, hope and doubt mingling in her expression.

"That's right. This is not something I would normally say to someone who has made the decision you just did this morning, but I am compelled to emphasize to you that the process of sanctification doesn't always feel very good. In fact, it hardly ever does. You must trust, however, that the God who made you knows what is best for you. Your love for your husband and child is but a cold ember in comparison to how passionately Christ's love burns for you."

Though a shadow flickered across Elena's face, she nodded. "Reverend, may I be baptized?" she asked.

"Of course, my dear woman," Fordham replied. Stepping back, he gestured that they should lead the way to the baptismal font. "I do have one more request for you, though." He spoke from behind them, his voice warm and flowing.

As Elena turned, her gaze met Jesse's, seeking security yet

communicating her desire to move forward. "What is it?" she asked, turning completely to face the reverend.

"Promise me that if you should ever like to sing in our choir, you will speak to Mrs. Pond."

Chapter 13

For Elena, the days leading up to Christmas were like nothing she'd ever experienced. Deep within her mind were both patchy memories of Christmases long ago when her mother was alive, and slightly more complete recollections of observing the holiday goings-on as a yearning but uncomfortable outsider at Olivia's home or Romy's. In later years Christmas had been just another day, perhaps on which an extravagant meal might be consumed and a few gifts exchanged.

But this . . . this. Elena looked at all the decorations her mother-in-law had painstakingly placed and positioned about the pristine sitting room. The dustless dining room. The gleaming foyer. The house on Adelaide Street had been transformed into a breathtaking, expectant announcement of the Christ child's birth. Delicious aromas had wafted from the kitchen for weeks now, and with the snow and cold temperatures outdoors and a cozy fire in the hearth, the home felt warm and welcoming.

How was it possible her life had changed so much in only three months? Had she really lain, starving and impoverished, in a hospital bed, wanting to die? Had she truly believed her soul was already dead and God, if he existed, did not care anything about her? How could she have come from one end of the spectrum to the other in such a relatively short time?

Amazing grace. Sanctification. The burning love of Christ.
These were mere word reasons to explain such a seeming impossibility, yet an actuality her spiritual self knew to be true. Since her baptism, she and Jesse had had many talks about faith, that riddling mystery that was at once simple and intricate.

In the past, she *had* believed. As a young girl, she *had* trusted until . . . until when? Until her mother's death? Fingering a silvery angel adorning the mantel, Elena searched her memory for the precise time—was it a single moment or a slow change?—that she had decided she didn't want any more to do with God. No, it hadn't been when her mother died. It had been later, when things had been happening in her home that were too awful to be true, and all the desperate prayers she'd prayed had bounced back down on her head like scornful pellets of hail.

She'd felt hurt and betrayed. Unloved. Desperate. The only answer she'd seen was to get away or be destroyed.

She walked to the window, staring outdoors but not really looking at the street and the snowcapped houses beyond the glass. Her deep sigh fogged the area before her, making the scene blur. Because her girlish prayers hadn't been answered the way she'd wanted, she had deliberately done away with God. She was beginning to see that was a different thing than having no belief in his presence. Over the years the shell encasing her heart had grown harder and thicker till it had been impossible to recall any of the childlike hope and belief she'd once had.

Meeting Stephen Villard so soon after she'd run away had only validated her judgment that she was better off taking the matters of her life into her own hands. The handsome, charismatic man who became her manager told her everything she'd wanted to hear . . . that she was beautiful, she indeed had talent, and that he would make her and her voice famous.

And so he had.

But what had she done except trade one set of troubles for another? At barely sixteen she had run away from home, a place of misery and sin, only to tumble headlong into a life of more misery and sin—this time of her own consent and making. *You didn't have to leave St. Louis,* she ruminated. *You could have told Romy or Olivia what was happening. . . . You know Granny Esmond would have fought tooth and nail for you. So would Mr. and Mrs. Schmitt. You were full of shame, but you were also full of pride, Elena. Always impetuous, always thinking things should be done the way you wanted them done, when you wanted them done.*

It was ironic that she had ended up doing not her will but Stephen Villard's. She felt restless as she turned from the window and went back to warm herself at the fire. Jesse and Bobby had gone to the train station to fetch Sara and Scott and the children, and Frances was working in the kitchen making preparations for their Christmas Eve dinner.

Yes, she had defied Villard in marrying Jesse. But for that she had forfeited dearly, and so had her loved ones. Would the penalty ever be paid? she wondered, feeling hopeless tears sting her eyes. Would she find strength in her new relationship with God, or did the sins of the past retain the power to destroy them all?

Like the dark, flapping wings of a raven, these anxious, disheartening thoughts intruded frequently on the peace and joy she was only beginning to experience. They came when she said her prayers and read the Scriptures. When she walked into church. When she held Bobby on her lap and tousled his blond curls. At moments when she and Jesse shared never-before-known unity. When she opened her mouth and sang, marveling at the miracle of her healing.

They also came in the new, unfamiliar manner of her mother-in-law. Queerly, Elena wished for a return to the open antagonism that had existed between her and Frances Golden until the evening they had passed bitter words. At least she'd known where she stood with the older woman. Something drastic had happened that night, but Elena was at a loss to define what that was.

No longer was Jesse's mother the fire-breathing dragoness she had initially shown herself to be. The hatred in her eyes had glassed over into a vacant expression, and her manner was now carefully polite. Jesse was concerned about her, and he hoped that having Sara, Scott, and the children here would help her.

A half hour later the travelers arrived. The children rushed in first, looking for their nana with excited calls and laughter. An apron-clad Frances stepped out of the kitchen with a pleased, reserved expression, bestowed hugs and kisses all around, then went back to her work, her three grandchildren trailing happily behind her to the warm, good-smelling kitchen.

Sara came in next, followed by Jesse and Scott, their arms laden to overflowing with bags and gifts. With warm affection, Sara greeted Elena, her full, round belly pressing against Elena through the voluminous wool cloak she wore. Was it possible to feel joy and wistfulness at the same time? Elena wondered, hugging her sister-in-law.

"Oh Elena, you're looking so . . . *well!*" beamed Sara, allowing Elena to help her from her outerwear. "On the way from the train station, Jesse told us some very exciting news about you!"

"Yes," Elena returned with a shy smile, adding, "but if there's anyone glowing here, it's you."

"Did you say 'glowing' or 'growing'?" With a rueful chuckle, Sara gestured toward her gravid abdomen. "In this red-and-white dress, I feel like a great big peppermint drop."

Having set down the load in his arms, Scott swooped over and dropped a kiss on his wife's lips. "Mmm, sweet," he pronounced with a rakish expression.

"You incorrigible man," his wife praised.

"Indeed," he agreed, his gaze warm upon her before he kissed her again.

"All right, you two," Jesse mock-admonished while shooting Elena a pleased glance, his eyes telling her of his approval of his sister's husband. "Ellie, you'd best take down all the mistletoe or we'll never have a clear doorway as long as they're here."

Jesse's words were every bit as jaunty as Scott's, and his deeper meaning was not lost on Elena as he gazed toward the sitting-room entrance. Last night after Frances had retired, he had kissed her passionately beneath the wooden beam, to which had been affixed a sprig of mistletoe. By the dim, flickering light of the fire he had told her, with words and without, of the depth of his feelings for her.

"I wonder if Mama needs any help in the kitchen." Sara appeared not to notice the blush on Elena's cheeks. The men, having sorted through the baggage, began up the stairs with the articles that belonged in the bedrooms.

"She told me she had everything under control," Elena replied, looking around at the immaculate, garland-festooned foyer and dining room.

"That sounds like Mama. She probably didn't let you help with anything, did she?"

Elena shook her head.

"Try not to take it personally. She's always been that way. I'll go say hello to her and offer to stir something, but she'll shoo me out of the kitchen and tell me to go put my feet up."

"I'll save you a chair in the sitting room." As Sara went toward the kitchen, Elena realized she was very happy to have her newfound friend here again.

In only a few minutes, Sara rejoined her, her slow, careful movements peculiar to those in the late stages of pregnancy. More than five years had passed since Elena had given birth to Bobby, but she remembered how heavy and unwieldy she had felt toward the end of her confinement.

"Jesse was right." Settling into the chair by the window, Sara allowed a long, unladylike sigh to escape. "Mama isn't herself."

A silence passed while Elena wrestled with a strong desire to unburden herself. Finally she said, "One night while Jesse was in Ann Arbor . . . well, your mother and I had words."

"Jesse told us that." Sara's face expressed sorrow. "I wish you could know what kind of person Mama normally . . ." Shaking her head, she trailed off before beginning again. "Elena, I am so sorry for the way my mother treats you. As unbelievable as this may sound, it goes against everything she believes in."

The words of that awful night replayed themselves in

Elena's head, and she found herself unable to sit still. Taking her feet, she began to pace, feeling her conscience prick her. "I'm not completely innocent," she acknowledged, having been wondering if she was responsible in some way for her mother-in-law's altered condition. "I said some terrible things back to her."

"I don't doubt she had them coming."

Just then, the children ran into the sitting room, interrupting the women's conversation. "Auntie Elena! Auntie Elena!" Elena found herself being hugged simultaneously by Benjamin and Pearl while Bobby stood, seemingly spellbound by the mountain his aunt Sara's lap had become.

"Nana says dinner will be ready soon," Pearl announced as Jesse and Scott joined them. Outdoors, the day had faded to violet black, and Jesse switched on the gas wall lamps. Moving to the hearth, he moved the spark screen aside and stirred the logs, appearing satisfied at the renewed blaze that resulted. He and Scott sat down, and for the next several minutes the two families enjoyed a time of conversation and closeness.

Later that evening, Elena silently marveled once again at how comfortably she and Jesse engaged with Scott and Sara. For a short time after the delicious meal, the candles on the Christmas tree had been lit, making the children's eyes and mouths grow round with wonder. Each taper had been carefully extinguished before it burned down too far, but the light from the fireplace continued to play against the shiny ornaments, evoking a quieter beauty. Though Frances's leaden presence had caused currents of tension, this was the kind of Christmas Elena had only read about in books.

Tonight the Gospel account of Jesus' birth had been read, several carols sung, popcorn and hot chocolate consumed. Later, the children were tucked comfortably into their beds; they were certain they would never fall asleep for the excitement of opening gifts in the morning. But like a trio of contented, milk-drunk puppies, they grew drowsy and dropped off, one by one.

Frances was the first of the adults to retire, slipping away not long after the children were put to bed. Soon afterward, Sara could no longer disguise her yawns. As Scott escorted her from the sitting room, he paused in the doorway beneath the mistletoe, pointed upward with a grin, and stole a kiss from his sleepy bride. Their footsteps were heard on the stairs and for a short time overhead, and then the house was quiet.

"I've never had a Christmas like this, Jess," Elena said softly once she and Jesse were alone. The fire crackled, and in its light her husband's face was so earnest and handsome that it made her heart hurt. Moving from her chair to the little footstool in front of his, she sat before him.

His hands welcomed her, settling over her shoulders and kneading muscles she hadn't known were tense. After a comfortable silence, he spoke. "When you know and love Christ, the holiday takes on a whole different meaning, doesn't it?"

A shiver went through her as she recalled his deep voice reading the account of the birth of Jesus from Luke. From Olivia and Romy and their families she had heard stories of God and his people, the Jews, as well as men such as Samson and Solomon, Daniel and King David. She knew about the story of Jesus' birth and had dutifully memorized John 3:16 to please Granny Esmond. But never had it all begun to come together as it did now.

Reading the Bible was something new. Both Jesse and Reverend Fordham encouraged daily reading from the Gospels, as well as Old Testament history, New Testament epistles, and the Psalms. Some parts were easier to understand than others, she quickly discovered. Jesse presented her with his well-worn Bible when they'd returned home from her baptism, and every day since then she'd been reading from its pages.

"Yes, the meaning of Christmas is completely different," she agreed, feeling her body grow languid from the pleasure his hands created in her neck and shoulders. "But I also meant the celebration tonight. The meal. When I was growing up—" she started, then stopped.

"When you were growing up?" Jesse's prompt came after a long silence, his voice gently determined.

The dark wings flapped, warning her with a silent, icy ripple of air. *Hushhh. Say no more, Elena. You already said too much the last time this came up.* Even so, the desire to unburden herself warred against the fear that made her heart race and trip.

"Ellie, look at me." His hand cupped her chin and turned her face upward, toward his. "I'm your husband. You're safe here with me. After all the water under the bridge, you have to know that I don't take lightly the vows we made. I love you." On his face was a lean, intense expression. "That means I accept *all* of you, Elena. Your past, present, and future, no matter what that includes."

Elena's heart beat harder, and she felt a fine sheen of perspiration break out over her body.

"Men's daydreams are grand things," he went on, the corners of his lips quirking into the beginnings of a smile. "But they're also straightforward in their simplicity. Whether it be slaying a dragon or fighting bare-handed against impossible odds, we want nothing more than to be heroes. I want to be your hero, Ellie."

"You already are," she whispered, feeling her throat catch. Suddenly, it was impossible to meet his gaze. Her hands trembled, and she buried them deeper in the folds of her skirt.

"Will you tell me what frightens you so badly?" His words settled over her with infinite gentleness. "Let me help?"

She shook her head, shook them off. "No. There's nothing."

Scenes from the past rose up in her mind, causing her heart to twist with anguish. From some things there was no salvation, no freedom, no release. Until her dying day, she would have to live with what she had done. How could she have been so spineless and weak? so cowardly? Though Pastor Fordham said there was no sin greater than the power of God's forgiveness, she wasn't sure God would *want* to forgive some sins.

"The enemy will try to use the past to paralyze you," Jesse went on. He stroked her hair. "But that doesn't have to happen. Don't let it happen. Ask for God's help. He will always provide a way for you to go."

Elena nodded numbly.

"What happened when you were growing up, Ellie? What were you running from?"

"My father . . . my brothers . . . they tried to . . ."

Closing his eyes, he said, "I suspected as much." Moving his hands to her shoulders again, he gripped her firmly. "But they can't hurt you anymore. You were taken advantage of—betrayed—but no longer. You're my wife, and until my dying breath I will protect you. There is *nothing* I wouldn't do for you." Bending, he kissed her forehead.

He prayed then, for God to heal the wounds of her past and to strengthen their marriage. With her whole heart, she wanted to believe that everything could be made as bright, shining, and new as he believed, but the dark thoughts fluttered even more furiously.

What about the hurts that can't be healed? The situations for which there are no solutions? You think believing in Jesus will set you free? Think again, foolish woman. You're not free, and you never will be! Your heart is divided. No matter what idealistic things Jesse says to you, he has his limits. He's a man, after all. He could never accept . . .

As he led her from the sitting room, after a lingering, breathless moment beneath the mistletoe, Elena fought against a renewed desire to try his devotion, to take a chance and pour out everything.

But she didn't. There were some things that could never be told.

❧

Jesse awakened the next morning feeling both tranquil and uneasy. He had slept well, having drifted off to sleep with the warm body of his wife curled against him. She must have risen quietly and gone downstairs, for he was now alone in the bed.

After spending several minutes in prayer, he revisited the conversation he'd had with her last evening. Though he regretted none of his words, he wondered if there was something more he could have said. Should have said. Would she ever be able to let down her guard and trust him completely? believe he would stand by her always?

He had often suspected the burdens she carried had to do with her father and brothers. She had furthered those suspicions right before her baptism, when she had choked out those damning items about the family into which she'd been born. *"One night,"* she'd begun, concluding with a tearful *"I had to leave."* She'd been sixteen years old. The thought of what had happened between "one night" and "I had to leave" made his gut tighten into knots.

From the frying pan, she'd jumped straight into the fire— into the clutches of Stephen Villard. Despite the objectivity Jesse tried to maintain, feelings of aggression mounted. To him, Elena's father and brothers were unspecified evil beings, but he had known Villard.

A large degree of his anger was directed toward himself. How could he have been so blind to the duress his wife had suffered under her manager? All the signs had been there. So much pain could have been averted if only he'd been a stronger, wiser man.

Been Elena's hero.

I'll do anything to make Elena whole again, Father, he prayed. *Anything she needs. Lead me to be the husband and father you intend for me to be. In Jesus' name, send your healing to this house. Help all of us to live in freedom, for your glory.*

He rose, dressing quickly in the chilly air. When he opened the door and stepped into the hallway, he heard the excited voices of the children carrying up the stairs, causing him to smile distractedly. He wasn't so old that he'd forgotten the thrill of Christmas morning.

The tantalizing aroma of bacon wafted to his nose as he descended the stairs, making his stomach growl despite the leaden thoughts weighing on his mind. Sara and Elena came into view, smiling and chatting in the sitting room. Scott was doing his best to keep three wound-up youngsters from worrying the packages beneath the Christmas tree. As he passed across the entryway to join the family, he observed that his mother already had the table set. Obviously, she had the granddaddy of all Christmas breakfasts underway in her well-stocked kitchen.

Retracing his last few steps, he walked through the dining room and pushed open the door to the kitchen. "Merry Christmas, Mama," he greeted his flush-faced mother. With one hand, she turned a slice of bacon in a black skillet; with the other, she expertly flipped a trio of pancakes on a smoking griddle.

She looked up. "Merry Christmas, Son." A faint smile crossed her face, then vanished.

Walking over to her, he bent and kissed her cheek. "It's been too long since I told you I love you."

"I love you too."

Taking the bull by the horns, he added, "I'm happy with Elena," he said softly, "and I want you to be too. God's doing wonderful things in her life."

"I know." Her low admission came after she transferred the cakes onto the plate in the warming oven. From her painted glass mixing bowl, she spooned creamy batter onto the griddle, creating three new circles.

"I want all of us to be happy together here."

She nodded mutely and moved the bacon around in the skillet.

"Mama," he said, taking her by the shoulders, "we've all been very concerned about you. Will you please tell me what troubles you?"

She blinked rapidly, her blue eyes unnaturally bright. "I've been thinking a lot about . . . your sister," she replied in a faraway manner. Did she tremble beneath his touch?

"There's no need for worry. Sara's in splendid health," he said, puzzled by his mother's depth of emotion for his sister's normal, healthy pregnancy. Sara had borne Pearl and Benjamin without difficulty, and there was no reason to expect there would be trouble this time around.

"Of course . . . you're right," she said with more vigor,

sounding almost like her usual self. "Goodness, I'm almost done in here. Tell the children to wash their hands. We can open gifts right after breakfast. There should be enough time to do dishes before we leave for church."

Jesse was heartened by her effort, but to his eyes and ears it didn't ring true. He did as she asked, herding his son, nephew, and niece to the water closet to wash and dry their hands before they all enjoyed another one of Frances's scrumptious meals. He watched her throughout breakfast, keenly aware of her heavy spirit. Elena seemed to be similarly affected, though she endeavored to make lighthearted conversation.

Dear Lord, what is the matter here?

As he finished his pancakes, Jesse realized he was experiencing anxiety about the gift giving that was about to take place in the sitting room. Did his mother have something for Elena? Did Elena for her mother-in-law? He wished he'd thought to talk to each of them separately long before this moment. For all their sakes, but especially for the children's, he prayed that an uncomfortable scene would not ensue.

After pleading to be excused, the children ran into the sitting room, followed by the slower-moving adults. Jesse led them in a prayer of thanksgiving, then asked the children to distribute the gifts. In some families he knew extravagance was the order of the day, but not in theirs. Simple, handmade, or thoughtfully selected treasures were lovingly given and received on this holy day of celebration.

Once the packages and bundles had been passed out, it was traditional for the youngest person in the room to open the first gift. After he or she thanked the giver, the person to the right was next to open one of his presents. This went on until they had gone around the room and everyone had opened a gift. The process was repeated until all the packages had been unwrapped and admired.

Robert, being the youngest, was first. Unabashedly, he chose the largest box in his pile and began tugging at the string.

"The tag," his grandmother prompted, raising her
eyebrows.

"Oh. Sorry. To Robert," he read proudly. "From Pearl and
Benjam. *Ben-jam?*" Looking up at his cousin, he expressed
amusement. "Is that your new nickname?"

"No, he wrote his name too big and ran out of space," Pearl
informed her cousin.

Benjamin made a disgusted noise. "That's because you took
so much room writing your name. There's only five letters in
Pearl, and you used more than half the tag—"

Jesse was grateful for the good-humored banter, which
eased a good deal of the accumulated tension in the room. Elena
fingered the small stack of bundles in her lap, meeting his gaze
with a warm, shy smile.

"I've never had a Christmas like this, Jess," he remembered
her saying last night in the firelight, her eyes dark and round.
Protectiveness for her rose inside him, and more than ever he
hoped this Christmas celebration would fill her with joy. He
smiled back, hoping she would be pleased with the small brooch
he'd selected for her in Ann Arbor, all the while hoping his
mother had done the right thing and given Elena something.
Anything.

Robert was overjoyed with the carved, brightly painted
train engine he received from his cousins. Its wheels turned
easily, and he gave the wooden locomotive a push across the
carpeted floor while supplying the energetic and hearty sounds
of its whistle. Benjamin—or Benjam, as he was now addressed—
was next to open a gift, then Pearl.

Laughter and exclamations abounded in the cozy sitting
room, making Jesse wonder, for all his worries, if this Christmas
wasn't turning out better even than last year's. *Of course it's better*,
he told himself as he watched Scott separate the layers of paper
enfolding a new gray scarf. *Last year you had no idea where Elena
was or if she was even alive, and now she's right here at your side.*

His mother was next to open one of her gifts. Without
fanfare, her capable hands untied the knot of a small, round

bundle. Holding up what appeared to be a blue crocheted ball with a little skirt around its middle, she lifted her gaze toward her daughter-in-law.

"It's a pincushion," Elena said nervously from beside him. "Your old one looked like it had seen better days."

"It has, at that." His mother nodded, the stiff set of her features softening faintly. "Thank you, Elena."

"You're welcome."

As an inaudible, collective sigh seemed to leave those adults gathered in the sitting room, Sara artfully selected one of her packages and made a production of guessing what its contents might hold. When at last she had exhausted a list of possibilities, she opened it and exclaimed prettily over the woven trivet Pearl had made.

What's the use of worrying? Jesse asked himself, feeling the tension drain from him. It was such a foolish venture, not to mention a waste of time. He remembered now, one day at the store, Elena asking him for a crochet hook, some fabric, and colored thread. He should have known she was thinking ahead to Christmas. She must have worked on her gifts while he was away in Ann Arbor.

In her chair beside him, she selected a small, neat package. He watched her profile, admiring the graceful movements of her slender fingers undoing the ribbon and smoothing aside the wrapping. Inside was a stack of snowy white handkerchiefs, their edges tatted with lace.

"Thank you, Mrs. Golden," she said graciously, though Jesse heard uncertainty in her voice as well. "They're lovely."

As his mother returned a cautious smile of her own, he thanked God once again for his goodness, and for all the miracles he had performed to unite this family.

Chapter 14

The next several weeks passed in a comfortable rhythm. On the sixteenth of January, they were all blessed by the safe arrival of Scott and Sara's daughter, Isobel. A delightful visit to their home ensued, and Frances stayed on for a month. Jesse made a few more trips to Ann Arbor to work with the director of his play, refining lines and rewriting one of the scenes. This left Elena and Bobby with a great deal of time alone to become better acquainted, and the bonds between mother and son grew steadily stronger.

At the beginning of February, Elena began singing with Dr. Suffington again. He did not seem surprised to learn she had recovered her voice, promptly filling her folder with difficult music, some of it Italian. She relished the challenge, pouring herself into the process of learning, improving . . . making music. She was *singing* again, and every time she opened her mouth, it was with the realization that this marvelous gift she had been given—this fresh start—was straight from the hand of God. The memories of her past outstanding performances, the ovations, the encores, were pallid, indeed, in light of this knowledge.

She had just finished rehearsing her music this late February morning, and was for some reason unable to stop thinking of her old friends. As she grew settled in her new life, more than ever she regretted letting her old friendships slide. Would Olivia and Romy welcome hearing from her? she wondered. Would she somehow be able to locate them?

Olivia had been living in a little town in Colorado the last time Elena had written her. She and her grandmother had moved west about a year after Elena had left St. Louis, taking their healing skills to a small farming and ranching community. Romy had gone on to teachers' college. Where were they now? What turns had their lives taken? Were they wives? mothers? How would she go about finding them?

You could write them in care of Romy's parents. Chances are, Mr. and Mrs. Schmitt are still living in the same place. A sudden series of unpleasant thoughts came to her. What if the Schmitts told her father where she was? And what if he or her brothers came looking for her?

She chastised herself for her ridiculousness as she put away her music and went to Jesse's writing desk. Mr. and Mrs. Schmitt would do no such thing, especially if she asked them not to. Didn't it make sense that if such a thing were going to happen, it would have happened long ago, when she was writing Romy?

She decided she would write Olivia first. A picture arose in her mind of her friend's shining gray eyes and simple, dazzling smile. She swallowed a lump in her throat and dipped the pen into the well, tapping off the excess ink.

To my dear friend Olivia,

Are you ready for a ghost to rise up from your past? First of all, this ghost must humbly beg your forgiveness for being invisible for so long. I am trying to recall how many years have passed since I've written. Too many, I know.

"What on earth has happened to you?" I can hear you ask in that motherly way of yours. "Where have you been?" Your letters to me back in the 70s were always so filled with concern. At the time I told myself I did not appreciate such care, but a part of me did long to be mothered.

You frequently exhorted me to be careful, but I was not. I quit writing you because I felt unworthy of your friendship. I fell far from grace, becoming the type of woman a decent person would give wide berth to. You know my name became popular for a time. There are many trappings and temptations that go along with that, and I succumbed to them all.

This will undoubtedly be a long letter (if you care to keep reading). I am well, but it is only by the grace of God. You might be interested to know that I recently surrendered my heart to Jesus Christ. Now I know why Granny Esmond made me memorize that passage in the book of John.

She paused, wondering how to summarize the things that had happened since she'd last written, then spent the next hour telling of her career, of Villard, of meeting Jesse, and then of all the things that had transpired since then.

Despite the wretched state into which I had fallen, God saw fit to spare my life and restore my marriage. Jesse and I are living, along with his widowed mother, in Detroit, Michigan (which is much colder and snowier than Missouri).

After a few more paragraphs she closed, hoping her old friend was not easily shocked. A letter to Romy followed, much the same as the one she'd written Olivia. Making out one envelope to Romy and one to Olivia, she sealed each letter in its envelope. She then composed a brief polite letter to the Schmitts, asking them to please forward the two letters, and enclosed them, with a little money for postage, in a larger wrapper.

A weary sense of satisfaction overcame her when she had completed that, and she went to the kitchen to make herself a cup of tea. Frances had gone to spend the day with a convalescing friend, and Jesse was due home from Ann Arbor late this afternoon. Glancing at the clock, she saw it was past noon and decided to make herself an egg salad sandwich. After a little more time had passed, she would put on her outdoor clothes and walk to the post office, trying to time her excursion with the dismissal bell at Bobby's school.

A warm feeling spread through her middle when she thought of how his face would light up when he saw her. *My life has never been this good,* she prayed with deep gratitude. *Thank you, dear Lord, for restoring my husband and son to me. If you are willing, please help these letters find Olivia and Romy. And please, God,* she added, finally summoning the courage to bring him a petition she had locked away in the furthest-flung places of her heart, *please watch over—*

Sudden guilt clenched her vitals and made her limbs go weak. She couldn't bring herself to do it after all. Accusing thoughts bore down on her like a chorus of strident voices telling her she was weak, ineffectual, powerless. Trapped.

Couldn't Jesse . . . ?

No. She immediately rejected that thought. There were things Jesse could not help her with, things that had to be just as they were. What she needed to do was concentrate on living in the present and to count her blessings. With shaking movements, she put on the teakettle, then cut two slices of bread for her sandwich.

Live in the present. Count your blessings.

The sulfurous smell of chopped eggs was unpleasant but helped her focus on the task at hand. Making a sandwich. She was thankful for this warm kitchen and its food, and for the knowledge that in a short while, she would be able to hug her son tightly against her breast.

If only . . .

Setting the knife back down on the cutting block with a sharp sound, she forbade herself to think further on any *ifs.* For if she'd learned nothing else in her troubled life, it was that wanting too much led only to ruin.

❧

"I have a proposal for you, my boy." Charles Suffington regarded Jesse with an enigmatic expression. The older gentleman had asked to meet Jesse for lunch again, this time at the Randolph

Hotel. This noon the dining room was nearly filled with businessmen and a scattering of well-dressed couples. The atmosphere was quiet and refined, the quiet hum of conversation and clinking of cups and cutlery a stark difference from the atmosphere of some of the less expensive, more boisterous eating establishments.

"What's your proposal, sir?" Jesse asked, suddenly wary. For the past hour they had been making pleasant conversation, with Suffington seeming genuinely interested in the production of his upcoming play. Jesse took a sip of coffee, wondering if his wily former professor had only been biding his time to spring whatever trap he had in mind.

"I suppose I could beat around the bush, but I won't. I want your wife to sing with my chorale."

"No."

"Now, now." Suffington raised his hands in a gesture of supplication. "Do me the courtesy of hearing me out."

Jesse forced down his annoyance. "I'll listen, but my answer will be the same. Elena's been through a devil of a time, and the last thing she needs is to return to the pressures of performing. For the sake of her health, I can't allow it. I *won't* allow it."

"She seems quite robust these days when she sings her lessons. And we both know what kind of talent she has." Suffington shrugged, moving his hands back to grip the edge of the table. Leaning forward, he spoke distinctly. "I could make her one of the great ones."

"She was one of the great ones. She doesn't want that anymore."

"Are you sure? Or is it that *you* don't want it? Maybe you would like her gift to languish as you have allowed yours to."

Jesse released a long, controlled stream of air from his nostrils. "If you were a younger man, Suffington, I'd see you outside for that remark."

The professor's neat silver beard wagged with delighted laughter. "Ah yes. When a fellow reaches my age he begins to take a few liberties." After his merriment subsided, he sought Jesse's gaze earnestly. "Now this is what I propose. Our spring tour starts in Detroit next month. From here we go to Chicago, then make our way south and east before going abroad. I want to showcase Elena here and in Chicago. This dream of mine could only be improved upon, of course, by your consenting to sing with her."

Jesse was speechless. Did Suffington's boldness have no limits?

"I recall our conversation of a few years ago, but your situation has changed drastically. I'm not asking you to tour the Continent with us, or even the States. Just two cities. If nothing else, think of the publicity. Getting yourself back into the public eye could be a marvelous boon to getting more of your work produced."

"Need I remind you that one of my plays *is* being produced?"

"One play . . . at a small theater in Ann Arbor. You told me you wanted to reach a large audience with your messages of God and salvation. You want your work to grip people's hearts and change their lives. This could be just the leg up you need to accomplish your goals."

How had Suffington remembered all that?

"You needn't fear that I have said anything to Elena about this. But I ask you to go home and give the matter serious consideration. It could be good . . . for all of us."

Jesse shook his head, appalled to find himself already thinking through the possibilities Suffington had just presented.

"I have one more question for you, Mr. Golden."

"You don't think you've already asked enough?" Jesse's tone was incredulous.

"It's about your mother."

"What about my mother?"

"May I call upon her? I realize I dropped away rather abruptly, but I did not want to apply any pressure to Elena, nor did I want your lovely mother to mistake my motives."

"Please be so kind as to tell me more about your motives." Jesse crossed his arms and leaned back in his chair, regarding Suffington with a critical gaze.

"Quite simple, really. I enjoy your mother's company very much," the urbane professor began, clearing his throat and revealing, to Jesse's surprise, a distinct flash of nervousness. "And if she has no objections, I wish to escort her to the upcoming concert of chamber music at Phoenix Hall. Mr. de Zielinski will be directing. Also, I should like to attend the opening of your play and would be honored to sit with your family."

The waiter appeared and cleared their plates, giving Jesse a few moments to think things over. "I'll talk to her," he conceded, avoiding answering directly. Would Suffington be good for what ailed his mother? he wondered. She had been much happier since Isobel was born, treating Elena with much more courtesy than she had before Christmas, but there still seemed to be something amiss. A void in her eyes, a blankness in her manner.

Everything having been said, lunch was concluded. For the remainder of the day, Jesse found himself distracted by the subjects Suffington had raised. Also, the opening of his play was fast approaching. A good performance—and good reviews— would help in the critical process of getting his name as a playwright established.

As dusk fell, once again his thoughts turned toward Suffington's wish for Elena to sing at his Detroit and Chicago concerts. Jesse's instinctive response was an emphatic *no*, but he told himself honestly that he did not know Elena's mind on the matter. She had not expressed any desire to perform; in fact, with his mother having been away so much, she seemed to be utterly content to devote herself to prayer and learning more of the Scriptures, practicing her music, and taking over the housekeeping tasks.

"This dream of mine could only be improved upon, of course, by your consenting to sing with her."

Had his problems with, then separation from, Elena soured him on performing? He could not deny that he and Ellie, together on stage, had had a remarkable chemistry that went far beyond the blending of their voices. After they had begun singing together, a grandiloquent reviewer in Philadelphia had written: "Seldom, if ever, will you see a couple that enthralls you, captivates you, and engrosses every fiber of your attention the way this leading man and lady do. Beyond the witticisms of this delightful, humorous love story, and even beyond the magnificent vocal talents of Jesse Golden and Elena Breen, *If Not for You* is a deeply satisfying theater experience for gentlemen and ladies alike. If you have not already seen this musical production, I urge you to run, not walk, for tickets to tonight's performance."

Oh yes. Life, in many respects, had been grand back then. Thrilling, exhilarating, heady. But with that was tangled so much sin. Before he'd left home to seek greater things in the world, he had given countless recitals and sung in many concerts. Suffington had not had international prominence then, but he was a respected vocal teacher who had put a great deal of himself into developing Jesse's musical career.

Jesse cringed as he recalled how he'd begun chafing under what he'd considered his limited circumstances and opportunities. At the same time he had grown rather rapidly in arrogance and self-importance. His training in classic opera had not been complete, but the idea of starring in one of the American musical plays, which were then quickly gaining in popularity, appealed greatly to him.

Suffington had urged him to be patient and continue building his skills and repertoire. His mother had wept and begged him not to do anything rash. Despite that, he had tried out for a theater company that was passing through Detroit. To his pleasure, he was taken on and began traveling with them. Only months later his popularity surged, and he jumped ship for a greater opportunity to star beside Elena Breen.

Sighing, he set the pen in its rest and pushed his pages forward. His mind was far too preoccupied to give justice to the scene he was writing. It was his mother's Ladies' Aide night, so Elena was rustling about the kitchen with Robert, preparing a simple evening meal. Robert's laughter carried from the kitchen, bringing a distracted smile to his face. His son had always seemed happy enough, but now that his mother had become a part of his life, the transformation in his personality was amazing.

Jesse wondered about his own relationship with Elena. For all the gains they had made, he still experienced times of uncertainty. Was she truly happy with him? with her new, slow-paced life? Did she secretly yearn to perform before an audience and receive the adulation and applause she once had?

He also wondered if they were only tiptoeing around the wreckage of their past, each shouldering his or her own private bag of debris. Though he felt certain of his calling to write plays, that didn't necessarily preclude him from singing more than in church on Sunday. Deep inside, he knew he'd been carrying an aversion to public performance since he returned to Detroit with Robert. Whether that was because thoughts of performing reminded him of his painful separation from Elena, or raised lingering guilt at his having strayed so far from the Lord, he did not know. He only knew that the idea of singing onstage made him feel very uncomfortable.

What do you say, heavenly Father? he prayed, bowing his head. *Am I letting my talents lie fallow, as Suffington believes? If making a few appearances would help in the process of getting my plays produced, would it be prudent to take this opportunity? What about Elena? Would she benefit from performing again?* Jesse let out a deep breath and paused. *Or am I looking at things all wrong? The voice you gave her brings such pleasure to those who hear her sing. . . . Is it your will for her to share that gift with others?*

❦

Elena bent her head and brushed her hair from the nape of her neck forward in long strokes. After straightening, she reversed directions and brushed her tresses away from her face. In the mirror, she was pleased to see that the shine and health of her hair had, for the most part, returned. Sara's beauty treatments had done wonders for her brittle, damaged locks. And while her skin was dry due to the wintertime cold, its ugly, scaly appearance had gradually faded away . . . once again thanks to Sara and her special blend of oils.

She fastened the top few buttons of her nightdress just as Jesse came in. After dropping a kiss on her cheek, he removed his jacket and pulled his braces down over his shoulders. With a sigh, he sat on the edge of the bed.

"Are you thinking about your play, Jess? You haven't been yourself today," she observed, going to his side. "I know you weren't satisfied with the second scene."

"That's not it." He turned toward her, his dark eyes shadowed.

"What is it then?"

"I have something to ask you."

Elena's heart thumped against her ribs. *Oh, dear Lord, what has he learned?* Was everything about to come crashing down upon the new life she had begun living? She should have known better than to believe someone like her could ever hope to—

". . . to sing with Dr. Suffington's chorale." Some of what Jesse was saying penetrated her careening thoughts. "Just two cities—Detroit and Chicago."

"Would you please . . . repeat that?" she asked, the turbulence of her mind and emotions having caused her to miss much of what he had just said.

"I'm sorry, Ellie. Please don't be angry with me. I do admit to initially telling Suffington no," apologized Jesse, "but then I realized you hadn't been consulted about the matter at all."

"About singing?" She hoped she didn't sound as confused as she felt. She toyed with the brush while the commotion inside her gradually began to settle. Would the day ever come when she would stop looking over her shoulder into the past? Was that even possible?

"Yes, with his chorale. What do you think about performing with them in Detroit and Chicago?"

"The first two cities of his tour," she put together, remembering having read about the group's itinerary one day while she was at the conservatory.

"He initially asked just about you, but then toward the end of our conversation, he hinted very strongly that he would like both of us to sing."

"Oh, Jess," she said, taking a little breath.

"Does that mean you would want to?" He watched her closely.

"Yes . . . and no . . . and yes and no."

At that, some of the tension seemed to leave him, and a faint smile curved his lips. "I know what you mean. I feel the same way."

"I miss singing with you," she said, resting her cheek against his shoulder.

In reply, he slipped his arm around her and pulled her close. "How much do you miss the stage?"

She chose her words carefully, wanting him to understand her heart. "Jesse, if I never appeared onstage again, I would be perfectly happy. God has been so good to grant me this life here with you and Bobby."

"Does that mean you've never thought of performing again?"

"I've thought about it," she said slowly, trying to keep thoughts of Villard at bay, "but I don't want that kind of life anymore. It almost destroyed me."

"It wouldn't have to."

"I suppose not."

A lengthy silence passed between them, growing longer as Jesse took his feet and began to pace. Finally he spoke. "Can I tell you something, Ellie?"

She nodded, concerned.

"There's a part of me that misses the excitement of being onstage, and I don't know how I'm supposed to feel about that."

"Performing's in our blood, Jess," she said with a wry smile. "That makes us different from other people, but I don't believe it necessarily make us bad. Lately I've been thinking that it's what a person does with his talents and desires that counts."

"But that's just it!" He made a helpless gesture, his palms raised up toward the ceiling. "What am I supposed to do? Write plays? Sing? Act? Perform with Suffington's chorale? Or stay home and be a responsible husband and father?"

Seldom had Elena seen Jesse this out of sorts. Was the pressure of his upcoming play weighing too heavily upon him, or was there something else distressing him? Something about her, perhaps? about their past? Quickly, she prayed for wisdom and understanding to help her husband. To help *them*.

"I don't know a more responsible husband or father than you," she spoke earnestly. "And where is it written that each person is allotted only one talent?"

"Tell me, then . . . what if using one talent helps another? Is that being self-serving? opportunistic?"

"I'm not sure what you mean by that."

"What kind of man does it make me if I sing for Suffington and take advantage of the advertising to further my chances of having more plays produced?"

Elena laid the brush on the bed and went to her husband, reaching her arms as far around him as she could. "Besides being a wonderful husband and father, a magnificent singer, and a brilliant playwright? A good businessman, I'd say," she said huskily, capturing his gaze.

"When you look at me like that, Ellie, I feel like I can do anything." His arms enfolded her, and he nuzzled her neck. "I feel like your hero."

"That's because you *are* my hero, Jesse Golden. I love you so much."

"I love you too, Ellie." As his hands moved up to stroke her hair, she felt the tightness go out of him. They continued holding each other, giving and receiving comfort, communicating their feelings for one another.

"If our singing in Suffington's chorale could help more of your plays be produced, I want to do it," she announced.

"But what if—"

"Let's not do any 'what-iffing.' Let's just trust that God will use this opportunity however he sees fit. We'll offer it to him."

"You're sure? Don't you think this might be too taxing for you?"

"The thought of being onstage with you again makes my heart sing." She raised her face toward his and smiled.

A slow, answering smile erased the worry from his features. "We were good together, weren't we?"

"We were indeed . . . and now we're even better."

"I don't want that to change." His tone and expression became urgent. "Promise me, Ellie, that if you change your mind, you'll talk to me."

"I promise I won't change my mind," she said mischievously.

"Elena Golden." A short chuckle rumbled in his chest. "What a wife you are."

"And what a husband I have."

"Suffington's not going to believe his ears when I tell him yes."

"It's another new beginning for us, Jess. Sometimes I just can't believe . . ." Sudden emotion overwhelmed her, and she melted against him.

"The past is behind us, Ellie," he said with tenderness. "Now the only place we have to travel is toward the future."

Chapter 15

March came in like a lion.

Frances could tell that neither Jesse nor Elena had antici-
pated the amount of public interest sparked by the announce-
ments and advertisements for Suffington's chorale. A reporter
from the *Detroit Free Press* and another from the *Sunday News*
came and did interviews, each releasing a column of several
inches about Elena's and Jesse's return to the stage. Jesse's work
as a playwright was also mentioned, prompting a sellout of tickets for the scheduled performances of his play in Ann Arbor.

Ten Long Steps was to open the third week of March, and
the chorale commenced its tour the first week of April. Though
Jesse and Elena were busier than ever with rehearsals and learning new music, happiness radiated from them. In fact, Frances
had to admit that she had seldom seen a husband and wife more
in love with one another than her son and Elena.

She'd initially had serious reservations about the two of
them appearing with Suffington's chorale, fearing that one or the
other, or both, would be tempted to return to a life of performing and touring. Jesse had gone to great lengths to assure her
nothing of the sort would happen; that he and Elena had agreed
to take this particular opportunity to expose his name more
widely, with the hope of garnering attention for his plays.

Knowing the objective of his dramas was to spread the gospel message, how could she make any argument? Frances sighed as she polished the mirror in the water closet, the sound of Jesse's and Elena's voices blending together making her feel curiously emotional. A few minutes earlier, she had quietly observed them from the doorway of the sitting room. The way they had looked at each other while they were singing had raised goose bumps on her arms. They were utterly compelling together, making her realize why, a handful of years ago, audiences had clamored to see their musical plays.

Gathering up her bucket and rags, she walked into the hallway. Elena was singing alone now, her voice resonating beautifully to the upper notes of the mournful ballad she had begun learning only this past week. For some reason, Frances's blonde-haired daughter-in-law no longer inflamed her the way she once had. Though she wouldn't go so far as to say she loved—or even liked—the girl, she found that she had developed a place of compassion in her heart for her.

And a reluctant admiration.

Of course Elena had no idea that her words on that ugly December night had scratched open a long-buried abscess inside her mother-in-law. Oh, the days and nights of pain the release of those poisons had caused! Emotions Frances had never allowed herself to feel ravaged her, taking her from despair to fury and back to despair. Memories of Uncle Clyde and the things he had done made her feel shaky, sweaty, nauseous. Unclean. Little Laura's face haunted her, as did the image of her still, silent body.

From the darkness of her bedchamber and all day long at her tasks she called upon the Lord for mercy, healing, and forgiveness. And for one black week after Christmas, she wondered if God was even there, and what use there was in her existence.

Then one day Frances realized that, although she could not discern the distinct moment at which it happened, the void inside her had slowly begun filling in. The heights of her fury were no longer limitless, and the depths of her despair not nearly so bleak and yawning. She recognized that God was in the process of binding up her wounds, though not in the way—nor nearly as quickly—as she would have liked.

Then Isobel had been born. The miracle of her new grand-daughter had given her fresh hope to press onward and the faith to continue clinging to the Lord. As she rocked the healthy infant girl in her arms, she'd wept many tears over her long-ago first daughter, Laura. Sara had been puzzled by her behavior, she knew, but Sara herself was highly emotional after having given birth and hadn't asked any questions.

After spending a month in Ann Arbor, Frances had returned home to see a new closeness between Jesse, Elena, and Robert. As opposed as she had been to Elena's becoming a part of their lives, what kind of Christian would she be if she didn't rejoice over her daughter-in-law's having surrendered her heart to God? Wasn't that the biggest objection she'd had to Jesse's having married her? That he'd wed an unbeliever?

The changes in Elena reflected a true conversion of heart. Gone was the suspicious, brittle young woman Jesse had brought home; in her place was a wife and mother who was trying to live out her vocations in a manner befitting one who loved Christ. Frances knew it was right for a husband and wife to be together. Quite simply, it was right for Jesse and Elena to be together. At the same time, however, Frances had begun feeling like a fifth wheel. An unnecessary fixture in this now complete and happy home.

She'd been trying to stay out of their way as much as possi-ble. She wanted to tell Elena she was sorry for having treated her so shabbily, but she couldn't seem to find the right words, the right situation, the right time. Frances believed the girl under-stood that an unspoken truce rested between them. That would have to be good enough for now, she thought, entering the kitchen with a heavy sigh. Perhaps there would be an opportu-nity in the future for the breach between them to be repaired.

She knew Elena favored a caramel cake she had once

made. Perhaps there was time yet this afternoon to get one baked and iced. After putting away her cleaning items, she washed her hands and pulled down two bowls, then gathered butter, sugar, eggs, flour, and the remainder of the ingredients she would need.

Jesse and Elena's sitting room rehearsal went on, filling the house with beautiful music. Sometimes Frances was overcome by the amount of talent her son possessed. He was every bit the vocalist his father was, and the plays he wrote were magnificent stories of intersection between God and man. She was so proud of him. As she listened to him and Elena singing, she predicted Suffington would not be content to settle for two cities. The old gentleman would want more from these two.

The butter was hard, and it took some effort to cream it with the sugar. Her arm grew weary while she worked, reminding her of the day she'd hurriedly mixed a batch of cinnamon-and-raisin scones while Dr. Suffington coached Jesse and Elena in the sitting room.

Last month Jesse told her the professor wanted to call on her. It was just as well Suffington had dropped away when Elena had quit her lessons, for Frances had been in no state of mind to think of entertaining his company. In fact, she still wasn't sure what she thought about his escorting her anywhere. She had said no to the chamber music concert at Phoenix Hall last month; to W. A. Mestayer's farrago of nonsense, *We, Us & Co.* at the Detroit Opera House; and to the appearance in the city of a live bear on roller skates.

When the silver-haired professor had come by the house to work with Jesse and Elena, she had offered him only tea. The second time she'd had a chess pie ready, and the third some lemon snaps. That day he'd asked her if he might accompany the family to the opening of Jesse's play, to which she replied she supposed so.

Whether it was because she had been so long out of sorts, or whether it was because Suffington had, in so many words, declared himself a suitor, things between them were no longer as relaxed as they once were. Why had she said yes to his attending the play with them? she wondered. What had she been thinking? He'd once mentioned he attended church, but that didn't necessarily mean he was a believer. What kind of mess had she gotten herself involved in now?

She separated seven eggs and began beating the whites, feeling as fragile as the empty shells lying beside the bowls.

❧

Jesse was nervous, tired, and energized all at the same time. Last evening's dress rehearsal of *Ten Long Steps* had not gone smoothly, but in the world of theater a bad dress rehearsal was often taken as a sign that the opening night would go well. Not believing in superstition, he turned instead to prayer, asking God's blessing over tonight's performance. Mentally shaking his head, he added an extra prayer for the leading man, who had been frantic over the loss of his lucky rabbit's foot.

A good review, coupled with the publicity and a good turn-out to Suffington's musical recital, could help launch his career as a successful playwright. He was well aware that success meant different things to different people. For him, being successful meant turning people's hearts toward God while they watched his plays.

During these past months, the significance of his task had grown in clarity. The initial indistinct calling he'd felt to become a playwright had evolved into his making a definite assent— saying yes—to the challenge and commitment of producing engaging, well-written plays that communicated God's truths through man's struggles.

Some might make the argument that entertainment existed for its own sake, to absorb a patron's attention for a time so as to lift his mind away from his worldly cares. Once Jesse might have been able to agree completely with that statement, but over the past four years especially, he had come to view time as a heavenly gift meriting careful stewardship. Adding more vapid theatrical material to a culture already saturated with too much would serve no good purpose.

He finished shaving by lamplight and wiped his face with the towel. Elena made a sleepy sound from the bed and squinted as she tried opening her eyes. Sara had put him and Elena in the guest bedroom in her and Scott's comfortable home; Robert was with Benjamin, and Frances had slept with Pearl.

"What time is it?" His wife's words were muffled by her yawn.

"A little after five."

"You didn't get in until late. . . . How come you're up so early?"

"I don't know. I heard Isobel cry awhile ago and just couldn't get back to sleep." He didn't add that his mind was racing with thoughts of last night's rehearsal, the actor who couldn't remember his lines in the third scene, and what kind of public reception *Ten Long Steps* would receive.

She propped herself up on one elbow, unaware of the fetching picture she presented against the fluffy pillows and counterpane. Tendrils of hair framed her sleepy face, and she stretched out her arm. "Come back to bed, Jess. Even if you don't nod off, you can rest for another hour or two."

His footsteps made no noise against the thick carpeting as he padded back to the bed. "I should just stay up," he protested, taking her hand. Its warmth and softness only added to the weariness he felt. "If I get an early start, I can get much more done today."

"And what good is that if you fall asleep during tonight's opening? Come lie down. Besides, your shoulder makes a very nice pillow," she added with a touch of sauciness in her early morning voice.

The thought of Elena snuggled against him tested his resolve, but he shook his head. "I don't think I could sleep anymore, even if I wanted to."

"All right then, I'll get up with you."

A moment later she was standing within his arms, her head

resting heavily against his chest. "You're tired," he spoke, knowing it would be better for her to go back to bed, yet at the same time drawing comfort and peace from her embrace. He stroked her hair, enjoying its silken texture. "Do you ever think of how far we've come since last fall?"

"Every day," she softly replied. After a long pause, she added, "Sometimes I can't believe God would be so good to someone like me. Not only did he spare my life, he gave me back you and Bobby . . . and my voice."

"That's because he loves you and has your best interests at heart."

"That's what Reverend Fordham said the day I was baptized. Do you remember what he said about the process of sanctification not feeling very good?"

"Yes."

"Why, then, does life seem to be getting more agreeable rather than more difficult? It feels like there have been good changes inside me, but maybe I'm not really growing in my faith after all."

"I see the process of sanctification in you already, Ellie. Now that you've accepted God's love, his light shines from your eyes."

"Do you really think so?" The breathless quality of her voice gave away how much she yearned for those words to be true.

"I know so." He tightened his arm, pulling her closer. "I also see your trust in the Lord growing every day."

Her voice quavered. "It's never been easy for me to trust. I'm sorry for that, Jess, for how much I've hurt you because . . ."

"Heroes are not only forgiving but are trustworthy men, as well." In response to her fading words he spoke lightly, though his senses were alert to the possibilities of the moment. Was this the day Elena would entrust her deepest secrets to his keeping? Silently he prayed that God would ready his heart to receive them, for he suspected the things she had to tell were far from pleasant.

Lifting her head, she looked deeply into his eyes. "You are my hero, Jesse Golden. There is no other man on earth for me. I wish . . . I wish you could understand how much I love you."

He wanted to answer that if she felt for him even half the way he did for her, he understood, but the kiss they shared made such words impossible.

And unnecessary.

❧

"Are you sure there isn't something you want to tell me? You've been beaming ever since you arrived in Ann Arbor."

"If I am, it's not for the reason you're thinking," Elena answered her sister-in-law with an indulgent smile, feeling her cheeks heat nonetheless. "But maybe one day soon, God willing."

Their gazes met in Sara's dressing-table mirror, in front of which sat Elena. Sara stood behind her, putting the final touches on the artful hairstyle she had just created for Elena. Carefully, she pinned a small, elegant hat in place on Elena's head, nodding with satisfaction when it was secure. "There, now. That's not going anywhere." Sara placed her hands gently on Elena's shoulders and bent forward until her face appeared next to Elena's in the mirror. "And neither are you until you tell me what makes you so happy."

"Can't a person just be happy?" Elena couldn't resist chuckling at Sara's persistence.

Sara raised her eyebrows and did not move.

"Oh, all right. I'm happy because I'm finding out just how much God loves me. Despite all my foolish mistakes, Sara, he's given me back my husband and son! I love your brother so much. In fact, I'm more in love with him than ever before. Then there's the opening of *Ten Long Steps* tonight, and Dr. Suffington's upcoming musical program. I can't believe Jess and I will be singing together again. It's as if all my dreams are beginning to come true. *That's* why I'm happy."

"And nowhere in all of this is a few missed monthlies? a touch of queasiness in the morning?"

"You are a badly behaved woman," Elena pronounced through blushing laughter. "And for your information, my monthly has only recently returned. For more than a year I did not have one."

"Oh." Sara's teasing manner was abruptly replaced by one of concern and loyalty. "I've heard of that happening in cases of poor health. Poor Elena, you were so sick when you first arrived. I'm sorry. I promise not to put any more pressure on you about giving Isobel a new cousin as soon as possible."

"Like you just did again?"

"I did, didn't I?" Sara's impish grin and giggle reappeared, and she pressed her cheek against Elena's for a long moment. "You might as well know that I've been praying for God to give you and Jesse another child."

Another child.

Joy and pain collided in Elena's heart as she was struck by a hail of thoughts. With new life there was always hope, but what was the result of hope too-long deferred? Would the secret, gaping places in her heart ever be satisfied by the good things God was giving her? Sometimes she told herself yes, they were, but at other times she recognized that her wounds were covered over by the thinnest of membranes.

Sara straightened, missing the effort it took for Elena to keep her composure. "We should get downstairs before Scott becomes impatient with us," she urged, her graceful fingers gathering the loose hairpins on the dressing table.

"I'm sure he'll forget any annoyance once he sees you," Elena replied, rising to her feet. "You look lovely tonight."

"Why, thank you. It's not just any day a girl gets to go to the opening of her brother's play."

"Or her husband's." Despite her sadness, Elena felt a surge of pleasure at Jesse's milestone accomplishment.

"Indeed. My brother will be so proud to have you on his arm." Sara returned the compliment with a warm smile before musing, "I wonder how Mama's evening with Dr. Suffington will pass? She was fussing with her dress more than usual."

"Who can say?" Elena remarked, glad for the change of topic. "But in a few hours' time, we'll all be back here comparing notes and congratulating your brother on the brilliant success of his play."

❧

As the first of the theater patrons began to appear, Jesse found himself pacing. He had promised himself he wasn't going to be one of those fretful playwrights who drove the cast and director to the point of madness with a score of last-minute thoughts and insecurities, and so far this evening he had managed to conduct himself with dignity. But as the hour to raise the curtain drew near, his nerves grew increasingly taut, as did his desire to make eleventh-hour checks on every part of the production.

So he paced about the theater instead, wishing Elena and the rest of his family would hurry and arrive. He had chosen seats near the back of the theater so he could best gauge the reaction of the audience. Though he reminded himself that whatever happened with this play was in God's hands, he couldn't help being strongly affected by the sense of responsibility he felt toward those who would fill the rows and view his work.

At long last, he caught sight of Scott entering the lobby, looking elegant in his dress clothing. And there were Sara, Elena, his mother, and Suffington. With relief, he went forward to greet them, comforted by the warmth of Elena's dark eyes and loving, intimate smile. Weight he didn't know he was carrying left him.

"We're so proud of you, Jesse," Sara praised, moisture welling in her eyes. Since giving birth to Isobel, she had been more sensitive than usual.

He accepted the congratulations and well-wishes of the group, cautioning them to hold their opinions until after the curtain fell. To that they redoubled their commendations.

"Let me show you to our seats," he said with a helpless

grin, holding up his hands to stop their words. The lobby was becoming filled with people, and he did not wish to draw undue attention. With Elena on his arm, he led them through the door to the chairs he had selected. His mother and Suffington entered the row first, then Scott and Sara, then Elena. Unable to sit, he remained standing.

His wife's eyes shone with compassion as she looked up at him. "Nervous?"

"As a cat."

"Oh, Jess," she said with gentle laughter, patting the empty chair on the end of the row. "Sit down and try to relax. Things are going to be fine."

"I haven't been backstage yet." Looking about, he saw that the theater was nearly half filled. A steady stream of people continued entering through the sets of doors that opened to the lobby.

"Then go tell the cast to break a leg," she said with understanding. "I'll be here waiting for you."

"I won't be long." It was a relief to be moving again, he thought, making his way around to the backstage door. In all his years of performing, he had never experienced such a case of nerves as he was having tonight. Taking a deep breath, he silently called on the Lord for peace.

It heartened him to see that the players were in good spirits. After wishing them well, he asked if they would bow their heads while he said a brief prayer. All complied, and he prayed for God to work through the small company to touch the hearts and minds of those present tonight with the message of unfailing love within the play. The leading man, still minus his lucky rabbit's foot, was already in character. When Jesse told him he'd prayed especially for him, the actor nodded gratefully.

He left the greenroom feeling more peaceful. The theater was nearly full now, and the lights had dimmed. He made his way up the side aisle and walked around his family's section of seating, approaching them from behind. At first he thought nothing of Elena's seat being empty, assuming she'd left to answer a call of nature.

There remained no sign of her, however, as the lights went down completely and the curtain arose. Had she become ill? The play began, but he could not concentrate on the performance. The stage lighting cast faint illumination on the faces of those in the audience, and he leaned toward his sister, indicating Elena's empty chair.

"She left without a word," Sara whispered. "But I'm sure she will return in a moment."

Finally, he could bear it no longer. He rose and went to the lobby, finding it deserted except for one doorman.

"You're Mr. Golden, the playwright, aren't you?" asked the attendant, probably a student from the university.

Jesse nodded automatically while he asked the young man if he'd seen a woman of Elena's description.

"Why, yes, sir," answered the adolescent, nodding toward the doors that opened to the street. "She left."

"She *left*?" Jesse was nonplused. "Did she say where she was going?"

"No, but the fellow with her seemed to be in a big hurry to be going."

A shock wave of numbness spread from Jesse's head to his toes.

"She didn't seem none too happy," volunteered the doorman, perhaps sensing Jesse's bewilderment. "The fellow tugged her right along, though."

"What . . . did . . . he . . . look . . . like?" Jesse managed to say through the gray fog that had become his thoughts.

"Tall man. Dark hair, swarthy complexion . . ."

Jesse listened to no more as his long legs carried him through the doors to the outside. With absolute certainty he knew Stephen Villard was the man who had come for his wife. Several carriages and teams were parked in front of the theater, but no traffic moved in the street. No persons were visible in the glow cast by the modern electric streetlights.

Where was Elena?

He thought he had succeeded in conquering his deepest fear, which was believing Elena would never truly be happy with him. Had her skills as an actress been so great that she had deceived him completely during these past weeks and months? Had she only been taking advantage of him, biding her time until she was well enough to leave? These thoughts and others like them revealed that his fears were not gone, but alive and well inside him.

No, he told himself fiercely. The doorman had said the tall man had pulled Elena along. She hadn't gone willingly.

But why hadn't she called for help? he asked himself, shaken by a reflexive shiver. She'd been sitting beside Sara and Scott. Surely Scott could have prevented his sister-in-law from being abducted in a public place.

But had an abduction even occurred? What if Elena had made plans to meet Villard here this evening and go away with him? Misery more awful than that he had experienced four years ago engulfed him.

When Sara and Scott appeared at his side a moment later, he found he was not able to speak.

Chapter 16

"I must say, you're looking considerably more healthy than the last time I saw you." In the moonlight, Stephen Villard's gaze was assessing, his voice sardonic. He turned his attention back to the team of horses he had whipped to a reckless speed. "Apparently you know how to land on your feet, after all."

"How can you do this to me?" Elena sobbed, shivering as the cold March air rushed toward her. In her effort to call his bluff, she had exited the theater without her wrap.

"How can I do this to you?" he mocked. "You were the one who all but ruined me."

"B-but I don't want anything to do with you anymore. Give me Beatrice and leave us alone."

"Give you Beatrice? I don't think so. Without the girl I have no bargaining power."

"You're a monster!" Fury and despair made her wish she could overpower him. Yet at the rate they were traveling, any rashness on her part could well lead to a crash.

"Careful with your voice," he cautioned, turning his head to reveal an impassive expression. He raised an eyebrow. "Now that we've resumed our partnership, we can't have you ruining your instrument."

"I will *never* sing for you again."

"Yes you will." He chuckled, the wind carrying the evil sound into the night.

A sick, helpless feeling clenched Elena's vitals. With it came guilt, shame . . . maternal protectiveness. "Where is Beatrice now?"

Villard gestured with his head. "Back there somewhere. I don't expect my sister will be driving this fast. She'll meet up with us later."

The events of the past half hour spun in Elena's mind. She'd been waiting for Jesse to return to his seat when someone tapped her shoulder and dropped a note into her lap. Sara was engaged in conversation with Scott and did not notice Elena unfold the small piece of paper.

Beatrice is outside, read the sheet.

In an instant, Elena was on her feet and moving toward the exit behind their section of seating. Waiting in the folds of the heavy maroon drapes hanging on the back wall was Stephen Villard. Even in the shadowed lighting, she'd recognized him immediately.

"What are you trying to do?" she'd whispered frantically as his hand clamped around her wrist.

"Don't you want to see the girl?" he'd asked in the superior way she remembered all too well.

"You're bluffing. She's not here." Without success, she'd tried to wrench free.

"I assure you, my dear, she is."

"I could scream, and you'd—"

"Go ahead." He'd cut her off, shrugging. "If you do, I'll leave, and you'll never lay eyes on your daughter again."

Desperation mounted inside her. Already it had been two years since she'd seen Beatrice. "How do I know you're telling me the truth?"

"You'll have to come and see. If she's not here, you can go back to your seat and watch your husband's dreary little play." Without waiting for an answer, Villard had begun pulling her along. The doorman in the lobby had looked up with mild curiosity as the dark-haired man had led her against the stream of last-minute patrons hastening toward their seats.

Just outside the door, on the steps, stood a hooded woman and a young girl whose covering had been thrown back to expose her hair and face.

Beatrice.

For a too-short moment Elena drank in the sight of her daughter's flaxen hair and wide brown eyes, until the woman had pulled the cowl over the girl's head and tugged her down the steps to a waiting carriage. The quizzical expression she had seen on Beatrice's face was like a knife in Elena's vitals, and she had started after her, heedless of Villard's previous threats.

"If you want to see her again, you'll come with me," Villard had pronounced, his grip like a band of steel as he forced her to a different carriage.

"Wait," she had cried, wondering where Beatrice had been taken, but it was too late. Somehow Elena had been shoved roughly into the seat, its hardness a tangible sign of reality in the midst of these unreal happenings. The horses had lurched forward.

Please, God, she prayed silently, the lights of Ann Arbor now far behind them. The way was lit sufficiently by moonlight, but the swiftness with which they traveled did not allow for error or mishap. This evening was worse than any of her nightmares come to life. Just as in her dreams, she was powerless against the forces opposing her. Burying her face in her hands, she sobbed wretchedly.

"Take this," came Villard's voice as something thumped against her side. A rough blanket. "And keep your mouth covered so the night air doesn't harm your voice."

With shaking hands, she draped the blanket across her chest and arms. In silent defiance, she breathed deeply of the chilly air. What did her voice matter when she was about to lose all that was dear to her? Jesse . . . Bobby . . . and yes, Beatrice too.

How can you lose Beatrice when you never really had her?

She'd found herself with child only a few months after

meeting Villard. The dark-haired vocal teacher, ten years her senior, had taken advantage of her desperate straits—and her innocence—in short order, all the while insisting that he had her best interests at heart.

I love you, Elena. I'll always take care of you, he'd professed with seeming sincerity as he assumed the role of her manager. *You're destined to become someone, and I'm the man to help you attain your dreams. I'll make you into a star like the American stage has never seen.*

Hungry for love as well as for food and shelter, she had fallen prey to Villard's attentions. Trusted in every one of his promises. It had become her deepest sorrow that she'd given up her child, merely because Stephen had deemed it best for her career. For them.

Only there had been no *them.*

It had taken her some time to see the truth, but she had eventually seen it. Stephen Villard had viewed her as nothing more than an opportunity to bring profit to himself. In the beginning, he had plied her with honeyed words and even sweeter promises.

She had been a few days shy of her seventeenth birthday when she'd given birth. Stephen had not proposed marriage, but insisted that she conceal her pregnancy so as not to interfere with her up-and-coming success. When it was no longer possible to disguise her condition, he sent her to his sister's house in Illinois until the end of her confinement.

Whereas Stephen could easily project an outgoing, even charming, social demeanor, his sister seemed incapable of producing so much as a smile. Sybil Reed lived on a tumble-down property on the outskirts of Chicago. Her husband had left one morning and never come back, leaving behind a dour-faced woman with four children to raise on her own, the youngest of which was less than a year.

Life at the Reed home was bleak. Things were kept in as much order as circumstances permitted, but Sybil moved through her days with an attitude of indifference. She cooked, cleaned, and wiped her children's noses with a blank, faraway expression. All attempts Elena made to befriend the woman failed, and finally she stopped trying. She quietly did the chores she was asked to do, and in her free time sang little songs and read to the cheerless brood of older children. The day she received a smile from little Gwen, then five, was the happiest memory Elena retained of the Reed home.

When Elena's labor came, the oldest boy was sent for the local midwife. Stephen was not there; he was in the city arranging auditions for her. After a few hours of the pains, water had begun trickling from her, and the labor had intensified. Sybil instructed Elena to make herself a pallet on the kitchen floor, then once the midwife arrived, had taken her children away for several hours.

The remainder of that day was one of Elena's worst memories.

Odel, the grandmotherly woman in charge of her care, was impatient to have her job finished and be on her way. Her disdain of Elena and Elena's unmarried state was plain. In all ways possible, Odel couldn't have been more unlike Granny Esmond, giving rise to fantasies in Elena's mind, between the contractions, of leaving the Reed home and making her way somehow to Olivia's grandmother. She had vowed she wouldn't cry out, but the pains were too strong, far beyond her imagining. She'd disgraced herself by screaming the last few hours before Beatrice's birth, to much eye rolling and derision by the heartless Odel.

The moment the baby had been laid in her arms, however, something inside Elena was forever different. The wrenching, burning pain she had experienced was rinsed away by a river of pure love for her daughter. She did not know what the future would hold, but Stephen had assured her he would handle everything, and she had taken him at his word.

Indeed, Stephen had come to his sister's later that day, elated that Elena had delivered. He'd been successful in getting her two big auditions and had scheduled them just a week hence. He'd expressed only mild interest in the blanket-wrapped bundle as he'd presented Elena with the arrangement to which he and his sister had previously come: Sybil would take the baby in exchange for a monthly stipend.

At first Elena was uncomprehending. Shaking his head, he'd repeated the deal he and his sister had struck, conveying his disappointment that she wasn't more grateful for all he'd done . . . for all he had sacrificed to give her every opportunity possible.

Once she understood he'd wanted her to give up the baby, she'd wept and pleaded, argued and threatened, and in the end had finally given in. With time and experience had come the knowledge that Stephen Villard was a master of manipulation, making the most of any situation at hand. But she had not known that then. Plying her with alternating doses of tenderness and reason, he'd convinced her that leaving Beatrice in his sister's care was the best thing for them all.

A week after giving birth, she had auditioned in Chicago and was signed by a well-known musical theater troupe. Because the company was traveling on to St. Paul the next day, she'd not had the opportunity to go back and hold her daughter one last time. Stephen had behaved in a particularly loving and attentive way during those next difficult weeks, assuring her that they would visit the baby whenever they were in the area.

Over and over she had told herself that Stephen knew best, that Beatrice was better off in a stable home with brothers and sisters. Elena's soreness faded and her milk dried up. She learned new songs and sang them on many stages around the country, gaining critical acclaim as her roles grew in prominence. In only a few years' time she became a leading player, captivating audiences with her powerful voice and stage presence. They did stop in at the Reed household from time to time, and her heart was wrenched each time she was forced to play the role of Uncle Stephen's female visitor before the daughter who had opened her womb.

Stephen kept reassuring her that with success came great happiness. While she did enjoy many of the perquisites that came with her achievements, she began to realize that accomplishment didn't bring the kind of satisfaction she'd been told it would. She also realized that Stephen's arrangement with his sister had nothing to do with love or anyone's well-being, and everything to do with himself.

The same went for his relationship with her. After Beatrice's birth he had not pressed her for physical attentions, and she had believed he was conducting himself as a gentleman during a time of confusing sadness mixed with excitement. Then one evening after a show she had seen him with a painted brunette on his arm. The next week, it was a lush blonde. Without words being spoken, she understood that their association had become one of business only. He was the manager; she was the talent.

Sometimes she wondered if he had looked into the future and known the hold he would have over her if they were bound together by a child. Stephen Villard was a man with no scruples and even less of a conscience. Whatever he had to do to keep her singing, he did. And in Beatrice, he had all the leverage he needed.

He had always held their daughter before her like a dangling carrot. *"Do this and I'll let you visit the girl. Don't get uppity with me, or I'll put her in an orphanage so far away that you'll never find her."* Later, when she became involved with Jesse and they had wed, Villard's threats became quietly sinister. *"Do you want me to expose your illegitimate child? Golden will leave you. Even if you don't care what happens to your stage name or reputation, there's not a man on earth who will raise a bastard child as his own."*

Villard slowed the horses to a brisk trot. Turning to her, he chuckled. "I have my lucky stars to thank for reading the article in the Chicago paper about your return to the stage. It even told me where I could find you tonight."

"What happened to your new girl?" she asked without rancor.

"Maggie didn't work out quite as I expected."

"Did you destroy her too?"

"Tsk, tsk, Elena. Is that all the better your opinion of me is?"

"You're an evil man," she said, turning to face him, her teeth chattering from the cold. "To you, people are just objects. You don't care about anything except making money. That's why you came after me, isn't it? You've got no one to turn a buck for you."

"A man must look after his interests."

"Give me Beatrice and let me be," she iterated. "I'll have nothing to do with you."

"You're in no position to be making demands. Not if you care about your daughter."

"I'll tell Jesse everything, and he'll—"

"And he'll what?" Derision dripped from his words. "Take in a whelp? A constant reminder of his wife's indiscretion? I don't think so."

"I wasn't his wife then. And he loves me."

"You might think he loves you, but you'll kill any affection if you tell him about the girl. You knew that before; that's why you never came clean with the truth. *That's* why you let him take your baby and leave. You might as well face it, Elena. I still own you, and I own the girl."

"You can't own *people!*" she cried, her words disappearing into the night. "Beatrice is your daughter. Doesn't that mean anything to you?"

"Her voice means something to me. It's quite good. In another year or two I can do something with that."

"I would give my life before I allow that to happen!"

"I was counting on that."

"Take me home," she said firmly, trying not to give in to the rising panic inside her.

"We should be to your husband's home by midnight or so, where you will gather your things—while I gather whatever I wish—and then you will be part of his life no more."

She had not thought it possible to be shocked by Villard's depravity, but open thievery atop his other sins was too much to comprehend. "You would steal from my husband?"

"He stole from me."

"No! You can't do this! I won't leave Jesse again! Or Bobby!"

"No matter what, it's always going to come down to one of your brats or the other."

"You can't make a mother choose between her children!"

"Oh yes I can. I did it once, and I'll do it again."

※

If not for Scott's strong arms and sense of reason, Jesse would have run down the steps of the theater and down the street to search for Elena.

"It's dark, and we have no idea where they've gone. The last train has run. We aren't going to find them tonight," his brother-in-law rationalized. "Place Elena into God's keeping and we'll begin searching in the morning. From what you've told me about this Villard character, he'll put Elena back on the stage the first chance he gets."

"Why did she go with him?" Jesse exploded, feeling a helpless sense of abandonment and anger.

Tears spilled from Sara's eyes, and she clutched her brother's arm. "Maybe he didn't give her a choice."

"She told me she loved me!"

"She does love you," insisted Sara, her words filled with emotion. "Just today she told me how happy she is and how much she cares for you. She was excited for your play, and she told me she looks forward to singing with you again as a dream come true. I don't understand this any more than you do, Jesse, but Elena's feelings for you are not in question."

"I can't go through this again." His chest caught, and he blinked hard against the stinging in his eyes. "My heart can't take it."

"You're not alone, Jesse, and neither is Elena," Scott reminded him, leading a brief, touching prayer for Elena's safety. Unable to accompany the pair back inside the theater for the remainder of the play, Jesse spent the next hour and a half alternately pacing the lobby and the front walk of the theater, desolation threatening to envelop him.

He happened to be crossing the lobby when a rumbling sound greeted his ears. Applause? He didn't have long to wonder as the attendant propped open each of the doors and the thunderous sound spilled from the theater to the entrance hall. Animated discussion accompanied the exiting patrons, and more than a few of the ladies dabbed at their eyes.

How he got through the next minutes he did not know. He accepted the congratulations of those who recognized him as the play's author, all the while straining for sight of his family. What was taking them so long? Finally he spied Scott's tall form and a flash of Dr. Suffington's silver hair. A few moments later, they had reached him, with an unfamiliar foursome in tow.

"Jesse, these are Elena's friends," Sara spoke wonderingly, shaking her head. She turned toward the pleasant-looking woman whose steady gray eyes seemed to look right into him. "What a small world we live in. I had no idea that Dr. Gray was Elena's friend Olivia. She delivered Isobel."

Bewildered, Jesse looked at the strangers standing behind his sister, two nicely dressed couples upon whom he had never laid eyes.

"Each of us is known as Dr. Gray," explained the blond-mustached gentleman holding Olivia's arm. "I'm Ethan and this is my wife, Olivia, who was Elena's friend from St. Louis."

"Jeremiah Landis," said the other man with curly dark hair, extending his hand after Jesse had shaken hands with the male Dr. Gray. Landis's theater dress did not disguise his strapping build, which only emphasized the delicate beauty of the brunette on his arm. "And this is my wife, Romy."

"We came to surprise Elena," said Romy, disappointment and concern lacing her clear diction. The schoolteacher, Jesse remembered.

"The director pointed us out to them." Sara supplied answers to the questions that buzzed in Jesse's head. "Some weeks back, Elena had sent letters for Romy's mother to forward.

It took some time for her to get them because Romy's father had passed on and her mother moved over the line into Illinois."

"Ethan and I live here in Ann Arbor." Olivia directed her words to Jesse, and as she spoke he found himself immediately liking the woman doctor's kind, direct manner. "I got my letter first, the same day I read the article about your play in the *Daily Argus*. I couldn't help but wonder about the Lord's timing in that."

"When Livvie contacted me," Romy chimed in, "I thought how wonderful it would be to attend the opening of your play and greet Elena in person. It's been hard to wait all these days, and I nearly wasn't able to stop myself from coming to your door. Jeremiah and I live in Detroit, not too far from you—Adelaide Street, is that correct?"

Jesse and Frances responded at the same time, which prompted Sara to realize she hadn't introduced her mother and Dr. Suffington to Elena's friends. With swift grace, she rectified her oversight.

Worry shone in Olivia's gray eyes as she glanced between Jesse and Scott. "Please tell us what's happened tonight. Elena *was* here, wasn't she?"

Scott nodded, and Jesse found he was glad to have someone else do the talking. "Just before the play started, the attendant saw a man take Elena from the theater."

"What man?" asked Ethan, his dark gaze assessing.

"Jesse suspects it was her former manager," Scott supplied. "A man by the name of Stephen Villard."

"Why would she go anywhere with him?" asked Romy. "In the letters she used to write, she didn't seem to like him very much."

Olivia appeared to be near tears. "Oh, Ethan, we should never have settled for that letter the Pinkerton agent brought us. I don't believe Elena wrote it at all!"

"What Pinkerton agent?" A mixture of frustration and confusion made Jesse's voice sharper than he intended. "What are you talking about? What's going on? What letter?"

"Before Livvie and I were married, I hired an investigator to search for Elena. That would have been in '81," Ethan clarified. "He later sent word that he had located her and included in his packet of information a letter that was supposedly from Elena, informing us that she had no desire to be contacted by her old friends."

Olivia's voice broke. "It was so difficult, but we believed ourselves to be respecting Elena's wishes by leaving her alone."

Romy squeezed Olivia's arm and spoke for her friend. "The agent learned that Elena had married you, and that she had changed her stage name from Elena Breen to Ellie Lundeen. She was in California then."

"That would have been after we separated." Jesse sighed, feeling weary beyond description. "I took our son and moved back to Detroit. She . . . came back only last autumn."

Romy nodded, appearing on the verge of tears as well. "We didn't know that until recently. She told us of her hardship and illness, and of the miracle of your finding her at that hospital." The dam burst, and Jeremiah came to his wife's rescue with his handkerchief. "Poor Elena," she managed amidst her sobs, "everything has been so hard for her. Her mother dying . . . that awful family of hers . . . and then she ran away . . ."

Olivia swept at the outer corners of her eyes with her fingers. "We always wanted to help her, but we never knew what to do. I wish you could have known Elena as a girl, Mr. Golden. She was as brilliant as the sun. When she smiled, you couldn't help but smile too. And when she sang . . ." Fresh tears escaped Olivia's eyes as she continued. "When Elena sang, it took my breath away. I understand now what incredible talent God gave her. Back then, I only knew that my friend was happy when she sang and that her gift made others happy."

Olivia's shoulders shook. "At the same time, there were so many shadows inside her. When it was time for her to go home, you could see them fall across her face. I ache to think of the sufferings she bore. Now that I look on those years as an adult, I can't help feel that we failed her."

"Nonsense," Jesse contradicted, his throat having grown thick at Olivia's distress. "Elena has never made anything but the kindest remarks about both of you. If anyone has failed her, it's been me. Even though I suspected Villard of being no good, I didn't protect her from him."

"I used to think Elena kept secrets," stated Romy, having recovered her composure, "but now I believe she wasn't trying to hide things so much as she was trying to put on a good front. She wanted to keep her pain from others."

"That's true," Olivia seized upon her friend's words with passion, "but she was stubborn too. God could have helped her, but she wouldn't let him. She had to do things her own way."

"Haven't we all been guilty of our own seasons of rebellion at one time or another?" Jeremiah gently pointed out.

Everyone fell silent. The few remaining theater patrons vacated the lobby while the doorman glanced up from his sweeping, his gaze curious.

Sara, always thinking, broke the silence. "We don't live far from here. Why don't you all come to our home, and we can continue our discussion there? If we put our heads together, maybe we can piece together more about Elena and try to figure out where she might be."

"Do you mind if I come along with you?" asked Dr. Suffington. "As soon as I get back to Detroit, I'll begin making some inquiries about this Villard fellow. Someone, somewhere has to have heard of him."

"We'd be glad to have you," replied Sara.

"I don't know what the constable could do tonight," asserted Ethan, "but we can go by and let him know what's happened. And I'll contact Pinkerton's in the morning. Are we certain Villard took her against her will?"

An enormous sigh left Jesse's lungs, deflated as he admitted, "No, I'm not certain."

"Of course she didn't go of her own free will," vouched Sara. "She would never leave the man she loves."

"She did once. If she even loves me at all," Jesse added

dully, a dreadful tangle of emotions rising inside him. Worry, dread, shame, insecurity. Had he been nothing more than a fool all these years? What if Elena's feelings for Stephen Villard were stronger than they were for him? Part of him wanted to trust that she hadn't been putting on an act during these past months, but at this moment it was easy to believe the worst.

Olivia reached in her bag, withdrew an envelope, and pressed it into Jesse's hand. "Read this. You'll see how much she loves you."

Jesse took the letter without looking at it, clutching it in his palm. "Why would she go with Villard then, when the man nearly killed her?" he burst out. "What kind of hold does he have over her?"

Ethan's words were thoughtful. "If he's as unscrupulous a fellow as I'm making him out to be, he may be blackmailing her in some way."

"We'll get to the bottom of the matter," averred Landis. "All of us together. There's no hold of the enemy so strong that the power of God can't break through."

Ethan nodded. "We start tonight, on our knees. Tomorrow the search begins."

Chapter 17

"Don't do this!" screamed Elena as Frances Golden's sideboard went over with an enormous crash. Pieces of glass and china sprayed throughout the dining room; a jagged shard of plate struck Elena's skirt and landed on her foot. Sick with fear, she hugged herself. "I beg you to stop this senseless ransacking!" she cried. "The Goldens are good people!"

His chest heaving from exertion, Stephen Villard looked up from his handiwork with a glittering gaze. Never before had Elena seen him physically out of control, but right now he acted as if he intended to turn this house into a pile of rubble.

"You've already taken everything of value," she entreated, fearing for Jesse's manuscripts. Fortunately, they were stored in the space behind the sitting room's built-in bookcase. Stephen had not noticed the clasp that allowed the outer bookshelf to arc out on hidden hinges. "What's the sense in ruining what little you've left them?"

Near the back door were pillowcases and boxes filled with silver utensils and serving pieces, cash, Frances Golden's jewelry, as well as various other items Villard thought might fetch a price. After breaking a window and letting himself in, he had marched through the house like he owned it, helping himself to whatever struck his fancy.

"Would you like me to set the place afire?" he said in a deadly cold voice, inclining his head toward one of the gaslight sconces.

"No!"

"Then keep your mouth shut." He picked up a dining-room chair and threw it against the wall, knocking down a picture. His voice grew louder, shaking with his anger. "Golden owes me. *You* owe me. You sank my career so low that I've got nothing left. And now, *miraculously*, your voice seems to have recovered—just like your health. How come you're singing again, Elena? I thought you never wanted to sing again."

If she hadn't been worried that her former manager might actually carry out his threat to start a blaze, she would have retorted that she never wanted to sing for *him* again. She would also have challenged him to tell her what he had done with all the money she had earned over the years. He'd always said he was investing it for her, but long before they'd parted company she had known it was gone. Spent. Stephen Villard's tastes had expanded in correlation to the income at his fingertips.

"Write a letter," he said abruptly, striding toward her with long steps. Grabbing her by the wrist, he dragged her to the desk in the sitting room. "To your husband. Tell him you're leaving, and this time it's for good. You don't love him. You want a divorce."

"Nooo!"

Her wrist wrenched painfully in his grip as she resisted sitting in the chair. He whirled toward her, his face inches from her own. "If you don't do exactly as I say, the house burns to the ground."

Numbness spread through her limbs as he forced her down hard into the chair. Spying a sheaf of papers toward the rear of the desk, Stephen grabbed several loose leaves. His gaze flicked over Jesse's neat script pages, which Elena recognized as a previous draft of *Ten Long Steps*. "I'll start the fire with this," he snarled as he threw the papers toward the fireplace, which was cold. Sheets scattered about the room, adding to the disorder he had already wrought.

Elena doubted there was a part of her that wasn't shaking. Thirteen years ago, how could she have failed to see the wickedness in Villard? Compared to her former manager, her father and brothers looked like decent men. She would have done far better to never have left Missouri at all. Perhaps this was her reward for living astray so many years. The time had come for her to reap the wages of her sin.

"Start writing, and be quick about it. The train to Chicago leaves in an hour. You'll get to see the girl then."

What were her options? At the realization that she was really going to see Beatrice again, emotion flooded through her. Yet at the same time, her soul cried out in anguish at the thought of leaving Jesse and Bobby behind. Again. Were Villard's words true? Did her life really come down to a choice: one child or the other?

Oh, God, please help me, she prayed silently. *Show me what to do.*

"Write!" Villard's neck veins stood out as he shouted.

Dear Jesse, she began, her penmanship looking like that of someone very old or very young.

Stephen Villard has come back into my life. I must go with him. Salty rivulets flowed down her cheeks. *Please forgive me, and do not try to find me.*

"You want a divorce," prodded Villard, standing over her shoulder. "Tell him you want a divorce."

"I don't want a divorce," she wept. "I love Jesse."

"You want a divorce, or he and the boy return to a pile of ashes."

"So you burn down the house." With feigned bravado, she set down the pen. Through her tears, she added, "If that's the worst you can do, then do it."

"You think that's the worst I'll do?" he asked in low, sinister tones. He shook her shoulder roughly. "Oh no, Elena. Setting fire to a house is nothing compared to what I will do. If I have to."

"W-what do you mean?"

"I want your voice." He took his hands from her shoulders but not before giving her one last shove. "You're going to make a comeback, and you're going to be even bigger than before. If you resist my plans, I'll be forced to make you cooperate."

"I can go to the authorities."

"While you're doing that, I'll put Beatrice on the streets to earn money."

The room seemed to tilt. "You wouldn't," she whispered with desolation, having no doubt he would do exactly as he said.

"I would."

Beaten, she picked up the pen.

"A divorce," he repeated.

I want a divorce, she wrote, while every fiber of her being cried out to the heavens that she did not.

≫

"What happened?"

Frances Golden's cry echoed around the ravaged entryway as Jesse hastened in behind her, Robert in tow. Beyond the foyer, she could see chairs tossed about the dining room and the oak sideboard lying on its face. Her hand closed around the house key in her palm, and she wondered why she'd bothered locking the door.

"Papa, what's happened to our house?" Robert parroted his grandmother's question, fear and uncertainty in his young voice. "Did a tornado come?"

"No, Son, it wasn't a tornado," Jesse replied, bending to lift Robert into his arms.

"Where's Mama? Is she here?" asked the boy, straining around Jesse's shoulders for a glimpse of his mother.

"I would guess not." Jesse's words were flat, unemotional.

Frances turned to look at her son, momentarily forgetting about the state of their home. He hadn't shaved this morning, and dark blond stubble covered his jaw. His gaze was burning and raw; the whites of his eyes were bloodshot from lack of sleep. Holding his son, he stared at the interior of the house as if he could not comprehend the sight before him.

Since Elena's disappearance last evening, Frances had been deeply concerned about Jesse. At first, her son had seemed determined to pursue Villard and retrieve Elena. Yet as the evening went on, despite the encouragement and assistance of Elena's girlhood friends and their husbands, he gave in to pessimism and despair.

Frances, Jesse, and Robert had taken the late-morning train back to Detroit. Jeremiah and Romy Landis had accompanied them on the forty-mile journey northeast from Ann Arbor. They parted company from the pair at the train station; Romy promised to come by later in the day, after they had been home to check on their three young sons, whom Jeremiah's parents had kept overnight. Dr. Suffington had taken the earlier train back, after spending the night in a hotel.

"Where is Mama?" Robert repeated the question he had asked a hundred times since awakening this morning. While the grown-ups had gone to the opening of Jesse's play, he and his cousins had been put to bed by Scott's younger sister, Marcia, who had come to Scott and Sara's home to watch the children. "Is my mama lost again?"

"Oh no. Your mother is not lost," Frances supplied with more enthusiasm than she felt. "She's gone away for a bit. I'm sure she'll be back before long."

The woebegone expression on her grandson's face made her anger flare more than did the wreckage of her home. Curiously, she recognized that her feelings were not directed toward her daughter-in-law but rather toward Elena's former manager, Stephen Villard.

In the conversation that had occurred around Sara's dining-room table last evening after the play, Frances had pieced together a far different picture of Elena than she had carried in her mind all these years. With great affection, Olivia and Romy had spoken, telling many tender and funny stories about their friend Elena Breen.

Why, Elena had been a dear young woman, Frances realized, if not spunky and a bit outspoken. An image of a young blonde girl came to mind: a frightened, unhappy woman-child who smiled and charmed and sang to disguise the ugliness of her reality. As if nothing were amiss, Elena had bravely carried on with her friends, soaking up the goodness they and their families offered before she'd had to return to her revolting circumstances.

Though Romy and Olivia recognized that Elena's home life had been unpleasant, neither of them seemed to know for certain what Frances knew: that Elena's father and brothers had tried to use Elena for their depraved desires. That Elena had viewed running away as the only option she had to preserve her virtue. But after leaving home, the lovely young girl with the black cherry eyes had fallen into the hands of yet another predator—Stephen Villard.

"You are . . . loose and a seducer of men. I'm sure you were no virgin when you took up with my son." With shame, Frances recalled the ugly words she had hurled toward Elena . . . and the way her daughter-in-law's chin had come up when she'd replied, *"As a matter of fact, I wasn't."*

How had she dared judge the wife of her son? As Frances lay in bed last night, consumed by remorse for all the ways she had failed to love Elena, she recalled how she herself had gone to the altar—and then to her marriage bed—every bit as sullied as she had accused Elena of being.

The truth was, they had both been victims. Their situations had been different, but each of them had suffered exploitation at the hands of evil men. Her heart rent, Frances had prayed last night for God's forgiveness as well as for another chance to treat Elena as a beloved daughter.

Jesse stepped into the sitting room and surveyed the mess while Robert stared about with wide, frightened eyes.

"We've been robbed," Jesse spoke, bending to upright a chair. "Look at the shelf. The clock is gone."

With a deep breath, Frances followed behind her son. Besides the clock, various knickknacks were missing and the jadeite bookends Gerald had bought for her an anniversary long ago. Pages of Jesse's work were strewn about the room, and the chair near the window had been gutted with the letter opener, its haft still sticking out of the cushion.

"Papa, I see your name," said Robert, pointing to a paper on the desk.

Unmindful of his steps, Jesse strode to the desk and unfolded the sheet upon which had been written *Jesse*. Seconds later, his face contorted with pain, and he dropped the note to the floor.

"Go to Nana." He passed Robert into Frances's arms without making eye contact, then disappeared from the room without so much as a backward glance.

Frances put Robert down and retrieved the paper. Its chaotic script and terse message got right to the point, but Frances couldn't believe Elena had suddenly been seized with the idea to divorce Jesse. After how far the two of them had come, there had to be more to this affair than what met the eye. She was silently thankful for the intersection of Elena's friends' lives with theirs, for she could see that after years of fighting for his marriage, Jesse was faltering. God had sent help just when it was needed the most.

This morning the men had made contact with the authorities. Additionally, Olivia's husband, Dr. Gray, had hired a Pinkerton investigator to search out Villard. Dr. Suffington was going to wire his contacts in nearby major cities. What was left for them now was the waiting . . . the most difficult job of all.

Frances sighed and gently laid her hand on Robert's shoulder. She had always thought of him as her grandson—and indeed he was—but for all the years of his life she had failed to recognize him as Elena's son. How might things have been different if, from the beginning, she had regarded Jesse's wife with dignity and respect? By her poor behavior and Christian example, she had been just one more adversity for Elena to contend with in a life already far too full of problems.

"Nana?" said Robert, his voice quavering. He looked up, his enormous chocolate eyes swimming in tears.

Frances knelt and swept him into her arms, aching to do the same for her grown-up little boy, whose brown eyes had brimmed with unshed moisture as he'd left the sitting room. Robert she could comfort, but there was little she could do for Jesse, a man who needed time and space to release his grief.

❦

Two developments resulted before the end of the day. The first came from a friend of Dr. Suffington's in Columbus, Ohio, a director of musical theater. He recalled crossing paths with Villard a few years ago, when he'd had urgent need for a soprano in the operetta he was producing. The principal had fallen ill just a few days before opening, and the understudy was not suitable. Unfortunately, the director was able to provide no more information about Villard than that he had behaved in an ugly and ungentlemanly manner when they'd rejected Elena as a possible candidate. Even at that time, her voice and health were in decline.

The second lead was more promising. It had come from the Pinkerton agent, who had promptly gone to work on his task, spending a productive afternoon making calls and ferreting out useful information. Villard had grown up in the Chicago area, he had learned, barely eking out a living giving piano and vocal lessons. His mother had been an actress and singer who died just as Villard and his sister were entering their adult years. His father was unknown.

Elena was the first talent Villard had represented, and he'd experienced astonishing success by catapulting her to fame as quickly as he had. No doubt his shrewd achievement had a great deal to do with the influence of his childhood environment and the occupation of his mother.

Jesse had listened impassively to these items of news Jeremiah Landis carried. The broad-shouldered businessman and his wife had arrived at sundown, aghast to see what destruction had been wrought to the Golden home. Refusing to take no for an answer, Landis had rolled up his sleeves and put his muscle into restoring the house to order. Romy donned an apron and began working beside Frances. The former teacher and mother of three quickly drew out Robert, even managing to make him laugh with stories about her own sons.

There was still much left to do, but with Jeremiah's and Romy's help, a great deal more was accomplished for the day than Jesse had expected. Getting Robert's room restored to normal had been Jesse's first undertaking. That completed, the women were now putting the youngster to bed, making a fuss over him to compensate for his mother's absence.

Without Landis's help, Jesse knew he would not have been able to upright the oak sideboard. The dishes were a total loss, but the large cabinet itself had not sustained mortal damage. With some sanding and oiling, it would hold a new generation of china and glassware every bit as proudly as it had the last.

"That's a solid piece of furniture," remarked Landis, wiping sweat from his brow.

Jesse nodded, feeling winded from his efforts. Adding to his exertion was the fact that he hadn't eaten all day. He couldn't. He hadn't slept last night either.

The blue-eyed visitor arched one brow. "I suppose we can be thankful that Villard didn't spend any more time here than he did." Bending, he gingerly began picking up the larger pieces of china that had been beneath the sideboard. "With the information Gray's Pinkerton agent has already gotten, I bet we'll find him in another day or two."

"And then what?" Jesse's heart felt like a hollow, echoing chamber.

"And then you get your wife back."

Jesse kicked at a curved piece of bowl. "What if she doesn't want to come back?"

"I read the note, but I hold with your mother's opinion. I believe Elena was forced to write what she did."

"What my mother doesn't know is that Stephen Villard was once Elena's lover."

Landis was quiet for a long moment. Finally he looked at Jesse. "That doesn't necessarily change the fact that she went with him unwillingly. Last night your sister told us of Elena's conversion. In the waters of her baptism, she was made a new creation."

"Maybe her past is too much to overcome."

"Too much?" the big man questioned gently. "More than what can be overcome by God's grace?"

Landis's point did not escape Jesse; he just could not bring himself to hope in anything at the moment.

"You're tired," empathized the other man. "And right now this must all seem like too much to bear. I know it's tempting to give in to despair . . . I know because I've done so."

"You don't know what I'm feeling. You've never been in my position."

"No, I haven't," Landis agreed. "But my first wife left me."

"Your first wife?" Jesse looked at his new friend.

"She walked off a pier—" pain shadowed the blue gaze that held steady—"taking her life and that of our unborn child." Landis didn't seem to expect Jesse to reply as he continued. "I won't trouble you with the rest of the story right now. However, I say this much because I want you to know I understand some of what you're experiencing—and because I want to urge you, by faith, to submit your intellect and will to the Lord. Don't live by what your feelings are telling you. Consider me the voice of experience."

Jesse nodded once.

Landis's hand was warm on his shoulder. "Among the many attributes of the Almighty is truth. Our God of truth will reveal truth. Because you and Elena are his children, the facts will come out. Pray for his will to be done and that he will supply the grace necessary to deal with what comes as a result."

Just then the women came down the stairs. Despite the interior deadness he felt, something stirred in Jesse's chest when his mother eyed the sideboard with a hopeful expression.

"Well, there's one thing saved," she said with pluck, tucking a strand of hair behind her ear. She turned to Jesse, looking full into his face, a tired smile playing about her lips. "God willing, Son, it's the first of many more good things to come."

࿐

Sybil Reed's house had changed little over the years. The kitchen curtains were new since the last time Elena had been here, and each of the children, of course, had shot up several inches, but not much else was different. Whatever Stephen's money had done, it had not changed his sister's circumstances nor the dwelling's atmosphere of broken-down sadness.

It didn't seem possible that more than a decade had passed since she'd come to this place and given birth, but Beatrice would soon celebrate her twelfth birthday. Sybil's youngest, Tad, was almost thirteen. Sally was fifteen, Gwen seventeen, and the oldest, Curtis, had left home. Feeling like a prisoner, Elena paced the house and bare dirt grounds, trying to catch sight of Beatrice whenever she could.

Her daughter appeared healthy, but like the Reed children, she was somber and kept her eyes averted, especially when she was around adults. This morning Gwen had plaited Beatrice's pale, silky hair, the darker under-strands providing pleasing color gradation within the braid. Beatrice was just beginning her ascent toward maturity, and her face was a lovely, heartrending combination of girl and young woman.

Elena's heart felt as if it had been torn into pieces. She missed Jesse and Bobby dreadfully, but at the same time she ached to be near her daughter. If only she could hold Beatrice against her, stroke those glossy strands of hair . . . tell her how much she loved her. Thanks to Stephen, the girl believed herself to be the youngest daughter of Sybil Reed.

The wind, surprisingly balmy this afternoon, blew into Elena's face, carrying the promising scents of spring. As she rounded the corner of the house, she wondered why she couldn't just take Beatrice and leave. Despite Stephen's vile threats, he hadn't chained either of them down. Tonight, when the household was asleep, she could awaken her daughter and they could walk toward the city. Surely a police station would give them asylum.

But how can you prove Beatrice is your child? No doubt Odel recorded the birth as Sybil's. You possess no papers or certificates, and in the time it would take to procure the truth, Stephen would take Beatrice and be gone. You would never see her again.

At the thought of Villard exploiting their daughter to earn his living, Elena was filled with a feverish panic. She had to protect Beatrice. She couldn't count on Jesse helping her, particularly since her daughter was half Villard's . . . leaving her with only one option to safeguard Beatrice: doing what Stephen said.

You cowered before Villard's intimidation once before. Surely you haven't forgotten! You gave up Jesse and Bobby, and if not for the grace of God, might never have seen them again. What happens if your voice fails for a second time? or your health? Villard will throw you out like yesterday's rubbish, and you can bet Jesse won't be waiting with open arms to welcome you back. You'll be left with no one and nothing.

No one and nothing.

She closed her eyes, the sun warm upon her face. *Dear God,* she began helplessly, not knowing what to pray. Was it too much to ask for both of her children? The past months of living in the Golden household had filled her with a sense of peace and order at a home well run. Though Frances Golden had not been warm toward her, she had learned much from Jesse's mother about caring for a family. Despite the tensions that had existed between her and Jesse's mother, the snug home on Adelaide Street had been warm and welcoming compared to this loveless place.

For the past two days Stephen had spent much of his time

poring over newspapers representing as many major cities as he could find, which he had picked up in downtown Chicago. Already he was making bold new designs for her career, planning to reintroduce her with a splash of publicity far greater than that which Suffington had already been responsible for.

I don't want this, she cried out to God. *I don't want to be on the road, living in hotels and rented rooms. I want a home—with my husband and my children.*

She heard the back door squeak open and shut; then Villard called her name. She saw that he was dressed in a fine suit, his look reminiscent of the days when her popularity was at its height. In the sunlight, his dark hair was glistening black, slicked to his head with oil.

"Get dressed," he ordered in clipped tones. "Something nice."

"I don't—"

Holding up his hands, he cut her off at the same time he adjusted his cuffs. "Be quick about it. We're going into the city."

"I can't . . . I don't feel up to it." She stalled, not wanting to leave Beatrice. During the years of touring, months had elapsed between visits to Illinois. She needed more time to think of a way out of her situation. If she took Beatrice and made a run for it, did that mean she forfeited Jesse and Bobby? At the same time, she couldn't leave her daughter to a childhood fate worse, possibly, than her own had been.

What was the solution? Was there even one to be had?

Villard went on as if she hadn't spoken. "Warm up your voice. You'll probably be asked to sing. You'd better hope your lessons with the high-flying Dr. Suffington prove to be what the newspaper said."

Seeing no alternative but to accompany him, she took slow, unwilling steps toward the house.

Chapter 18

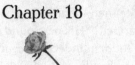

The pounding against the front door was urgent. Three days had passed since Elena's disappearance. Finally having collapsed into a deep sleep, Jesse could hardly drag himself out of bed and down the stairs. After fumbling with the lock, he opened the door to a clean-shaven and bright-eyed Jeremiah Landis.

"Get your things—we're getting close!"

"Is it Elena?" called Frances from the staircase. "Is she back?"

"Not yet, Mrs. Golden," replied Landis, stepping inside and closing the door. "But we'll have her home soon. Dr. Gray telephoned with the news from the agent late last evening. I let you get as much sleep as I could, Golden, but now it's time to get up and go to Chicago."

Though it was still dark, Jesse rubbed his eyes, trying to force himself into a wakeful state. The cool outside air against his face had done nothing to dispel his drowsiness.

"I'll put on some coffee while you get ready." Already his mother had moved into the dining room and had lit the lamps. "Will your wife be accompanying you, Mr. Landis?"

The dark-haired man shook his head. "She's staying behind, and so is Olivia. Your son and I will meet up with Gray. The agent located Villard's sister."

"Elena's there?" Slowly, a feeling of vitality was beginning to replace Jesse's sluggishness. Landis's words the other evening had seeped into his despair, renewing his hope for a continuing bright future with Elena. With God's help, he would fight for his wife and his marriage against any and all obstacles—even Stephen Villard.

Especially Stephen Villard.

"She's unharmed?" His newfound optimism was dealt a blow at Landis's sudden, indecisive expression.

"I believe so," Landis replied after a longer than necessary pause.

"What is it?" Seemingly of their own accord, Jesse's hands were on the lapels of Landis's coat. "So help me, Landis, you're going to be sorry if you don't spit out whatever you're holding back."

Jeremiah's large hands closed around Jesse's wrists, forcing them down. "There's no need for violence. I'll tell you what I know." Jeremiah's clear eyes, level with his own, communicated empathy.

"You'd better," protested Jesse, pulling free of the other man's grip. Breathing hard, he fought against the riotous emotions inside him.

Jeremiah inclined his head toward Frances. "Do you want to include her?"

Following Landis's gaze, Jesse looked over his shoulder and saw his mother standing at the entrance to the dining room, her hands at her throat. The light from the wall sconces spilled around her form, giving her a youthful, vulnerable appearance.

Jesse nodded and extended his arm toward her. Since Elena's disappearance at the theater, his mother had been a source of remarkable strength and caring, expressing support not only for him and Robert but, astonishingly, also for Elena. For their marriage. After years of contention where Elena was concerned, her transformation was startling.

"What is it, Mr. Landis?" Fear was evident in Frances's voice as she took her place beside her son.

"Elena and Villard had been at his sister's home, but neither was there when the investigator arrived," reported Landis.

"Where did they go?" Jesse's voice was sharp.

"I'll get to that. But there's something else you need to know. I was going to tell you on the train, but I may as well have out with it now."

Jesse swallowed against a cold lump of fear forming in his throat. Had Landis been untruthful? Had something happened to Elena? If Villard had harmed her in any way . . .

"Many of your household items were found at the home of Sybil Reed, Villard's sister," Landis went on. "That leaves no doubt that Villard was behind the robbery and wreckage here at your home."

Jesse nodded impatiently, not caring about the things. He needed to hear about Elena.

"Bear with me a bit longer," requested Landis, taking a moment to look first at Jesse, then at Frances.

"Go ahead, Mr. Landis." Frances's voice was calm and clear. She placed her arm around Jesse's waist, as if her limited physical strength could brace him for what was to come.

Jeremiah nodded. "Villard's sister was out when the agent arrived at the home. The oldest daughter admitted that Villard had been there with Elena and that her uncle had brought the stolen items with him. She seemed relieved to confess everything, and the agent has been in contact with the U. S. Marshal's office." Landis paused, then sighed. "It seems what he did here the other night is only the tip of the iceberg."

"Where is Elena?" ground out Jesse, losing his patience.

"She is presumed to be with Villard. The pair are temporarily unaccounted for."

A foul word skidded free of Jesse's tongue as the fear and frustration inside him mounted.

"What else has this Villard done?" asked Frances.

Showing no reaction to Jesse's language, Landis replied, "He's been holding Elena hostage for the past twelve years."

Hostage? Jesse wanted to hoot in disbelief. When he'd met Elena, she'd been the most emancipated woman he'd ever met. To describe her as free-spirited, independent, and self-assured painted a placid picture of the vivacious performer with whom he had fallen in love. That Villard had some kind of sway with Elena was obvious, but that the man held her captive was ludicrous.

Perhaps she had gone with him of her own accord after all. Maybe her request for a divorce wasn't as far-fetched as people seemed to think. Doubts and suspicions cluttered his mind again, giving rise to a host of skeptical replies.

" . . . their daughter," Landis was saying, to which Jesse's mother gasped and began weeping.

"What are you saying?" Through the commotion of his thoughts, he had grasped nothing but the two final words of Landis's previous statement.

"They have a daughter together." Landis was patient in his reply.

"Who has a daughter together?" bellowed Jesse, hating how dim-witted he sounded not half as much as he bristled against the sympathetic expression on the other man's face.

"Elena has a daughter, Jesse," answered his mother through her tears, "with Stephen Villard."

A roaring began in his head. Elena had admitted to an affair with Villard. But giving birth to a baby as a result was another matter entirely. Where had this child been all these years? Were there more children? What other secrets had his wife brought into their marriage? How many more revelations would come to light?

"Oh my," his mother wept, "that explains so much."

Landis nodded. "From what Villard's niece told the Pinkerton agent, Villard uses the girl to get Elena to do his bidding. She'll be twelve this summer. The pregnancy and birth were kept secret, and Villard's sister took the baby to raise as her own."

"Oh, the poor dear."

"Which poor dear is that, Mother?" asked Jesse.

"Why, Elena, of course."

"What about the child she left?" Jesse's words were scalding. While he reeled with shock at the news Landis carried, he was angrier than he could ever recall being. "For years you were outraged at the fact Elena left Robert. Now we learn she's done it before. I ask you, what kind of mother leaves her children?"

"Jesse, calm down," his mother beseeched, glancing nervously over her shoulder toward the stairs. "Robert could wake up and hear you."

"He may as well learn the truth. It's over. He has no mother. Elena can have her divorce." Taking a step back, he wanted to leave . . . to be anywhere else but here.

"Before you give up, why don't you learn the truth?" His mother stood up to him, unflinching, pinning him with her gaze. "The whole truth, Jesse. Go with Mr. Landis and find out why Elena made the choices she did. You might be surprised at what you find out."

"I can't believe you're defending her!" he shouted, pouring out his wrath. "Whose side are you on? You've always hated her."

"You're right. I have behaved terribly for years." His mother's chin went up in that tenacious manner he knew so well. "But I was wrong. Your wife is a courageous woman who has tried on her own to make the best of adversities we can only imagine." She laid her hand on his arm. "She loves you, and I know you love her. With God's help, you can overcome anything. However, each of you must cooperate with the grace he provides. Go to her. Help her."

Hurt flashed in his mother's eyes as he roughly pulled his arm away, but he was too upset to care. How much more did he have to take as far as Elena was concerned? He had honored their marriage vows in every way humanly possible, yet with his faithfulness and heartache came no reward—only the discovery of more deception.

"I checked the paper," interjected Landis in a subdued tone, "and the Michigan Central runs a seven o'clock out of the Third

Street station. Dr. Gray will meet us there. We'll be in Chicago by six tonight, and God willing, by that time the Pinkerton agent and a deputy marshal will have located Villard. The niece thought he was taking Elena to the city for some auditions." Reaching inside the lapel of his coat, he pulled out his watch. Squinting, he checked the time. "It's going on five-thirty. Get your things together, and let's be on our way."

For a long moment, Jesse nearly replied that he wasn't going anywhere. His rage at being deceived . . . *betrayed* . . . burned within him. How many nights had he held Elena with loving patience, expressing his heartfelt willingness to share the painful burdens he knew she carried? He would have accepted anything—even news of an eleven-year-old child born out of wedlock—if she had only trusted him enough to confide in him.

But she hadn't.

Thinking back on his marriage, he realized that Elena had never trusted him. It wasn't that she had never given *of* herself but that she had never completely given *herself*. Who was this woman he called wife? Who was Elena? With bitterness, he realized he was as far from knowing the answer to that question as he had ever been. Why had he been so foolish to believe that a future with the complex creature called Elena could hold anything but sorrow and misery?

"Jesse?" came his mother's voice, interrupting the downward, turbulent spiral of his thoughts.

"I'll be back in a few minutes." His words were curt as he turned and went up the stairs. He would go with Landis . . . if only to tell Elena good-bye to her face.

He'd had enough.

❧

The independent melodies of violin, flute, and cello mingled discordantly as the first musicians arrived and began warming up in the large concert hall of the New Olympic Theater. As Elena waited with Stephen Villard to see the manager, she wondered if

Villard recalled that this was the establishment at which she was scheduled to sing with Suffington's chorale just two weeks hence.

Villard's extravagant new plans did not allow time for her to be cast in a musical theater production. He believed she could fill an auditorium by singing a recital of popular music and was pressing one entertainment-hall manager after another to engage her for such an event.

After observing her former manager for the past few days, Elena believed he had become mentally unbalanced, evidenced by his desperation to generate money any way he could. In the beginning of her career, Villard had been cunning and calculating, smoothly playing his well-thought-out strategies. Now, even more so than in the days of her decline, his manner betrayed his need.

Since yesterday afternoon they had visited several theaters. During the meetings he was able to solicit, urgent words tumbled off his tongue while his eyes burned with intensity. Elena had no doubt that the managers they visited had perceived and reacted to this, giving him answers he hadn't wanted to hear . . . answers that further inflamed him to achieve his purposes.

The graceful notes of a piano and unconnected rhythm of deep, booming drums added to the cacophony from the orchestra. Years ago her pulse would have quickened to the air of anticipation and preparation for the upcoming performance; now she hated the memories the sounds evoked. If only she could change the past. She wanted to shout, run, kick something, yet she did nothing more than stand docilely at Stephen Villard's side, waiting for the manager to see them.

You're getting nothing more than what you deserve, Elena, a cruel voice inside her derided. *Why don't you look at the truth? You traded away Beatrice in order to stand on stages across the country and sing to strangers. For a short time you thought Jesse could free you from that, but with him you created another child and abandoned both of them as well. You've made your bed; now it's time to—*

"Villard?" spoke a short, portly man past his middle years.

His small, assessing eyes flicked over them. "I'll see you," he said in clipped tones, taking charge of the brief, one-sided conversation. "Later. Here are two tickets. Find me after the show." With that, he hurried away.

Stephen's face flushed a dull red as he silently gripped the tickets. He hadn't been snubbed, but neither had they been received warmly. Would this be enough to make him reconsider his plans? Elena wondered. She wanted nothing more than to leave, to go home, but where was her home? Did she even have one?

There was no reason to return to St. Louis. And if not for Beatrice, Sybil Reed's dwelling was not anywhere she desired to be. Nor could she go back to the house on Adelaide Street in Detroit, not if she cared about protecting her daughter from Stephen. Having come full circle, she was back to having no place . . . no one.

You are mine . . . your home is in me, came the faintest whisper of a thought.

"Move along. You heard the man," muttered Villard, taking her elbow in a manner that was far from gentle. He propelled her toward the door. "We may as well find something to eat while we cool our heels."

If I'm yours, God, then where are you? Where do I belong? Where is the help you promise to your followers? she wanted to cry out as they walked down the sidewalk, Villard's fingers digging cruelly into the tender flesh of her upper arm. As she thought of the long evening ahead, wings of despair unfurled themselves over her distress. She was trapped. There was no escape for her. Tears clouded her vision as she thought of Jesse and Bobby . . . of innocent, young Beatrice.

Everything was on her shoulders—again. To guard against the pain of it all, she steeled herself by trying not to feel, though at the same time she couldn't help but wonder what good her conversion to Christianity had done. Did God listen to random prayers and answer only the ones he fancied? Was his love as real as Sister Evangeline, Reverend Fordham, and the Bible proclaimed, or was her experience of his presence only wishful thinking on her part? or emotionalism? In none of the events of the past days had she seen any indication of God's love for her. She felt abandoned and alone. She might as well handle things on her own again for all the good her newfound faith had done her.

"In here," ordered Villard, inclining his head toward an inexpensive eatery.

She winced as he yanked her toward the door, knowing she would have bruises atop bruises from his tight hold and callous handling. How she would get through the remainder of this day, she could not imagine.

Once again, the thought of the rest of her life was too much to bear.

❧

The commanding features of United States Deputy Marshal Jacob Beyer held no good news. When the lawman had introduced himself at the train station, Jesse had taken one look at his face and known that Elena and Villard were still at large.

The all-day trip to Chicago with Landis and Gray had seemed like an eternity. The pair had allowed Jesse his self-imposed solitude and had not set about trying to cheerfully convince him things were going to be just fine. Given the untimely demise of the first Mrs. Landis and her unborn child, perhaps Landis, especially, knew better than to build false hopes.

"Do you want a bite to eat?" asked Beyer, directing them toward the railroad diner. "I'll fill you in on what's happened today. Agent Houle will be meeting us here directly."

"A bowl of soup might hit the spot," remarked Landis, putting his hand on Jesse's back and gently setting him into motion following the marshal. "We didn't have much on the train."

Once they were seated in the busy café and four steaming cups of coffee had been set before them, Beyer took a long pull of the brew and wiped his mustache before addressing the men. From beneath dark brows he studied Landis, Gray, then Jesse.

"Once we got ahold of Sybil Reed—that's Villard's sister—she didn't bother trying to hide anything," Beyer began. "She tried to make a run for it this morning, but we had her in custody before noon. Her story matched up with what the oldest girl told us yesterday. Seems your wife—before she was your wife—Mr. Golden, spent some weeks at the Reed home before giving birth to a daughter named Beatrice. That would have been back in '74. The record book says the delivery was attributed to Mrs. Reed, but Reed confessed that the child was born of Elena—and that the baby was sired by her brother, Stephen Villard. In exchange for a monthly allowance, Reed agreed to bring up the girl as her own."

Jesse's spirits felt as if they could go no lower. In what kind of tawdriness had Elena been involved? How could she have, in essence, sold off her firstborn child in order to pursue her career? It made him sick to think that the bright, beautiful singer over whom he'd lost his head and heart had, in reality, been an absentee mother.

"There didn't seem to be any evidence of mistreatment amongst the children in the home," Beyer added, "but I must say they are a sad-looking lot."

"What do you mean by that?" asked Gray.

"Whatever Villard had been paying his sister, it wasn't enough. The place is about falling down around their ears, and the youngsters were dressed right shabby. To hear his sister tell it, Villard had blown through his money and has been sponging off her for some time."

"Where's the girl now?" Jesse found himself asking, though he told himself he didn't care.

"She was placed with a good woman in town until we can reunite her with her mother."

"What about the rest of the children?" Landis interjected, concern written on his rugged features.

"They're being looked after by their sister, who seems to be a far sight more capable than the mother. However, if Sybil Reed is willing to testify against her brother, she may get off lightly.

Apparently your wife is not the only soul Villard has exploited for his own gain."

Gray was following the marshal's words closely. "How close are you to finding him?"

"I've worked with Houle before. He's a resourceful agent." Beyer raised his brows and nodded. "If Villard's in the city, it's just a matter of knocking on enough doors until we find the right one." Looking up toward the door, he added, "Here's Houle now."

A tall, rangy man removed his hat and walked toward their table. Jesse felt the few sips of coffee he'd drunk churning like lye in his stomach. When he'd wed Elena, he never dreamed their marriage would end up the way it had, its contents torn apart, visited by lawmen, investigators, strangers, and surprise children.

"Evening, Beyer," greeted the agent as he drew near, taking the empty chair.

The physician extended his hand and came partway to his feet. "Houle? I'm Ethan Gray. Thanks for getting on the case as quickly as you did and for getting the U.S. Marshals' office involved."

Once the round of introductions was concluded, Houle pulled a piece of paper from his breast pocket and unfolded it upon the table. A list of theaters and addresses was written in neat script down its face in ink; in pencil, many additional notes had been made in the margins. Without preamble, he began. "An hour ago I visited the New Olympic Theater, where Villard visited this afternoon with Elena."

"How did she appear?" asked Gray. "Had she been harmed in any way?"

"The manager reported her to be in good health, though he commented that she was as forlorn-looking as he's ever seen a body look. She didn't say a word."

"What happened?" queried Landis.

Houle shook his head. "Nothing. Apparently Villard's gotten himself a bad reputation with some of the fellows in town over the past few years. He and Elena were turned away."

"Where do we go from here?" asked Gray, studying the list. "There's still a lot of ground to cover."

Beyer set down his coffee cup. "As soon as we eat, we'll split up; that way we'll get twice as much done." Turning his head, he spoke to Jesse. "We're going to find your wife, Golden. God willing, sooner than later."

Jesse nodded, unwillingly touched by the news that Elena had appeared despondent in Villard's company. Even so, he told himself, none of this would have happened if she'd only opened her heart to him. That was what hurt worst of all—the knowledge that she hadn't trusted him.

"I have a feeling Villard's still in town," Houle said thoughtfully, cradling his chin between his thumb and the side of his forefinger. "He's desperate to get work for Elena, but he won't settle for just anything. He's aiming for a certain standard."

Gray's brow was furrowed. "What if he doesn't find what he's looking for? He'll leave the city."

"That's possible," Houle conceded, "which is why we've got our task cut out for us tonight."

"I can only imagine what Elena's going through." Landis shook his head sorrowfully. "Romy's been beside herself with worry."

Gray shook his head with concern. "Olivia hasn't stopped crying since the night of the play. She feels responsible, in part, for Elena's plight."

"Why should she?" Agitation forced Jesse's voice to a higher than normal pitch. "Elena has always made her own choices."

A look passed between Gray and Landis while Beyer drained the remainder of his coffee. Houle sighed and folded his hands over the paper. "I can understand how upset you must be by all this, Mr. Golden, but from what I've learned so far, I'd have to say most of your wife's decisions have been made under duress. Villard is heartless. He has no qualms whatsoever about using his daughter to manipulate Elena."

"You all seem to forget that I knew Villard too." Jesse's

words spilled from him in a river of frustration. "I never liked him, but I have trouble understanding how he could wield so much power over a sharp, intelligent woman like Elena."

"Two words, Golden," Beyer put in. *"Shame* and *intimidation.* That combination could make a coward out of the most courageous man."

"But Elena told me she found a new life in Christ!" Jesse countered. "She said she had given the reins of her life to God to lead her where he would."

"Perhaps he is doing exactly that," ventured Landis. "And us, as well, to be a part of his plans for her new life."

Jesse let out his breath, unable to reply. What kind of men were Landis and Gray? he asked himself hotly. Out of love for their wives, they had set aside everything to help him, a stranger, find his wife. That was simply not reasonable.

"If you need some time to sort things through, Elena and Beatrice are welcome to stay with us in Ann Arbor," offered Gray.

"Or with us and the boys," volunteered Landis. "We'd be delighted to have them."

"You don't even know Elena," Jesse said weakly. "Why would you—"

"We know she needs help," interrupted Landis, "and that's enough."

Jesse's mind seemed to go blank while Ethan Gray indicated agreement, giving Jesse's shoulder a brief squeeze. At the same time, U. S. Marshal Beyer took the paper from beneath Houle's hands and began scrutinizing the notes, asking questions and making comments.

Do you trust me, Jesse?

The voices of the men became indistinct as he perceived a voice in his mind asking a question which, at this moment, he did not want to answer. What *was* trust? Did it mean confidence? faith? hope? Right now, he felt none of those things. They were lost, along with his marriage. Along with his wife.

"Here. Take this." Leaning toward him, Landis pressed a

handkerchief into Jesse's left hand. In a low voice, Romy's husband added, "Hold fast, Golden. God knows."

Jesse stared at the white linen for a long moment, uncomprehending, then awkwardly wiped his face.

He hadn't known he was crying.

Chapter 19

The audience in the New Olympic Theater responded with delight to Gilbert and Sullivan's comic opera, *The Mikado*. With feelings of unreality, Elena wondered how so many people around her could be laughing when she was sure she would never smile again. In the plush chair beside her, Stephen Villard sat with his face cast in stone.

Almost as if she were someone else, she watched the production move toward its conclusion, doing her best to ignore the strained, impatient man sitting to her right. On a good day, Villard didn't like waiting for anyone or anything, and Elena could only imagine to what level her former manager's tension had risen through the course of this evening.

What was Jesse doing tonight? she wondered, tears springing to her eyes yet again. Did Bobby miss her? Though she tried not to think about them, she grieved for her dear husband and son, failing to be consoled by the fact that by forsaking them, she had saved her daughter from misuse.

Now Elena was certain that Beatrice would always believe Sybil Reed was her mother. As deeply as Elena desired to nurture her daughter, Villard had always opposed such a thing, as well as revealing to Beatrice her true parentage. He would remain Uncle Stephen to Sybil's children . . . and to his own child.

Finally, with grand flourish, the opera came to an end. Wild applause broke out in the auditorium, intensifying as the actors took their bows. Elena studied the beaming actress who had played Yum-Yum, wondering if she had borne any children . . . and where they might be.

This time when Villard grabbed her arm, she couldn't stop the soft cry that escaped her. The curtain had fallen, and the houselights were up. People were laughing and talking and leaving their seats, waiting to merge into the crowded aisles. Shooting her a malevolent look, Stephen towed her into the aisle. With no courtesy for the departing stream of patrons, he pulled her in the opposite direction, toward the front of the theater, the process seeming to take forever.

"Where's the manager?" he demanded of a hapless stagehand when they drew near. "I want to see him immediately."

The young man shrugged and scurried behind the curtain, causing Villard to spit out a bitter curse. As he fumed aloud about incompetent help and being forced to sit through the entire opera, he drew curious looks from the musicians who were packing up instruments and gathering sheets of music.

"Stephen," Elena whispered as loudly as she dared, trying to draw back. She was rewarded with a sneer and a wrenching pull on her arm. This time her cry of pain was not disguised.

"You are going to sing here," he raged, "and I don't care what I have to do to make that happen."

"You, there!" The conductor emerged from the pit, his deep, German-accented voice carrying clearly. "Unhand the woman."

The foul phrase with which Villard responded caused the well-dressed orchestral leader to stiffen, his shoulders going back with outrage. "Get the police!" His full voice caused gasps from the remaining patrons toward the rear of the theater. Advancing on them with a rapid gait, he again ordered Villard to let go.

Elena heard her former manager's sharp intake of air as he reached into his vest and withdrew a knife and held the glittering blade aloft. There came an immediate babble of voices, a shrill scream, then quiet.

"Why don't you give me the knife and the woman, and you can be on your way?" Though the conductor was of an intrepid nature, he'd stopped in his tracks when he saw the weapon.

Villard made no reply. Pain shot through Elena's shoulder as he dragged her up the stairs to the side of the stage. Fleetingly, she thought she should feel fear, but oddly, things were happening so quickly it was all she could do to keep her feet. In an ungainly manner, her aggressor pushed past the heavy outer drop. Though the backstage activity appeared to have come to a halt before they appeared, at the sight of an armed man, people panicked and ran.

"What are you doing?" From the nearest wing came the theater manager's forceful, rapid voice.

Villard swung his head around. "I'm through waiting. I want Elena booked here."

"The schedule's full."

"Make room. Get rid of someone. I don't care what you have to do."

At that moment, Elena tried breaking free, but Villard's reflexes were too quick. He recaptured her before she had gone even one step, pulling her full against him, the arm wielding the knife tight against her throat. "Let me go!" she sobbed helplessly. "Just let me go!"

"United States Deputy Marshal Beyer. Hold it right there, Villard," came an unfamiliar, commanding voice at the same time the curtain began to rise. A second later, three pairs of legs came into view, then as the curtain ascended, a trio of men whom Elena had never before seen.

"Hand over the knife and it'll go better for you," ordered the man who had identified himself as Beyer, pulling a revolver from the holster beneath his coat. He took a step forward. "Release Mrs. Golden."

Villard's arm tightened around her neck, cutting off Elena's voice and nearly her ability to draw air. Taking a step backward, he warned, "I'll kill her before I let anyone come near."

"It doesn't have to be this way," countered Beyer, holding his hands before him in a conciliatory fashion, the gun seeming to lay casually in the palm of his right hand.

"Put the gun on the floor," snarled Villard, retreating a few more steps. "Out of your reach."

Elena felt light-headed as she watched the lawman kneel and place his weapon on the floor, then kick it toward center stage. When Villard had first begun shouting, his voice was loud in her ear. Now he sounded as if he were speaking from a distance. Imaginary quicksand enveloped her legs as he dragged her back a half dozen more steps, pulling her behind a tall set. "Don't move, any of you!" Villard commanded.

Her captor's breath came in great gasps as he paused, then continued in his cumbersome flight toward freedom, farther into the shadows. "Come on!" he said through gritted teeth into Elena's ear. In his haste to flee from the law, his arm pressed deep into the soft flesh beneath her chin, cutting off her air completely.

I am going to die, Elena thought as she fell slowly into a black abyss. At the edge of her consciousness she was aware of a jarring clatter, a cutoff cry, and a searing pain in her side.

Then there was nothing.

※

A young, solemn-faced police officer caught up with Jesse and Agent Houle as they exited a playhouse not far from the New Olympic. Deputy Beyer had given the officer a list of possible places to find them, and the officer was fortunate enough to locate them on his second stop. Stephen Villard had been apprehended, he reported, and Mrs. Golden found. If he was in possession of more information than that, he did not divulge it.

Jesse felt numb inside as he and Agent Houle entered the lobby of the New Olympic Theater. People milled about, talking in loud, excited voices. Leading with his nightstick, the officer threaded his way through the throng until they reached the doors to the auditorium, where he greeted a fellow uniformed officer standing guard. Once their business was stated and identification established, the other policeman let them enter.

As the doors swung shut behind them, the noise decreased to a low rumble. The theater lights were up, as was the main curtain, which lent an eerie atmosphere to the empty, echoing seating area. A few small groups of people stood on the stage talking quietly. Jesse caught sight of Jeremiah Landis's strapping build at the same time the dark-haired man noticed him.

"Golden!" Landis hailed. "She's back here."

The moment of truth is coming. When he'd learned Elena had been found, that single thought had roared through Jesse's head like the winds before a storm. In only a few moments he would have to make a decision. Would he leave her here? say good-bye? take her back? Maybe it wasn't up to him. She might have already chosen Villard and the girl, Beatrice.

The thought of Elena's having a child by her former manager continued to produce a raw shaft of pain through his chest. Climbing the stairs to the stage, he realized afresh how he had been played for a fool for all these years.

"Thank God you're here," exclaimed Landis, "and thank God Gray was here!"

"What happened?" asked Houle, eyes narrowed, his gaze scanning the stage.

Jesse was glad for the investigator's forthright question. He couldn't seem to think clearly; things were moving too rapidly.

Landis's words seemed to tumble one over another. "The theater manager said Villard was here with Elena tonight, wanting to engage her for a show. He lost control—Villard, not the manager—and pulled out a knife. We arrived right when this was happening, and Beyer drew his gun. Villard tried to escape, taking Elena as hostage."

"Where are they now?" Houle's next question caused Landis to point toward the rear of the stage.

"Villard's back there. Gray is with Elena in the greenroom. She was cut."

"I'll kill him!" Jesse's low utterance reverberated around the theater as he started in the direction Landis had pointed, intending to seek vengeance from the man whose hold upon Elena had intruded upon her life . . . his life . . . their marriage.

"Hold on, Golden," said Landis, taking his arm. "He's already dead, and it's not a pleasant sight."

The news stopped Jesse in his tracks.

"Villard's arm was around Elena's neck as he was dragging her away. Gray thinks she blacked out, and her deadweight caused him to lose balance. Beyer went running when we heard the crash. Apparently, Shakespeare plays tomorrow night, and one of the swords from the prop table somehow impaled him. Elena sustained a flesh wound. Come back here; I'll take you to her."

"I . . . I . . ." Jesse faltered, feeling suddenly overwhelmed. *Lord, I don't know if I can do this. I don't know what to do.*

Misunderstanding his hesitation, Landis added, "I'm not withholding anything from you. I saw Elena myself, and she had already regained consciousness. Providing no infection sets in, Gray says she'll be fine in a matter of days."

With leaden limbs, Jesse allowed himself to be led to the room where performers relaxed before or after appearances. Ethan Gray looked up when they entered, giving Jesse a brief nod. He was kneeling before a sofa upon which lay Elena. Her eyes were closed, and her skin was pale. A blanket covered her body.

"I didn't have my bag," the physician said regretfully, "but I've been able to make do surprisingly well with what they had on hand here."

"Jesse?" Elena's eyelids fluttered. Before Dr. Gray could stop her, she tried to sit up, which caused the blanket to fall and her features to be contorted by pain.

"Now, now. There'll be none of that," Gray admonished

gently as he helped her lie back down. "I just got your bleeding stopped."

Jesse was shocked by the sight of the enormous red-stained bandage around Elena's middle before the physician positioned the blanket back over his patient.

"Jesse?" she repeated weakly, insistent, her eyes closed tightly against her discomfort. Her breaths came shallow and rapid, and she pressed her hand against her side.

"He's right here," supplied Landis, giving him a nudge.

Just then the door opened, admitting Olivia and Romy. Frances brought up the rear, weariness and worry etched into her fair features. With loud cries, Elena's friends rushed tearfully to her side, a bittersweet reunion taking place while Jesse looked on.

"Son?" Touching his arm, Frances looked up into his face.

Tears he didn't know he was suppressing stung his eyes and thickened his throat.

His mother wrapped her arms around him, laying her head against his chest. He felt her silent weeping against his body, and in reply, his arms came up to enfold her. Despite their difficulties over the past several months, a flood of love for her washed away all the friction, the tension, the strain.

"How did you get here?" he was finally able to ask.

With the back of her hand, Frances wiped her eyes. "We couldn't stand being left behind, so we took the ten o'clock train this morning. Olivia telephoned Romy with the plans, and Romy came to pick me up. Robert's staying next door with Mrs. Cox. When we got here, we went to the police. They said something about a stabbing but wouldn't tell us any more than that. They brought us to this theater." A fresh swell of tears made her eyes swim. "How is Elena?"

"She was injured. Dr. Gray thinks she'll recover."

"Is she well enough to travel back home?"

He shook his head. "I . . . I don't know if I can . . ."

"If you can what, Son?" His mother's voice was gentle, but woven into her words was the filament of resoluteness he had always known to be a part of her. "Elena is your lawful-wedded wife. You married her, for better or worse, till death do you part. Those were your words to me once. Do you remember?"

But, he wanted to protest, *she wasn't honest with me. She didn't tell me everything. She had a child by another man!*

"Step outside with me for a few moments," Frances said, her eyes communicating something strange and urgent. "I want to tell you something."

After glancing toward the couch, Jesse nodded and followed his mother through the door. Elena was so tightly surrounded by her friends and their husbands that he wasn't even able to see her.

When the door latched quietly closed, Frances took his arm and led him down the hall, away from the stage people who lingered about.

"Son, I want to tell you what can happen to a woman when she's afraid . . . when she carries a burden of shame."

"Please stop making excuses for my wife." Jesse's words flared hot, and he took a step backward, feeling betrayed by her disloyalty. "I'm not an unreasonable man, Mother, and Ellie has never had reason to be afraid of me. At the very least, she could have told me about the girl! I would have helped her." A sob clutched at his chest. "I would have."

"Did you think your father an unreasonable man?"

"Father? What's he got to do with this?"

"Just answer me, Son. How do you think your father would have reacted if I'd told him I had given birth to a child before we were wed?"

Jesse answered reflexively, recalling Father's kind, generous nature. "He would have loved you anyway. But that's not the point! Elena didn't—"

"There is a point to be made here, and I want you to listen well." Taking a deep breath, his mother squared her shoulders. "Jesse, I *did* give birth to a child before I wed your father. A little girl." A ragged sigh escaped her. "I named her Laura."

"You . . . *what?*" Was there no end to the secrets kept by the women in his life?

"Your father never knew." With a look of sorrow, Frances shook her head, tears spilling down her cheeks. "As much as I wanted to tell him, I could never bring myself to do so. When I was a girl, my uncle . . . violated me for years. You're the first person I've ever told."

Anguish sluiced through him at the thought of his dear mother being abused in such a way, and he reached out to her, pulling her trembling form close. How had she managed, all these years, to shoulder this terrible burden alone?

"Oh, Mama. I'm so sorry." His voice was hoarse as he tried to absorb her grief, standing in for his father in a way that would honor the memory of Gerald Golden. For several minutes he held her as she wept against him, his soul tearing in two.

Beyer had spoken true words this evening when he'd said that shame and intimidation could make a coward out of the most courageous man. Shame and intimidation. Indeed, they had held his own mother captive for most of her life—his *mother*, who was one of the two strongest, most capable and unshakable women he knew.

Elena was the other.

If his mother had suffered such a horror in silence, wouldn't it follow that other women—even valiant, spirited women such as his wife—would feel bound to make the same choices? The anger and feelings of betrayal gripping him loosened as he began—finally—to comprehend the reasons for Elena's inability to trust him with the truth of her past. During all the years of his parents' marriage, his mother had not been able to entrust his father with her secret either.

"Where is your daughter?" he finally asked as gently as he could. As if an electric light had been switched on, he exclaimed, "My sister!"

"Laura was born too soon." His mother's reply was muffled against his chest. "She lived only a short while." Looking up into his face, she added, "But Elena's daughter is alive and well, and she's going to need a good home."

Just then, Beyer called, "Mr. Golden?"

Turning, with Frances still in his arms, Jesse beheld a young, tender girl—the very image of Elena—standing beside the imposing lawman. Her blonde hair gleamed in the dimly lit hallway, and a too-big cloak covered her form.

"I hope you don't mind my taking the liberty of retrieving Miss Beatrice tonight," said Beyer, sounding surprisingly tentative, "but I thought it best that she be reunited with her mother. Young lady, this gentleman is your mother's husband, Mr. Jesse Golden."

Though a faint, timid smile curved the girl's lips, her words carried clearly. "I'm pleased to make your acquaintance, sir." Her dark eyes appeared enormous in her winsome face.

At the surprisingly familiar sound of her voice, Jesse's insides turned to melted butter. This child was Elena's daughter, and his heart responded accordingly, without hesitation. Releasing his mother, he walked forward. "And I'm very pleased to make yours, Beatrice."

"Though she is not aware of her father's identity, apparently she's known for some time that Elena is her mother. Sybil Reed's oldest daughter told her." Over the glossy fair head, Beyer's gaze met Jesse's, his brows rising with significance.

Jesse understood at once the sensitive nature of his meaning. He would not reveal Stephen Villard as the girl's father. That was for Elena to make known at a time and place of her determining.

Going down on one knee, Jesse looked into Beatrice's face. "You've had quite a day, haven't you?"

She nodded solemnly, studying his features.

"How would you like to make your home with your mother and me in Detroit? We have a nice little house in the city, and behind me is my mother, the best cook in all of Michigan." As he continued, Jesse was aware of Frances's noisy, joyful weeping. "Elena and I have a son, Robert, who will soon be six, and a nephew and two nieces in Ann Arbor, who will be delighted to meet you. Pearl is only a little younger than you."

"Are you my father?" Her questioning gaze met his directly.

He shook his head, at the same time arriving at a decision. "But I would very much like to be. Shall we go in and see what your mother thinks about that idea?"

"Yes, sir," she replied, taking the hand he offered.

As he stood, he noticed Beyer surreptitiously wipe his eyes just before he honked loudly into his handkerchief. On silent feet, Agent Houle had come up behind them, and he nodded toward Jesse with approval.

The occupants of the greenroom looked up when he opened the door, stepping away from the sofa in one movement as if a curtain were drawing back, allowing him access to Elena.

"Jesse," she sighed, her wan face lighting at the sight of them. "And Beatrice, too? How did she get here?"

"The marshal brought her," Jesse replied, leading Beatrice to the sofa.

"Oh." Elena extended her arm, her face crumpling.

Without hesitation, Beatrice's slender fingers slipped through Elena's. "I know you're my mother," she said, "and I'm glad. Even though I wasn't supposed to talk to you, I always liked it when you came to visit. I'll miss Gwen . . . but I want to go live with you." She glanced up at Jesse before continuing. "Mr. Golden wonders what you think about the idea of him being my father."

From Beatrice's face, Elena's gaze went to Jesse's, her countenance expressing astonishment, regret, and wonder. Closing her eyes for a long moment, she opened them again as if she couldn't believe the sight before her.

"Beatrice . . . my precious daughter," she began in a voice filled with emotion, "I think that a girl couldn't ask for a better father than Jesse Golden . . . nor could a woman ask for a better husband. I love you both so much. I love all of you. I don't understand . . . after what I've put everyone through, I just don't know how you can . . ."

"How soon can we go home?" posed Beatrice with an artless, charming smile, bringing a welcome wave of laughter to the room.

"Is tomorrow morning soon enough, young lady?" asked Dr. Gray with a tender expression.

"Yes, sir," Beatrice replied as Olivia and Romy closed around her, introducing themselves and telling stories of how, at her age, they had known her mother.

In the hubbub of noise and joy, Jesse knelt beside the sofa and brought his face close to Elena's. "I love you," he whispered, kissing her softly, pressing his forehead against hers.

"I'm sorry—," she began.

"Shh. You don't have to be sorry." He cut her off with another kiss. "I want you to know, Ellie, that I understand why you had trouble placing your trust in me."

Elena's dark eyes shimmered and her voice shook slightly. "It wasn't because of you, Jesse, it was because I—"

"Because you were wounded. You were hurt very, very deeply by people you should have been able to trust. Not surprisingly, even your trust in God was shaken." With two fingers he smoothed a tendril of hair that lay along her temple. "Poor Ellie . . . you have been through so much."

"Yes, I have." The quaver in Elena's voice disappeared as she continued speaking, her soft words ringing with passion. "But don't feel sorry for me, Jess. Look where I am! God not only spared my life, but he gave me back my husband and both my children. I don't understand why terrible things happen to some people and not others, but the Lord showed faithfulness to me even when I was unfaithful to him. Please don't feel sorry for me . . . if it took all that to bring me to this place, I'd go through it again. You're worth it, Beatrice and Bobby are worth it, and knowing Christ is *more* than worth it. After all, what did I suffer that was greater than his torture and death at Calvary?" Her last words were choked, and she swallowed hard.

"Ellie . . . ," he began, trailing off, his emotions having never experienced such a day as this. Her hair was soft against his fingertips, her breath gentle against his face. Finally, he began again, praying that he could express the way he felt. "I hope you can believe that your welfare means more to me than even my own. I love you, my wife, and I intend to make that evident every day of our life together. I pray that I will be a man worthy of your trust." He looked deeply into her eyes, seeing his face reflected in the radiance of her love.

"Jesse?" she asked.

"Yes?"

"You *are* my hero," she whispered, her face alive with bliss.

He kissed her again.

Epilogue

"Oh, Elena, aren't you nervous?" asked Romy, wringing her hands as she watched Sara affix a lovely seed-pearl hat to Elena's upswept mass of blonde curls. "I could never sing before such a crowd. I just peeked out there, and people are already taking their seats. It's supposed to be a full house!"

Filled with quiet excitement, Elena smiled at her lovely, pint-sized friend, with whom she had been reunited just two weeks earlier. She had been shocked to learn of the terrible accident Romy had suffered, and doubly astonished to discover that the former schoolteacher wore an artificial limb beneath her skirts. Romy walked as normally as any two-legged person and had borne three hale sons in as many years.

"Romy, you're forgetting that Elena has acted and sung before audiences for years," gray-eyed Olivia supplied, nodding with satisfaction as Sara gave the ornamental hat a final adjustment and stepped back to survey her handiwork. The sounds of various orchestral instruments resonated through the thin walls of the small dressing room as the musicians ran through their warm-ups.

Elena stood and took a deep breath, smoothing the folds of her dress. Though she still felt a few twinges from the injury at the side of her waist, the wound was nearly healed. Lifting her eyebrows, she smiled. "If it makes you feel better, I do confess to feeling a few butterflies each time the curtain goes up."

Romy's laughter was still as lilting as it had been when they were girls. "A *few* butterflies? Elena, you and Jesse are the featured attraction for the opening of Dr. Suffington's big tour tonight! If I were in your shoes, giant African moths would be flapping around in *my* stomach. You know, the ones as big as dinner plates!"

"I'd have to perform surgery," Olivia quipped, not able to suppress her answering mirth.

"Livvie, I still can't believe you're a medical doctor," Elena marveled, almost in awe of her friend's having realized such an accomplishment. As the three of them had renewed their friendships over the past weeks, she'd learned that Olivia had completed her medical education at the University of Michigan in Ann Arbor.

"And she's wonderful at what she does!" Sara turned her beaming countenance toward the physician. "Dr. Gray, you made having little Isobel so much easier."

"Why, thank you." Ever humble, Olivia accepted the compliment as something precious, receiving Sara's words with as much grace as she would a gift.

Elena recalled the afternoon tea she'd had with Olivia and Romy at the Landis's lovely home last week. As she and Romy had spoken of their children, Olivia had grown increasingly quiet. Finally, in tears, Livvie had confessed that she and Ethan had thus far been unable to conceive, and that she feared she might never become a mother. They had all wept, sharing Olivia's sadness. At the same time, Elena had experienced profound humility at the fact that the Lord had restored both her children, as well as her husband, to her. She did not deserve such goodness, but she accepted God's grace with all the gratefulness her heart could offer.

After a short time, Livvie had dabbed her eyes and said, "There's so little we really control in life. At the time of his choosing, the Lord brings us into existence, and at his appointed time we leave this world. We know he offers heaven—all eternity!—as a glorious reward for those who remain in his friendship. But rather than spending our energies seeking to know, love, and serve him while we live out these short years on earth, why do we so often go our own way? try to control our own lives apart from his wisdom? or worse yet, rebel against him?"

"I don't know," Romy had spoken slowly, "but after my accident, I could not accept that I had lost a limb. For months

I set my face against God. I confess that I behaved frightfully. But at the same time, I was miserable without him."

"Well, I've behaved frightfully my whole life!" Elena had declared, which somehow transformed their sorrow into peals of tension-relieving laughter, made all the funnier by Elena having to press her hands against her injured side.

A knock sounded at the dressing-room door, pulling Elena back from her thoughts.

"Five minutes!" an unfamiliar male voice called, causing Romy's hands to flutter, Olivia to smile with encouragement, and Sara to squeal quietly.

"Oh, Elena!" her sister-in-law marveled, eyes shining. "I can't believe I finally get to see you and Jesse onstage together. Mama has been telling *everyone* she knows—and even complete strangers—about the show. Between her pride in you and Jesse, not to mention in Dr. Suffington, she's probably responsible for half the ticket sales! And speaking of Dr. Suffington, I wouldn't be surprised if he up and proposed to Mama one of these days. Since we came back to Detroit, those two have been spending almost every day together."

Warmth rose inside Elena's chest at the thought of her mother-in-law. Not only had Frances Golden begun embracing her with heart and arms wide open, but Jesse's mother had also accepted Beatrice into their home, lavishing love, care, and attention upon the girl. It was beyond what Elena could ever have conceived in her wildest imaginings. If Dr. Suffington were to propose, she would be the first to congratulate her mother-in-law.

"There's been a lot of interest in Jesse as a playwright too," Olivia commented. "His reviews in Ann Arbor were wonderful."

"God's generosity can't be outdone," Elena said softly, having heard Reverend Fordham say the very same thing in church last Sunday.

"He longs for us to trust him completely," Romy added, "and as we do, we will become more and more open to what *he* has in mind for us . . . which is infinitely better than what we can do for ourselves."

"All ready in there, Mrs. Golden?" Jesse's voice greeted them at the same time he rapped against the door. Sara turned the knob and admitted her brother. Elena's breath caught at the sight of her husband in a black, double-breasted evening jacket.

"Shall we?" he invited, extending his arm toward his wife.

Elena's heart swelled as she passed Olivia, Romy, and Sara on her way toward Jesse, whose eyes shone with love for her. Each of these persons was more dear to her than she could put into words. She felt her eyes mist over as she took the strong, steady arm of the man whose name she had just learned meant "God exists" in Hebrew.

I believe you exist, Father, and I thank you for my life, she prayed silently as they began walking toward the stage. *From this moment until you call me to yourself, thy will be done.*

Thy will be done.

Acknowledgments

Once again I have been blessed with many generous and helpful behind-the-scenes persons as I put together *Elena's Song*, thereby finishing the Abounding Love series. I am profoundly grateful to everyone who has assisted me in this endeavor . . . especially my loyal, tolerant, and long-suffering family and friends.

I want to mention my gratitude for the information given to me by Dr. Cumella regarding starvation, and for the nurses of Remuda Ranch, who patiently answered my additional questions. Becki Hughs also was a valuable resource for helping me define Elena's character and providing me with additional insight into undernourishment.

And what would I do without Elaine Challacombe, curator of the University of Minnesota's Wangensteen Historical Library? With each of my projects, she has bravely gone into the noncirculating stacks and emerged with historical treasures that enhance the stories I write. Thank you, Elaine!

From Detroit, Ruth McMahon assisted me with historical data, helpful connections, and copies of period newspapers. Without her help, I would have had a much more difficult time retrieving that information. I am indebted to Ms. McMahon for her prompt and always cheerful replies to my queries.

I would be remiss to fail mentioning my appreciation for the Centennial branch of the Anoka County Library. The librarians there have always gone out of their way to search for the obscure books of which I perennially seem to be in search, followed by their kindly generating (dozens of) interlibrary loan requests. Mary, Cheryl, Chad . . . thank you.

Elena's Song contained many different elements, one of the most predominant being vocal music. Though I studied piano for many years, I was smart enough to know how much I *did not know* about music . . . so I turned to the experts. To Denise Meuer and Lora Loahr: Thank you, thank you, thank you! I truly could not have written this book without your help. Yet another person who blessed this venture with her time, talent, and expertise was Doreen Hutchings, professor of vocal music at Northwestern College, Roseville, Minnesota. I would also like to acknowledge—albeit posthumously—Manuel Garcia, an indisputable master of nineteenth-century vocal music. His writings were a godsend for this manuscript.

To my ever-faithful proofreaders, Mary Epps and Paula McGrew: thank you yet again. To Bernie and Sharon of The Habit coffeehouse: thank you for the delicious scones and mochas, and for letting me occupy one of your tables for hours on end. Even though I gained ten pounds while writing this book, and my children took to calling your wonderful establishment "Mommy's Bad Habit," my laptop computer and I plan to visit you frequently when I begin my next manuscript. (This time, hold the whipped cream.)

I want to acknowledge the important role of my church family in my writing ministry, and thank them for their prayer support. Fr. James Larson—thank you for your spiritual guidance and faithful prayers for me. For my close friends who pray me through every chapter, please know how much this means to me. I love you dearly.

To Claudia Cross, my agent, must go a heartfelt thank you as well. Your steadfast support of my writing gives me the courage to keep pressing onward.

May God continue to bless HeartQuest books and the wonderful team of persons behind the scenes. Kathy, Becky, Anne, and Travis: you have been an incredible source of encouragement to me. I want you to know that my gratitude for being a part of Tyndale's HeartQuest line is as fresh as it was the day I began.

A Note from the Author

Dear Reader,

Whew! Now we both finally know what happened to Elena! While I envisioned her story being starker and grittier than the first two books of the Abounding Love series, I had not conceived of all the events that eventually made their way into *Elena's Song* until I sat down and began writing.

The Scripture focus I selected for this book was Isaiah 1:5-6: "Must you rebel forever? Your head is injured, and your heart is sick. You are sick from head to foot—covered with bruises, welts, and infected wounds—without any ointments or bandages."

Doesn't this describe Elena to a tee? She was so badly hurt, so deeply wounded, yet she persisted in running away from the One who had the power to bind her injuries and heal her of every affliction. It took a special person—Jesse—to reflect Christ's love and care for her, and to demonstrate unconditional love in tangible ways. Eventually, Elena responded to this love . . . which was really the love of Christ being ministered through her husband.

We all know people who live lives of outright mutiny toward God. They are easy to dismiss and dislike, and perhaps even easier to despise. It is a rare individual who will take the time to peer past the disagreeable veneer of this type of person to see what God sees: a soul lovingly created in the image of the Creator. What we must bear in mind is that no one, not even the most unlovable person, is beyond hope or salvation. If this sounds like a challenge . . . it is! It does not come from me, however; it comes from God himself.

It is with a mixture of feelings that I conclude the Abounding Love series. I will be sad to leave Elena, Romy, and Olivia behind, yet at the same time I look ahead to the future and all the stories just waiting to be written.

May you know great peace with the Lord, and may your seasons of rebellion be fewer and farther between as you grow in faith, knowledge, love, and obedience.

Your sister in Christ,
Peggy Stoks

About the Author

Peggy Stoks lives in Minnesota with her husband and three children. A former registered nurse, she now enjoys working from home. Writing fiction gives her the opportunity to blend her faith in God, her love of history, and her knowledge of health, illness, and injury.

In addition to being an avid reader, Peggy enjoys a wide variety of outdoor activities. She is especially thankful for the woods near her home, where she takes many long walks. Peggy is an active member of her church family and has recently begun sharing her piano talent with its outstanding music ministry.

In the future, Peggy hopes to continue crafting rich and satisfying novels that weave together timeless truths about people, faith, and God. It is her most fervent hope that her work gives readers food for thought and inspires them to grow in holiness.

Peggy's previous books include *Olivia's Touch* and *Romy's Walk*. She has also written several novellas, which appear in the HeartQuest anthologies *Prairie Christmas*, *A Victorian Christmas Cottage*, *A Victorian Christmas Quilt*, and *A Victorian Christmas Tea*.

Peggy welcomes letters written to her at P.O. Box 333, Circle Pines, MN 55014.

Visit www.HeartQuest.com for lots of info on
HeartQuest books and authors and more!

www.HeartQuest.com

CURRENT HEARTQUEST RELEASES

- *Magnolia,* Ginny Aiken
- *Lark,* Ginny Aiken
- *Camellia,* Ginny Aiken

- *Letters of the Heart,* Lisa Tawn Bergren, Maureen Pratt, and Lyn Cote

- *Sweet Delights,* Terri Blackstock, Elizabeth White, and Ranee McCollum

- *Awakening Mercy,* Angela Benson
- *Abiding Hope,* Angela Benson

- *Faith,* Lori Copeland
- *Hope,* Lori Copeland
- *June,* Lori Copeland
- *Glory,* Lori Copeland

- *Winter's Secret,* Lyn Cote

- *Freedom's Promise,* Dianna Crawford
- *Freedom's Hope,* Dianna Crawford
- *Freedom's Belle,* Dianna Crawford

- *English Ivy,* Catherine Palmer
- *Finders Keepers,* Catherine Palmer
- *Hide and Seek,* Catherine Palmer
- *Prairie Rose,* Catherine Palmer
- *Prairie Fire,* Catherine Palmer
- *Prairie Storm,* Catherine Palmer

- *Prairie Christmas,* Catherine Palmer, Elizabeth White, and Peggy Stoks
- *A Kiss of Adventure,* Catherine Palmer (original title: *The Treasure of Timbuktu*)
- *A Whisper of Danger,* Catherine Palmer (original title: *The Treasure of Zanzibar*)
- *A Touch of Betrayal,* Catherine Palmer
- *A Victorian Christmas Keepsake,* Catherine Palmer, Kristin Billerbeck, and Ginny Aiken
- *A Victorian Christmas Cottage,* Catherine Palmer, Debra White Smith, Jeri Odell, and Peggy Stoks
- *A Victorian Christmas Quilt,* Catherine Palmer, Peggy Stoks, Debra White Smith, and Ginny Aiken
- *A Victorian Christmas Tea,* Catherine Palmer, Dianna Crawford, Peggy Stoks, and Katherine Chute

- *Olivia's Touch,* Peggy Stoks
- *Romy's Walk,* Peggy Stoks
- *Elena's Song,* Peggy Stoks

COMING SOON (SUMMER 2002)

HEARTQUEST BOOKS BY PEGGY STOKS

Olivia's Touch—Olivia Plummer desires nothing more than to honor God by using the healing touch he has given her. Eastern-trained doctor Ethan Gray, disillusioned by the pampered rich of Boston, risks his medical career to set up practice in rural Colorado. There he can help people who are truly in need. Immediately upon his arrival, he clashes with the town's "healer," Miss Olivia Plummer. But when his hand is injured, Ethan is forced to accept Olivia's help. Watching her work, he finds himself captivated by her bravery, her beauty, and her passion for helping the sick. And Olivia is drawn to Ethan's disarming tenderness. Still, he stubbornly refuses to support her efforts to obtain a state medical license. Must Olivia choose between the promise of love and fulfilling God's call on her life? *Book 1 in the Abounding Love series.*

Romy's Walk—Since moving to Washington Territory, teacher Romy Schmitt has secretly harbored tender feelings for the kind, handsome storekeeper Jeremiah Landis. But Jeremiah has secrets of his own. When a tragic accident forces Romy and Jeremiah to reveal their unspoken feelings, they make a hasty pledge that will take a lifetime to live out, testing their courage and faith. As Romy struggles to overcome her sense of loss and accept the gift she has received, Jeremiah's past threatens to shatter their newfound love. Together, they must learn how to surrender to God's plans, no matter what the cost. *Book 2 in the Abounding Love series.*

Wishful Thinking—Betsy Wilcox's heart has betrayed her. She believes herself to be long past the fluttering hearts that beset the very young. But her new neighbor, an exuberant and winsome widower, makes her feel like a girl again. Only when she faces the threat of losing him forever does Betsy realize the depth of her love for this dear, godly man. This novella by Peggy Stoks appears in the anthology *Prairie Christmas.*

The Beauty of the Season—A determined suitor risks everything to help a vulnerable young woman overcome her wounded past. This novella by Peggy Stoks appears in the anthology *A Victorian Christmas Cottage.*

Crosses and Losses—On Christmas Eve in snowy St. Paul, Minnesota, a cherished Crosses and Losses quilt opens the door of healing and love for a grieving young couple. This novella by Peggy Stoks appears in the anthology *A Victorian Christmas Quilt.*

Tea for Marie—In rural Minnesota, love springs unexpectedly from the ashes of disaster. This novella by Peggy Stoks appears in the anthology *A Victorian Christmas Tea.*

HEART
QUEST®

OTHER GREAT TYNDALE HOUSE FICTION